D0047068

A Cat in the Stacks Mystery

CLAWS FOR CONCERN

Miranda James

BERKLEY PRIME CRIME
New York

BERKLEY PRIME CRIME
Published by Berkley
An imprint of Penguin Random House LLC
1745 Broadway, New York, NY 10019

ISBN: 9780425277799

Berkley Prime Crime hardcover edition / February 2018
Berkley Prime Crime mass-market edition / June 2019

Printed in the United States of America
1   3   5   7   9   10   8   6   4   2

Cover art by Dan Craig, Inc. / Bernstein & Andriulli
Cover design by Katie Anderson
Book design by Tiffany Estreicher

This book is dedicated with great respect and admiration to Bill Scruggs, truly an inspiration.

ACKNOWLEDGMENTS

Thanks as always to my wonderful and enthusiastic editor, Michelle Vega, also an inspiration. I am grateful for all the help offered by Jennifer Monroe and the team at Berkley Prime Crime with every book. My agent, Nancy Yost, is always looking out for my best interests, and I couldn't have anybody feistier or funnier in my corner. Thanks also to the rest of the team: Sarah E. Younger, Natanya Wheeler, and Amy Rosenbaum. Y'all are the best!

Most of all I want to thank the many wonderful readers who are such ardent fans of Charlie and Diesel. I am truly humbled by your response to these books, and I will always do my best to create stories that you will want to continue reading. Thank you for giving me so much in return.

ONE

I couldn't stop checking the clock on the wall nearby. "Come on, three o'clock," I muttered under my breath. "Get here already."

The wretched clock refused to cooperate. It read two forty-seven, and the second hand seemed to be taking way too long to sweep around the clock's face. Thirteen minutes until I could pack up and head home.

Diesel, my Maine Coon cat and near-constant companion, warbled anxiously from the area next to my feet under the reference desk. He always picked up on my emotions, and I forced myself to calm down. There was no point in getting a nearly forty-pound cat all wound up. Nor myself, actually.

"It's all okay, boy," I told him in a low voice before I reached under the desk to scratch his head. "We'll be home soon." I think the cat knew what—or really, who—was waiting for us at home, and he was as eager as I to be there.

Clock check. Only eleven minutes to go. I could leave now if I really wanted to. I volunteered at the Athena Public Library. I did not earn a paycheck from the place. I knew, though, how much the director, Teresa Farmer, and the other staff appreciated my help on Fridays, and I wasn't going to cut my time short. I settled back into my chair for the remaining minutes and glanced around me.

On this late July afternoon, the only people I saw in the library were adults, mostly my own age or older. Some, no doubt, sought relief from the punishing heat. The soaring temperatures taxed air conditioners, and there were many elderly people in Athena who couldn't afford to cool their houses. I knew most of those who came into the library to get relief, at least by name.

One man was a definite stranger, however. I first noticed him a week ago. Tall, a bit stooped, with a shambling gait, he looked to be about ten years older than me, so that put him in his midsixties, though he might have been older. I'd not had any interaction with him last week, and he had not come near the reference desk today. He had glanced my way a couple of times, his expression a puzzled frown.

I wondered whether he knew me or thought that he might. I had never seen him before that I could recall, though there was an elusive familiarity about his face. Maybe I had run across him thirty years ago, I mused, before I left Athena to move to Texas for graduate school in library science. I couldn't place him, but I hadn't spent much energy trying. I had learned over the years to let such things resolve themselves on their own schedule. The answer to this particular puzzle, if I knew it, would occur to me in due course.

Earlier today I had thought about approaching him and simply asking him who he was, but I hesitated to follow through on that. He appeared reserved and perhaps shy, and I didn't want to intrude if he truly had no desire to talk to people. I glanced his way again, and he looked up for a moment. Then he dipped his head down, focused once more on the book in his lap, and I read that as a clear signal that he did not want to be interrupted.

Diesel chirped and laid a large paw on my knee, as if he were asking me the time, and I checked the clock. Two minutes to three. Bronwyn Forster, one of the full-time librarians, should be here to relieve me any moment now. Sure enough, when I looked toward the area where the offices were, I saw her emerge from the doorway and head toward us.

After we greeted her, and she and I exchanged places, Diesel stayed with Bronwyn while I went to gather my things. He had to be sure to get his full quota of rubs on the head and under the chin before we left. Bronwyn, like the other staff and many of the patrons, never hesitated to oblige him. No wonder he loved coming to work with me.

Back at the desk again, I spoke to Bronwyn. "Would you mind keeping him with you for a minute? It's so hot outside, I want to get the car started and cooling off before I put him in it."

Bronwyn gave me her habitual sweet smile. "Of course, Charlie. Diesel won't mind getting loved on for a couple more minutes."

I heard a happy warble from behind the desk and knew Diesel would be content until I was ready to take him out. "Back in a minute, then." I headed for the door.

The second I stepped outside the heat swarmed around me like a cloud of gnats. I could feel the sweat starting to form as I made my way through the parking lot to the far side where the staff usually parked. This morning I had found a spot beneath the largest tree that cast shade over the lot. That meant the inside of my car was a few degrees cooler than it might have been otherwise.

I backed the car out and drove it around the lot to the closest spot to the front door. I left the engine running and went into the building to retrieve my cat. The moment I called, he came running around the desk toward me.

I scooped him up in both arms and backed out the door, with one last farewell to Bronwyn. The temperature was too high today—hovering around the century mark— to let Diesel walk over the hot asphalt and concrete. In weather like this I carried Diesel to and from buildings where the sidewalks and parking areas were in the direct sunlight. I didn't want him blistering the pads of his feet.

The drive home took less than ten minutes, and once I had the car parked in my garage, I let Diesel out of the backseat. He preceded me into the kitchen where I knew we would find the object of our intense interest.

When I stepped into the room I saw my daughter, Laura, sitting at the table, feeding my grandson, and chatting with Azalea Berry, my housekeeper. Diesel approached Laura slowly. When he reached her side, he looked up at her and chirped twice.

"Hello, handsome boy," Laura said. "We're almost through here, and then I'll let you see him. How about that?"

Diesel warbled in happiness. He loved the baby and could sit near him and watch him for long periods of time. Until both he and the baby fell asleep, that is.

I greeted both women and put my things on the small table by the door. I moved closer to Laura and my grandson and watched for a moment. Then my vision blurred, and I had to slip my handkerchief out of my pocket to wipe my eyes.

"How is young Master Charles Franklin Salisbury?" I asked, my voice husky.

Laura laughed as she looked up at me. "Like his grandfather, always ready for a meal."

Azalea chuckled at that. "That baby sure is a chip off this old block." She slid a sly glance in my direction. "How about something for you, Mr. Granddaddy?"

I grinned at the silly nickname Azalea gave me not long after baby Charlie was born. We were all giddy with happiness over the arrival of this child. I hated that his grandmother and his great-great-aunt weren't alive to see him, but I knew they were watching over him. I sometimes felt their presence here in the kitchen. Like now, when a whisper of air passed my right ear.

"I wouldn't mind a cold glass of water," I replied. "This horrible heat wave makes me thirsty."

"I'm glad to hear you ask for water instead of a diet soda." Laura smiled at me. "You were drinking way too much of it. It's good that you've cut back."

After a satisfying couple of sips from the glass Azalea handed me, I raised an eyebrow at Laura and sniffed. "You wouldn't say that if you hadn't had to give up the exact same beverage while you were breastfeeding my grandson."

"Ha-ha," Laura replied. "By the time this young man is off the breast, I will have completely forgotten what the ambrosia tasted like." She sighed. "No wine until then, either. *That* I will definitely go back to, believe me."

"I didn't think you had to cut caffeine out completely, though," I said as I took a seat across the table from Laura and baby Charlie.

"No, I don't, but it needs to be limited," Laura said. "I still have a little, mostly coffee or tea, but nothing like what my intake used to be."

I recalled her teenage years—and probably the years spent in California while she pursued her acting career—when she seemed to live on diet drinks, salads, wine, and cheese, with the occasional hamburger and french fries on the side.

"How is his rash?" I nodded toward the baby.

"Almost completely cleared up," Laura said. "His doctor said that infant acne is fairly common and usually clears up on its own."

"I don't remember whether you or Sean had that," I said. "I don't think you did, though."

"It's all due to maternal hormones," Laura replied. "His little face will be completely smooth again in another day or two."

Diesel chirped as if to acknowledge gratification at this news.

Azalea placed a stack of mail in front of me. "You hit the jackpot today."

"Half of it at least will go in the recycling bin." I eyed the pile with a jaundiced glance. There were three catalogs, several circulars, and four letters. I pushed the catalogs and circulars aside and picked up the envelopes.

"When I was a little girl," Laura said, "you used to give me all the mail you didn't want so that I could pretend it was my mail."

"Yes, I did." I laughed. "You would sit and read through it so solemnly."

Laura rolled her eyes. "I must have been adorable, thinking I was important enough to have mail like my father."

"You were, and still are, adorable," I told her.

"Mushy," Laura said, but she smiled.

The first two letters were junk mail. The third was a legitimate bill. The fourth, however, seemed to be of a personal nature. The return address and my name and address were all handwritten.

I glanced at the return address. The name was Jack Pemberton, and the town was Tullahoma, a smaller town about eighty miles southwest of Athens. I didn't recognize the sender of the letter. I couldn't recall ever having met someone of that name.

Curious, I opened the letter by tearing a small strip off one end. I extracted the pages inside, along with what looked like a bookmark. Pemberton might be a writer, I decided. Was he trying a direct-mail approach to selling books?

I examined the bookmark first. One side showed two images of book covers, both with slightly lurid illustrations. I laid the bookmark aside and opened the letter. I scanned it quickly, impatient as usual to figure out what the import was. Then I went back and read it more carefully.

I frowned and laid the pages aside.

"What is it, Dad?" Laura said. "Bad news?"

"Not news at all." I laughed, suddenly struck by the seeming absurdity of the letter writer's intent. "A man from Tullahoma wants to write a book about me."

"About you? Why?" Azalea asked, obviously puzzled. Then suddenly her face cleared and she scowled. "About all your murders, you mean."

TWO

############

"They're not *my* murders, Azalea." I shook my head. "I may have helped solve them in some way, but I didn't go looking for trouble to get into. I can assure you of that."

"You might not have gone looking for it, but you didn't run away from trouble when you found it, Dad." Laura cocked an eyebrow at me. "I know it's not by choice, but you have to admit you got a lot of satisfaction out of figuring them out when the killer wasn't immediately obvious."

"I will admit that," I said. "I've been reading mysteries for nearly fifty years, so it's pretty hard to resist one when it practically falls into your lap."

"Or you stumble over the body." Laura grimaced. "Not something I want to experience ever again myself. Once was enough for me."

"I know, sweetheart." I remembered how upset she had been when she found her former boyfriend dead, the victim of murder.

"Kanesha might not be too happy to see you getting all the credit in a book, either." Laura wiped the baby's mouth, refastened her blouse, and then laid Charlie on her shoulder to burp him.

Laura referred to Kanesha Berry, chief deputy in the Athena County Sheriff's Department, and the official investigator of murders in the county. She also happened to be my housekeeper's daughter, a situation that Kanesha had never regarded with good grace.

Azalea snorted at Laura's observation. "That girl better thank the good Lord Mr. Charlie's been willing to help her out. Some of those murders were downright strange." She favored me with an oblique glance when she hit that last word.

"Strange murders or not, Kanesha got the credit in all those cases," I said. "I may have helped her solve them more quickly in some instances, but I have no doubt whatsoever that she would have figured them out all on her own. I also have no doubt that she would have preferred it that way."

"Then what are you going to tell the man who wants to interview you?" Laura asked.

"I haven't decided yet," I responded. "I want to talk it over with Helen Louise first."

Helen Louise Brady, owner of the best French bistro south of Memphis, was my best friend and also my girlfriend. Some might consider the word *girlfriend* old-fashioned, but I was an old-fashioned kind of guy in many respects, including romantic relationships.

"Now that she's cut back her hours at the bistro," Laura said, "you at least have more time to talk, instead of only late at night after the bistro's closed or when you go in there for a meal."

"You'd think so." I tried not to sound irritable. "But

Helen Louise is having a harder time letting go of some of the responsibility than she expected."

"I thought she had worked everything out," Azalea said. "Isn't that young man been working there doing good as a baker?"

"Henry?" I said. "Yes, he's doing fine, but I think he's getting a bit exasperated with Helen Louise. She tends to hover and hang around later than she says she will."

"She's put so much of her life into that place," Laura said as baby Charlie emitted a burp. She and I exchanged smiles.

Azalea took Charlie from Laura and rocked him gently in her arms. She crooned a lullaby to him, her voice low, while she carried him out of the kitchen into the living room. One part of the room looked like a nursery, with a crib and various baby paraphernalia gathered around it. The living room was close enough to the kitchen for Azalea to be able to hear Charlie in case he needed her and quiet enough for the baby to sleep without being disturbed by her activities.

"As I was saying," Laura continued, "she's invested everything—heart, soul, and pocketbook—in the bistro. I can understand why she's reluctant to let anyone else take charge of *her* baby."

"I know, and I agree," I said. "The problem is, Henry is a more than capable manager, and he's got Debbie and that new girl, Tina, to help him. Plus, Henry is extremely talented in the kitchen. I know he's getting a little frustrated, though, and I'm afraid Helen Louise is going to lose him if she doesn't step back the way she promised."

"Have you discussed this with her?" Laura asked. "Does she know Henry is unhappy?"

"Sort of, and yes," I said.

"Sort of discussed it, and yes she knows Henry is unhappy," Laura said. "Is that what you mean?"

I nodded. "I've tried to talk to her about the situation, but she basically brushes me off. I haven't pushed her because I know this is difficult for her."

"Sometimes you have to push anyway." Laura shook a finger at me. "*You* don't like confrontation. That's what's holding you back. If you don't push, and she keeps hedging, nothing is going to get resolved."

"No, I don't like it." I sighed. "But you're right. It's probably time to force the issue. Otherwise Henry might end up leaving. He has a bit of a temper."

"Many creative people do." Laura smiled. "I certainly do."

In a dry tone I responded, "I remember many occasions when you had a *bit of a temper*. Like the whole time you were a teenager."

She stuck out her tongue at me, then grinned. "I really could be a brat, couldn't I?"

"I plead the Fifth," I said. "You'll get your turn. Just wait until that little imp in the living room hits thirteen."

"That *angel child*, you mean?" Laura shook her head. "No, not my boy."

"Let's revisit this conversation in thirteen years," I said.

Laura giggled as she pushed her chair back. "I don't think that will be necessary. I would love to stay and talk more, Dad, but I really need to get to the grocery store and do a few other things before I come back to pick up Charlie. Lord bless Azalea, I don't know what I'd do without her."

"She'd have a fit if you let anyone else look after him," I said. "Besides me, that is."

Laura kissed my cheek before she grabbed her purse and headed for the front door.

I sat, savoring the quiet for a moment, and then I realized it was too quiet. I hadn't heard a chirp or a warble or a meow out of Diesel during the conversation with Laura. Normally he would have followed her to the door but when I checked, he wasn't even in the kitchen.

I knew where he probably was, however. Whenever Azalea or I had charge of baby Charlie, Diesel stayed somewhere near the infant when at all possible. He must have left the room with Azalea, and I hadn't noticed it. When I tiptoed into the living room, I found Azalea asleep in the rocking chair by the crib. Diesel lay stretched out beneath the crib, snoozing. Baby Charlie slept soundly as well. I tiptoed back out and retraced my steps to the kitchen.

The water had quenched my immediate thirst, and now I craved caffeine. I found a pitcher of tea in the fridge and poured myself a glass. Nobody made better sweet tea than Azalea, but because of the sugar content I rationed myself to no more than one glass a day. Between Azalea's Southern soul food and Helen Louise's haute cuisine, I found myself battling the bulge more than ever.

Well, at least I won't die hungry, I told myself. Nevertheless, I resolved to go up and down the stairs a few extra times a day.

I resumed my place at the table and picked up the letter from Jack Pemberton. I read it more slowly this time, and as I did, the name of a person Pemberton mentioned as a reference jumped out at me. *Ernestine Carpenter*. Apparently she was a retired schoolteacher in the Tullahoma area, and must be a person of good character. Otherwise, why would Pemberton mention her?

Ernestine Carpenter. For some reason, the name rang

a bell. I knew I had heard it somewhere, in the not-too-distant past, but where? On what occasion?

I tried to dredge up the memory while I sipped at my tea, savoring the taste and the coldness. My memory stubbornly refused to cooperate, though, and I decided I'd do better to occupy my thoughts otherwise.

Idly I pulled out my phone and tapped the icon for my e-mail. I usually didn't read messages on my phone, preferring my laptop for the task. At the moment, despite my pledge to get more exercise, I felt too indolent to haul my carcass up and down the hall to the den where my laptop lived most of the time.

Other than a few friends from my many years in Houston, I had few e-mail correspondents. I spent more time deleting unwanted messages than I did reading anything I actually wanted to see. I purged several messages before I got to one from a dear friend here in Athena, Miss An'gel Ducote.

Miss An'gel and her younger sister, Miss Dickce, were the two grande dames of Athena society. Their family were among the founders of the town, and Ducotes had been leading citizens ever since. The sisters, in their early eighties, were the last of the direct line, however. They had recently taken a young man from California named Benjy Stephens, a connection of an old friend of theirs, as their ward, however, and speculation was rife around town that he would one day inherit the Ducote millions.

Miss An'gel, after observing the niceties, got right to the point in her message.

Sister and I would be delighted if you and Helen Louise could join us for tea on Sunday afternoon. A dear friend will be visiting, and you really should

meet her. You have something in common, but I
won't tell you what until after you've met. Don't
forget to bring Diesel! Shall we say three p.m.?

I had no plans for Sunday afternoon but knew I would
have to check with Helen Louise. She wasn't supposed to
be at the bistro then, but I couldn't be sure she wouldn't
decide that something there needed her attention.

As I was about to reply to Miss An'gel, I received a
notice that I had a new message. From Miss An'gel,
no less.

Forgive my lapse, Charlie, but I forgot to tell you our
dear friend's name. Miss Ernestine Carpenter.
She's looking forward to meeting you.

Mystery solved, I thought. I remembered now that
Miss An'gel or Miss Dickce had mentioned the woman in
a recent conversation, though I couldn't quite recall the
context.

The Ducote sisters knew Miss Carpenter, and Miss Carpenter knew Jack Pemberton. *Curiouser and curiouser.* At
least I would be able to meet Miss Carpenter and find out
directly what she knew about Jack Pemberton and maybe
even why he was so keen to write a book about my experiences.

I replied to Miss An'gel and told her we would be delighted to join her, her sister, and their guest for tea on
Sunday afternoon. I assured her Diesel would be with us.

That accomplished, I put my phone down and had a
few more sips of tea while I contemplated a call to Helen
Louise. I had a feeling she might not be happy that I had
accepted an invitation for the both of us without consult-

ing her first, but I figured this was as good a time as any to confront her about really committing to her decision to cut back on work.

After a few more sips of tea, I picked up the phone and called her.

THREE

|||||||||||||||||||||||||||||||||||||||

To my surprise—and relief—Helen Louise didn't sound at all annoyed with me for accepting Miss An'gel's invitation to tea on Sunday without consulting her. She brushed aside my apology.

"No, I don't mind, honey, in this instance," Helen Louise said. "It will be a pleasure to see Miss An'gel and Miss Dickce and to meet their friend. Now, what shall we have for Sunday dinner? Is everyone planning to be there?"

Okay, so no confrontation at the moment. It could wait. I felt a bit cowardly, but after all, it would probably be best to have that conversation when we were face-to-face and not over the phone.

"Far as I know," I said. *Everyone* meant—besides Helen Louise, Diesel, and me—my two children, their spouses, my grandson, and my two lodgers, Stewart Delacorte and his partner, Haskell Bates.

"Alex must be about ready to pop," Helen Louise said, referring to my son Sean's wife, who was nearing the end of her pregnancy. "I know she'll be happy to have that baby out."

"Yes, poor girl, I think she's pretty miserable," I said. "Ever since her doctor told her she needed to stay home and off her feet these last few weeks, she hasn't been happy not being able to go into the office." Alex, like my son, was an attorney, and they shared a practice with Alex's father, a near-legendary figure in Athena.

"She and Sean will be even busier when the baby arrives," Helen Louise said. "They still haven't given any hints as to what it will be?"

"Not a single one," I said. "I don't think they actually know. I think Sean only pretends to know so he can tease me."

Helen Louise chuckled. "Yes, he would do that."

"As long as the baby's healthy," I said, "I don't care whether it's a boy or a girl."

"I have a feeling we're going to know pretty soon," Helen Louise said. "Now, about the menu. Here's what I was thinking."

We spent the next several minutes discussing food choices. Helen Louise insisted on preparing the meal herself—with help from her two assistants, namely Diesel and me. Once we had the menu fully planned, we said good-bye. Helen Louise had to get back to work.

After I put my phone down, I sat and listened for a moment. The house was quiet as I walked softly back to the living room to check on its occupants. Azalea, Diesel, and baby Charlie still slept. As long as everyone was resting, I thought I might as well have a brief nap before dinner. I made my way up the stairs to my bedroom. Shoes off, I stretched out on the bed. After a few minutes I drifted off to sleep.

When I awoke about an hour later I discovered that I

had a large, furry companion in bed with me. Diesel lay lengthwise alongside me, his head on his pillow, his body facing me. As I shifted in the bed to turn toward him, his eyes opened. He yawned and stretched before he meowed a couple of times. I stroked his head for a moment, and he began to purr, making the deep, rumbling sound that was the reason for his name.

I checked the time on the beautiful watch Helen Louise had given me last month for my birthday and was not surprised to see that it was nearly five thirty. I rubbed Diesel's head a few more times before I told him it was time to get up. He chirped as if to disagree.

"No, no arguing, we'd better get up." I turned to sit up on the side of the bed. After a yawn and a stretch, I went into the bathroom to splash water on my face and comb my hair. When I returned to the bedroom Diesel sat by the door into the hall, ready to accompany me.

I could hear Azalea singing one of her favorite hymns, "In the Garden," as we neared the kitchen. Listening to her brought back memories of my childhood, going to church with my parents, attending gospel singing events. I felt a wave of nostalgia for my parents and that bygone time. I wished my parents could have lived to see their great-grandchildren, but they had been gone more than twenty years now.

Azalea broke off singing when Diesel and I entered the kitchen. She rarely sang when I was in the room with her, unless it was to baby Charlie.

"That was lovely," I told her.

"Thank you," she said. "Miss Laura came and got baby Charlie a few minutes ago." She gestured to the oven. "Your dinner's about ready. Chicken and rice casserole. Give it about ten more minutes." She looked down at Diesel. The cat had come to a stop near her and stared hopefully up at her. She wagged a finger at him. "You can't have any, Mr. Cat. There's onions in it, and they're not good for you."

Diesel uttered a plaintive meow.

"No use complaining to me, Mr. Cat," Azalea said. "Next week I'll make something with chicken and no onions. No garlic, either. Then you'll be able to have some. Okay?"

Diesel warbled happily, and Azalea let a smile hover briefly on her lips. She turned to me. "You got this cat spoiled worse than any child, Mr. Charlie."

"I didn't do it all by myself," I said. Azalea had not taken to my cat when I first brought him home. Eventually, however, Diesel wore down her resistance, and I often caught her talking to him when she thought no one could hear her. She also slipped him tidbits from the stove, and I pretended not to notice, most of the time.

Azalea ignored my comment. She pointed to my phone. I had left it on the table when I went upstairs. "That was making noise a few minutes ago."

"Thanks." I picked up the phone and checked the screen. I had missed a call from Teresa Farmer. I listened to her brief message, asking me to return her call at my earliest convenience. She sounded a bit harried, so I called her right away.

"Hi, Teresa, this is Charlie," I said. "What's up?"

"Oh, Charlie, thank you for getting back to me so quickly," Teresa said. "Look, I hate to ask you this, but I'm in a bind over staffing tomorrow. Lizzie has come down with some kind of virus and went home sick about twenty minutes ago. I don't think she'll be able to come in tomorrow, and I have to be in Jackson tomorrow for my cousin's wedding. I'm one of the bridesmaids, and I'd hate to let her down at the last minute."

Lizzie Hayes was one of the full-time staff, along with Teresa and Bronwyn Forster. All three were librarians. The other workers were all part-time. Having two full-timers out at the same time made staffing difficult.

"Would you like me to come in and help out?" I said. "I'd be happy to. I don't have anything special planned for tomorrow, so it's not a problem."

Her relief was obvious when Teresa replied, "Thank you, Charlie. I hate to impose, but I'd feel so much better if you could be there with Bronwyn. Saturdays can be so hectic in the summer. I know she'll appreciate it, too."

"I remember all too well how Saturdays can be," I said, recalling my own days as a public library branch manager in Houston. "Diesel and I will report for duty at nine tomorrow morning."

After expressing her gratitude at least three more times, Teresa ended the call. I set aside the phone. "Looks like we'll be working at the library with Bronwyn tomorrow, boy," I told Diesel. He chirped in response. He knew he could count on Bronwyn for attention when the patrons weren't claiming it.

Azalea bade us good night, after reminding me to keep an eye on the casserole. I stood near the oven to make sure I didn't wander away and get distracted. I didn't dare let Azalea's food burn.

Diesel loped off to the utility room, and I heard him scratching around in his litter box. He rejoined me in the kitchen moments after I opened the oven door to take out the casserole. I sniffed appreciatively at the delicious odor, and Diesel did the same. He meowed again, but I told him firmly that he couldn't have any as I set the dish on a large trivet on the table.

I foraged in the fridge and found some bits of chicken that Azalea had probably set aside just for Diesel. I warmed them in the microwave while I took out the makings for a salad. A few minutes later both cat and human were happily eating their dinners.

I spent many Friday evenings on my own—with Diesel, of course—because Friday evening was a busy time at the bistro. Stewart and Haskell occasionally joined me, but this particular evening, they were in Memphis visiting friends for the weekend.

During the meal, aside from occasional remarks in response to more muttering from Diesel, I thought about the letter from Jack Pemberton. I didn't want to respond until I had a chance to talk in person with his reference, Miss Carpenter. I also wanted to discuss the subject with Helen Louise, but that would have to wait until Sunday.

I hadn't sought the limelight in the aftermath of the various murder investigations I'd been party to, and luckily for me the local paper hadn't played up my role—for the most part—outrageously. I was happy for Kanesha to get the credit. After all, she was the professional. I was content with being an advisor of a sort.

As I continued to think about the idea of a book about my experiences, I felt increasingly uneasy. I suspected that, were I to cooperate and give the writer full details of my sleuthing activities, I would end up regretting it. I didn't want strangers nosing around in *my* life.

Struck by the irony of that all of a sudden, I had to laugh. I had certainly nosed around in the lives of other people the past few years. Had karma decided this book project would be my comeuppance for playing amateur detective when I probably should have been minding my own business instead?

FOUR

‖‖‖‖‖‖‖‖‖‖‖‖‖‖‖‖‖‖‖‖‖‖‖‖‖‖‖‖‖

Diesel and I arrived at the public library the next morning promptly at eight forty-five. Bronwyn Forster admitted us and then locked the front door behind us.

"Good morning, Charlie, Diesel," Bronwyn said. "Thank you again for helping out like this. I'm so glad you'll both be here today." She scratched Diesel's head, and he rewarded her with a happy warble.

"Our pleasure." I indicated the container of cat litter I was carrying. "Let me just stow this away and clean out his box, and I'll be back to help you get ready to open."

"While you do that, Diesel and I will finish turning on the lights and making sure the computers are ready." Bronwyn smiled. "Come on, Diesel, you can help me."

Chirping and meowing, the cat followed Bronwyn while I took care of Diesel's litter box in a small storage closet in the staff area at the back of the library. When I returned from completing that chore, the librarian and the cat awaited me near the reference desk. While Bronwyn and I discussed sharing duties at the desk during the day, Diesel stretched out nearby and commenced cleaning his front paws.

"We'll have two assistants today," Bronwyn said, "so they should be able to handle the circulation desk and any shelving that needs doing." She smiled. "We'll be busy enough answering questions and helping people with the computers."

"Nothing like a busy Saturday at the public library," I said, remembering hectic past days at my branch in Houston.

"It's supposed to be near a hundred degrees today," Bronwyn said, "so I imagine we'll have a full house by midafternoon."

"I'm sure we will." I would love to win the lottery just so I could afford to pay for adequate air-conditioning and heating for all the families and the elderly in Athena who needed it. And feed them as well.

Bronwyn checked her wristwatch. "Time to open the gates." She flashed another smile before she headed to unlock the front door.

I joined Diesel behind the reference desk and watched as a dozen or so people streamed through the door. Among the group were the two library assistants, a couple of teenage girls, who went to clock in before starting work.

Upon seeing me at the desk three children immediately asked if Diesel were with me. Hearing his name, the cat came out of his relaxed state and walked around the desk to greet his young admirers. After a couple minutes of feline adoration, the children let Diesel go, and he returned to my side. This scene would replay itself throughout the day, with both children and adults. Diesel was a popular attraction whenever we worked at the library.

After I answered three questions and pointed one of the questioners to a particular database, I had time to look up Jack Pemberton in the library's online catalog. I wanted to see whether the library held any of his books. If one was available I figured I might as well read it to help me with my decision. If Pemberton's work turned out to be cheap sensationalism, I wanted no part of it.

A quick search revealed that the library did have one of his books, published a couple of years ago. The title was *Hell Has No Fury*. I wondered if the title referred to the old adage "hell hath no fury like a woman scorned." That, in turn, was a misquoted version of a line from a play by the English poet and playwright William Congreve. I concentrated for a moment, trying to remember the original. When the words failed to come, I resorted to the Internet and found them in a few seconds.

Ah, yes, from the play *The Mourning Bride*. The original read: "Heaven has no rage like love to hatred turned, Nor hell a fury like a woman scorned." I congratulated myself on at least remembering the Congreve connection.

Then I had to laugh at myself a little. I had quickly wandered from my original purpose. Not unusual behavior for me. I went back to the online catalog to the record for Pemberton's book. There was no summary but the subject headings told me that the murder took place in Mississippi. Unfortunately for me, however, the book was checked out. I debated whether to place a hold on it, but the book wasn't due for another ten days and I couldn't count on its being turned in on time. I needed to make a decision before then.

I had another thought. Our local independent bookstore, the Athenaeum, opened at ten. I would call there later and ask whether they had any of Pemberton's books in stock. If by chance they did, I could run by after Diesel and I left the library at five and pick one up. The bookstore stayed open until seven on Saturdays.

For the next half hour we had a slow trickle of patrons in and out of the library, mostly to return books and movies and to check out more of the same. I checked my watch and noted that there was still a quarter of an hour before I could call the bookstore. When I glanced toward the door a moment later I saw the older man I had noticed yesterday entering the library.

He hesitated a few steps inside the door before he turned to approach the reference desk. Once again I had that vague feeling of familiarity as I regarded his face. I wished I could figure out who it was that he reminded me of, but I still couldn't quite grasp it.

"Good morning," I said when he reached the desk. "How may I help you?"

He flashed a brief but nervous-looking smile, then cleared his throat. "Good morning, sir." His voice was soft, his tone diffident. "Sorry to bother you, but I was wondering if you could tell me if you've got any old phone books for the town."

"It's not a bother at all," I told him cheerfully. "That's what I'm here for. We do have old phone books. Let me show you where they are."

"I sure would appreciate it," the man said.

I nodded as I moved from behind the desk to escort him to the room where we kept the objects of his request. Diesel stirred from his latest nap and followed me. As he emerged from behind the desk, I could see the man's expression change. He took a step backward, as if in fear.

"It's okay, he won't bite or scratch you," I said. "Will you, Diesel?"

Right on cue, Diesel warbled, sounding indignant, if that were possible.

The man looked uncertainly at my cat but he didn't

step any farther away. "What kind of cat is that? I never did see one that big, except a bobcat once."

"He's a Maine Coon. They're the largest breed of American domestic cats. He is much larger than average, though. Most male Maine Coons are around twenty-five pounds at maturity, but he's close to forty."

Diesel watched the man intently for a moment before he moved closer. He stopped and looked up at him. He meowed as if to reassure the stranger. The man tensed briefly, then relaxed. He stretched out a tentative hand and touched Diesel's head.

"He's very friendly," I said. "Maine Coons are laid-back and sociable. He enjoys coming to the library with me because he can get extra attention. The children love him."

"I reckon I can see why." The man stroked Diesel's head gently several times. Diesel rewarded him by purring. "Goodness, he sounds like a truck engine."

"That's how he got his name, Diesel," I said.

The man chuckled. "Nice to meet you, Diesel."

The cat chirped for him in response.

"He acts like he knows what I'm saying."

I grinned. "I think most of the time he does. He's a smart kitty, believe me. Now, let me show you those phone books."

The man nodded and followed as I led him to the area where the phone books resided. I explained that they were shelved in chronological order and that there were gaps, unfortunately, but the collection covered most of the last five decades.

"That should do me just fine," he said. "Thank you again."

"My pleasure. Let me know if you have any other questions." I looked down at my cat. "Come along, Diesel, back to the desk."

Diesel glanced between me and the stranger a couple of times. Did he want to stay with the man? After a moment, though, he decided to come with me.

Back at the desk I found two women waiting. I answered their questions in turn, suggesting the resources they might try in order to find what they were seeking. I offered to assist them, but each declined.

By now it was a few minutes past ten, and as Bronwyn approached the desk, I asked whether she would mind taking my place for a few minutes. I explained that I wanted to make a phone call, and she waved me away with a smile. Diesel, happy to see his friend, remained with her.

I walked into the staff area of the library and pulled out my cell phone. I had the bookstore in my contacts list, and moments later I was speaking with the owner, Jordan Thompson.

"Hi, Charlie," she said. "Any chance you're coming by today? I have a few books here for you to look over."

"You always do." I chuckled. "Actually, yes, I am planning to come by, especially if you have books by a certain writer in stock. I know you have a small true crime section. Have anything by Jack Pemberton?"

"Let me check," Jordan said. "The name rings a bell. I don't read true crime myself, but we have some customers who buy hardly anything else."

I waited while she tapped at the keyboard. I could hear the clicking over the phone.

"We do stock his books," Jordan said. "I remember who he is now. He's from Tullahoma, I think, so he's practically a local writer. Let me see." She paused a moment. "I have two in stock, according to the computer. *Hell Has No Fury* and *Murder at Dawn*. Would you like me to add one of them to your stack?"

"Yes, I'll take *Hell Has No Fury*," I said. "According

to our online catalog it's about a murder in Mississippi. I'm working at the public library today until five, but Diesel and I will swing by on the way home."

"Great," Jordan said. "I'll see you then."

Briefly I wondered how many books Jordan had set aside for me. Probably anywhere from three to a dozen or more. She knew my favorite authors and always set aside their books for me, plus she often suggested new writers she thought I might like. I appreciated the level of customer service she and her staff provided, and I enjoyed visiting the store and browsing the shelves.

I pocketed my phone and headed back to the desk. A few paces out of the staff area, I heard an "excuse me, sir." I turned to see the man I'd helped with the phone books approaching. I stepped toward him, noting that he held one of the phone books in his right hand. The book was open, and he had a finger of his left hand on a page.

"How can I help?" I asked when I reached him.

He moved to stand beside me. "Can you tell me how to find this address?" He held out the book, his finger pointed at an entry.

I bent closer to read the small print. When I saw the name and the address, I felt a shock. It was my address, and the name, Delbert Collins, was that of my late aunt Dottie's husband.

FIVE

||||||||||||||||||||

For a moment I couldn't respond. *Why is this man interested in my address?*

"Can you read it okay?" the man asked. "I had a little trouble myself, the print being so small the way it is."

I cleared my throat. "Yes, I can read it. It's not far from the library." I hesitated, worried that my next words might offend him. "Maybe a little far to walk on a hot day, though. May I ask why you're interested in this particular address?" I stepped back, and he closed the phone book, one finger inserted to hold his place.

He regarded me briefly, then his gaze dropped when he began to speak. "My mother used to know Mr. Collins a long, long time ago. I reckon he must have passed on or else sold his house because I had to look in an old book to find his name." He tapped the cover of the phone book, and I saw that it was dated eight years ago.

Aunt Dottie was still living when that issue was published. Even though Uncle Del had died more than twenty years ago, the listing in the phone book remained in her husband's name. That was the custom, of course, and Aunt Dottie had never changed her entry.

"Yes, I'm afraid Mr. Collins has been gone a long time now," I said. "I'm sorry, but I never introduced myself. I'm Charlie Harris." I was hoping he would tell me his name now.

"Nice to meet you, Mr. Harris," the man said. "Bill Delaney." He stuck out his free hand, and I shook it.

"Nice to meet you, too, Mr. Delaney."

"Is Mrs. Collins still living?" Delaney asked, his gaze once again lowered.

Was he really that shy, I wondered, that he didn't want to look directly at me? Or was he afraid I would read his thoughts?

I shook my head. "No, she passed away about seven years ago."

"Did they ever have any children?" Delaney asked. "Would you happen to know?"

He seemed overly interested, at least to me, in Uncle Del and Aunt Dottie. I decided I wasn't going to reveal my connection to them—and to the house—until I knew more about Delaney and the reasons for his interest.

"No, they didn't," I said. That wasn't completely accurate, because they had had one child, a daughter named Veronica, who died in childhood, but I didn't see any point in revealing that to a stranger.

"That's too bad," Delaney said. "Sure would've been nice to talk to Mr. Collins about my mother. When you get to be my age, you know, there just ain't that many folk around who knew your parents in the old days."

"I know what you mean." My parents would have been in their late eighties by now, and most of their friends in Athena were gone.

"Well, I reckon that's that." Delaney shrugged. "Thanks again, Mr. Harris, for helping with the phone books."

"You're welcome," I replied.

He nodded and walked away. Obscurely troubled, I stood there for a moment and watched his retreating back. I couldn't explain it, but I had a feeling there was more behind Delaney's interest than simply wanting to find someone who had once known his mother. But I had no idea what that *more* could be.

Back at the desk I found Bronwyn engaged in a conversation with one of the regular patrons, an anxious-looking young mother with twins about seven years old tugging at her blouse. Bronwyn flashed me a grin as she left the desk to assist the mother. I noticed that Diesel was under the desk, well away from any questing hands. He remembered the twin boys and had obviously decided that retreat was the order of the day. I didn't blame him. They appeared to me to be even more energetic than usual this morning.

"It's okay," I told him in a low voice. "They're gone now."

Diesel meowed, and I nodded. He emerged from beneath the desk and resumed his usual spot by the chair. He stretched out and relaxed.

For the next two hours, I helped a number of people find the resources they needed. I also helped a youngish couple, new in town, with information about obtaining their library cards. I pointed them to the circulation desk where one of the part-time assistants stood.

"This young lady will take care of it for you," I told them.

During a brief lull after that, with the thought of library cards in my mind, I wondered whether Bill Delaney had registered for a card. I logged into the circulation module and did a quick check.

I found him right away, although there were several

other Delaneys in the database. I looked at his address and frowned. I recognized it. He lived in a small apartment complex with only a few units in a run-down section of Athena. From what I could recall, the complex appeared not to be well-maintained.

I closed out the circulation module. I really shouldn't have been prying into the man's business, but Bill Delaney had aroused my curiosity—and now my sympathy as well. He must be on a severely limited income if his address was any indication.

Bronwyn appeared at the desk while I was wrapped in thought and startled me.

"Easy, Charlie," she said. "Didn't mean to make you jerk like that."

"No problem," I said. "My fault for woolgathering on the job."

"Would you like to have lunch now? It's a few minutes after noon," Bronwyn said.

Diesel had already perked up with Bronwyn so close, but at the word *lunch* he warbled.

I laughed. "I guess Diesel's ready, at any rate. Yes, we'll go ahead and eat now. Give me a holler, though, if you need me." I pushed back the chair. "Come on, boy. Snack time."

Diesel knew where we were headed, and he loped in front of me into the staff area. I found him in the small kitchen staring hopefully at the refrigerator.

I retrieved the food and drink I had brought and took everything into the small lounge next to the kitchen. Diesel parked himself by my chair, and one large paw rested against my thigh seconds after I took my seat. He chirped.

"Yes, there's something for you." I unwrapped a few pieces of boiled chicken from the foil I'd used and pinched off a large bite of breast meat. He grabbed it and moved under the table to eat while I unwrapped my own meal, two ham-and-cheese sandwiches with lettuce and tomato on wheat bread. While we ate, I looked at my phone, checking for messages and e-mails, but found nothing.

I set the phone aside. I found my thoughts returning to Bill Delaney. That nagging sense of familiarity simply wouldn't go away but the puzzle refused to resolve itself. The more I worried at it, I thought, the more elusive the answer became.

Feeling too fidgety to take the full time allotted me for lunch, I cleaned up the detritus of our meals. I had to assure Diesel twice that there was no more before he would stop meowing at me. While I washed my hands and prepared to return to work, he sought out his litter box.

He joined me at the reference desk briefly, but when he realized Bronwyn intended to go eat her lunch, he trotted off after her. I had asked her before not to feed him, but unless I stood over them, I had no way of knowing whether she would honor my request. Diesel could look pitiful when he wanted to, like all cats determined to con food out of a human. Bronwyn was no doubt every bit as susceptible as I was.

We saw a steady parade of patrons through the doors that afternoon. One of the numerous book clubs around town that gathered in the library's public meeting room came in for their monthly meeting. I knew most of the members from my volunteer work there, and I greeted them as they passed by the reference desk. I bade them good-bye a couple of hours later when they began to trickle out. By that time it was after four, and the Saturday regulars who had spent most of the day with us began to pack up their things.

Among those leaving I spotted Bill Delaney. I hadn't had another opportunity to talk to him. I wasn't sure what

I would say to him, however, if I did. I simply couldn't help being curious about his interest in my uncle Del. Aunt Dottie had often told me, when I was a child, that I had enough curiosity for seventeen cats. I didn't think I had changed much in that respect in the last four or five decades.

Diesel and I helped Bronwyn prepare the library for closing, and soon after Bronwyn locked the doors, Diesel and I headed toward the town square where the bookstore was located. Though the square was busy with traffic, I managed to find a parking spot in front of the store.

Jordan Thompson, a tall redhead, glanced up as the cat and I walked through the door. A smile split her lovely face, and she came from behind the counter to greet Diesel with a few rubs of the head. He rewarded her with a mixture of chirps and trills. Two other customers, hearing the cat, looked at us to discern the source of the odd noises. They both smiled in our direction before they resumed their browsing.

"I'm glad you could come by today, Charlie." Jordan walked back behind the counter and pulled a stack of books from a shelf. She set the books on the counter for me to examine. I was happy to see among them new books by Ellery Adams and Julia Buckley, the latter author being a recent discovery. I set those two aside as definite yeses. Jordan talked to Diesel while I delved further into the stack.

The next book I picked up was *Hell Has No Fury* by Jack Pemberton. I began to thumb through it. He had dedicated the book to his wife, Wanda Nell. That was a Southern name if ever I heard one, I thought with a smile. After the dedication page came a page of acknowledgments, and that I skipped. On the next page, there was a quotation, the line from Congreve's *The Mournful Bride*, the source of the book's title. I took that as an encouraging sign. The man was obviously literate if he was quoting Congreve. I sampled the first couple of pages and decided I liked Pemberton's style.

I held up the book with the title facing Jordan. "Have you met the author?"

Jordan nodded. "Yes, he's been here twice to sign books. Really nice guy. He teaches high school English in Tullahoma."

An English teacher. That explained the Congreve quotation.

"Why this sudden interest in true crime?" Jordan asked. "I don't think you've ever bought any from me before."

I didn't want to share the real reason for my interest with her. Time enough for that later, if I decided to cooperate with Pemberton on his book idea. So I prevaricated. "His name came up in conversation recently, and I was curious."

"Let me know what you think," Jordan said.

"I will," I replied. I examined the three other books she had set aside. I passed on two of them but the third I decided to give a try.

Jordan rang me up, and a few minutes later Diesel and I headed home. Jordan had managed to slip him a few of the cat treats she kept on hand for his visits, and he was a happy kitty. I would have said spoiled, but that was redundant, of course.

After a full day at the library I was ready to get home and relax. Dinner and maybe a glass or two of wine, then I'd settle down with Pemberton's book and read until bedtime and my regular Saturday late-night phone call with Helen Louise.

We were half a block from home when I noticed a man walking down the sidewalk, his back to the car, in front of the house. He glanced at the house for a moment but continued on his way.

By the time I reached the driveway the man had reached the corner and began to cross the intersection. From the back he seemed familiar, but I didn't realize who he was until I pulled into the garage.

It was Bill Delaney.

SIX

‖‖‖‖‖‖‖‖‖‖‖

So Bill Delaney walked by the house. There was nothing wrong with that. I already knew he was curious about the former home of my aunt and uncle. I just wished I knew what the true connection was between Bill Delaney and Uncle Del.

Diesel hurried into the kitchen ahead of me. After I put away my things, including the bag of books from the Athenaeum, I went into the utility room to replenish Diesel's water and dry food. When I finished that, I found him in the kitchen in front of the fridge. He knew it was dinnertime.

Tonight's meal was about as simple as they came. I cooked a hamburger and made myself a salad. When Diesel smelled the ground beef cooking he headed for his food bowl. He didn't care for hamburger.

He did keep me company while I ate, however. He remained by my chair until I finished, and then he watched—or should I say *supervised*—while I cleaned up after myself in the kitchen. After that we retired to the den. He stretched out on the sofa, his head rubbing against my thigh, while I settled in to get started on Jack Pemberton's book.

I soon became engrossed in the book and read it straight through, with only a couple of brief breaks to stretch my legs and retrieve a drink from the kitchen.

Pemberton told the story of a woman who had evidently been a black widow—a woman who marries a man, disposes of him, and then moves on to the next target. By the time she met and married her fifth husband, she had amassed a significant amount of money. She always chose wealthy, older men as targets. Number five, while older and wealthy as per usual, turned out to be harder to kill than the previous husbands. He was either extraordinarily lucky or much shrewder than he appeared, I decided, because he lived to see his wife go to prison for four murders.

I laid the book aside, rather surprised to discover that it was nearly ten o'clock. Pemberton definitely knew how to tell a story, I thought. He also told it with good taste, without descent into cheap sensationalism. He appeared also to have shrewd insight into abnormal psychology, and into human behavior in general.

Diesel warbled sleepily when I roused him and told him it was time for us to go upstairs. He had turned onto his back, his spine twisted into what looked to me a painful angle but one apparently quite comfortable for him. He shifted until he sat upright and then stretched and yawned. I waited for him to finish before I turned out the lights in the den.

He followed me around the first floor while I checked the doors and windows. He placed a paw on the door to the back porch. "Not tonight," I told him. "You've had a long nap but I'm ready for bed. After we talk to Helen Louise, that is."

He chirped at the sound of Helen Louise's name and forgot about visiting the back porch. He trotted happily upstairs with me and waited on the bed while I undressed and put on my sleeping clothes, a pair of gym shorts and an old T-shirt.

I slipped into bed, and Diesel stretched out beside me. The clock now read ten thirteen. Helen Louise ought to be calling soon. The bistro closed at nine, and usually she and her staff were finished cleaning by ten. She lived only a few minutes from the square and would call once she reached home.

Five minutes later my cell rang, and I answered it. "Hello, love. How was today? Busy?"

"Extremely, sweetie," Helen Louise replied. "Summer visitor trade on top of many of our regulars." She paused, and I could hear her yawn. "Sorry about that, but I am completely worn out. These long days really take it out of me."

"Good thing you've got tomorrow to rest and recuperate," I said. "And on Monday Henry and the crew will open, so you don't have to set foot in the bistro until the afternoon."

Helen Louise chuckled. "Is that a gentle reminder that I shouldn't go in Monday morning to help out?"

"Yes, it is," I replied, my tone light as I continued. "You know Henry is utterly reliable and totally competent, and I don't think it will hurt to let him know you trust him."

"By not hovering over him, you mean." I heard her sigh. "I know, love, but after being in charge for so long, it's hard to delegate."

"You can do it," I said.

"We'll see. So how was *your* day?"

"Fine. Busy, but not as tiring as your day," I said. Once she changed the subject I knew there was no point in going back to the discussion of her work hours. "Nothing exciting. There are a couple of things to tell you about, but they can wait until tomorrow. Right now, you need to go to bed."

"Not going to argue with you." I heard another yawn, and I yawned in response. "Good night, love."

I bade her good night, and we ended the call. I laid my phone aside on the nightstand and adjusted my position in bed. Before I switched off the bedside lamp, I glanced at Diesel. He regarded me sleepily, his head on his pillow. His tail thumped a couple of times against the bedspread, and then his eyes closed.

Smiling, I turned off the light, got comfortable, and soon drifted into sleep.

A few hours after an enjoyable Sunday dinner with my children, their spouses, and baby Charlie, Helen Louise, Diesel, and I drove out to Riverhill, the antebellum home of the Ducote sisters, for afternoon tea.

On the way I told Helen Louise about Jack Pemberton's book. "I really enjoyed it," I said. "I didn't think I'd care for true crime, but the way he told the story, it read almost like a suspense novel. Well-paced with believable characters."

"I'll borrow it, then, if you don't mind," Helen Louise said. "I haven't had much time for reading all these years, and now that I actually have hours to fill away from the bistro, I'm looking forward to rediscovering books."

I smiled. "I have a large library at home entirely at your disposal."

"Yes, you do." Helen Louise punched me playfully in

the arm. "You have more books than I have cookware, cookbooks, and bottles of wine combined."

From the backseat Diesel meowed as if in agreement. When he was younger he tried to climb in between me and any book I started to read, and given his size, he easily obscured even the largest, thickest book in my collection. It took me six months to gently dissuade him from the habit. In the end I think he realized that that was one battle he was never going to win. Now he settled for simply being next to me when I paid attention to a book instead of him.

"Occupational hazard, I suppose, for a librarian." I had loved books from childhood, when my parents read to me before I was old enough to read on my own. Once I discovered that I could actually buy books at a bookstore, rather than only borrowing them from the library, I turned into a collector of sorts. I had to own copies of books by my favorite writers because I never knew when I might want to reread one of them.

Helen Louise and I discussed books the rest of the way to Riverhill. When we neared the magnificent old Greek Revival mansion, I saw a late-model, bright red Jeep parked in the circular driveway in front of the house. I parked behind it, and by the time Helen Louise, Diesel, and I exited the car, Miss An'gel was standing on the verandah calling a greeting to us.

The elder of the sisters, Miss An'gel had never been less than impeccably dressed whenever I saw her. She once told me that she and her sister, Miss Dickce, had inherited a large collection of classic haute couture from their mother and grandmother—names like Worth, Chanel, and Balenciaga, among others. Today looked like a Chanel day, I decided, after noting the simple black dress and pearls Miss An'gel wore.

"Come right in, all of you," Miss An'gel said, after first giving Diesel several pats on the head. "Helen Louise, it's lovely to see you away from work and looking so relaxed."

"Thank you, Miss An'gel." Helen Louise laughed. "I need to hear that because I confess I've been having a hard time letting go of the reins."

"Not surprising," Miss An'gel replied as she ushered us through the front door and closed it behind. "You created a highly successful business, and you want to ensure its continued success." She cast a sidelong glance at me. "Now, however, you have a handsome distraction who deserves more of your time, I daresay."

"He certainly does," Helen Louise said. As I began to blush, Helen Louise looked down at my cat. "Don't you, Diesel?"

The cat warbled loudly, and Miss An'gel joined Helen Louise in gentle laughter. I smiled.

"We're in the front parlor." Miss An'gel led the way. "Sister and I are delighted that you could come this afternoon. Our dear friend Ernestine Carpenter has been looking forward to meeting you."

We followed our hostess into the elegant front parlor at Riverhill. After numerous visits here I had become somewhat accustomed to the sight of the furnishings, many of which were well over a century old. Miss Dickce rose from a sofa that faced the door to come forward, hands extended. First Helen Louise, then I, gave her a quick peck on the cheek. Then Miss Dickce focused her attention on Diesel for a moment.

The other occupant of the sofa stood as well. She appeared to be nearly as tall as Helen Louise and I and probably in her early seventies. Perhaps a decade younger than the Ducote sisters, I reckoned. Her shrewd gaze swept over us, and I smiled. She smiled back and stepped forward.

Miss An'gel performed the introductions. Miss Carpenter immediately took a shine to Diesel, and he to her. When she resumed her seat, he sat on the floor by her legs and enjoyed her attention.

"It's a pleasure to meet you, Miss Carpenter," I said, after the first formalities were out of the way, including the obligatory remarks about the weather.

"We have actually met before," Miss Carpenter said, "though I doubt if you remember it because of the occasion. Your aunt, Dottie Collins, was a dear friend of mine. I attended her funeral, and we spoke briefly at the time."

"I'm sorry," I said. "I remember so very little of anything that happened at Aunt Dottie's funeral. I was in such a fog at the time that it is all still a blur in my mind."

Miss Carpenter regarded me with obvious sympathy. "I completely understand. You were overwhelmed, I know. Your wife had passed away not long before that, if I remember correctly."

I managed to nod, too overcome at the moment to say a word. Odd how those sharp, stabbing pangs of grief hit you sometimes and rendered you almost unable to breathe, let alone speak. I closed my eyes briefly, drew in a deep breath, then exhaled and opened my eyes. "Yes, that's correct. I'm glad to get the opportunity to meet you again under happier circumstances."

Miss Carpenter smiled and patted my arm. "I am, too."

I felt able now to resume our conversation. "Miss Carpenter, I understand you are a friend of Jack Pemberton, the true crime writer."

"Yes, I am. Please, call me Ernie." She flashed an attractive grin. "I have a feeling we're going to be friends, and my friends call me Ernie." She patted the sofa beside her.

"I will, if you'll call me Charlie," I said as I joined her. Helen Louise and the Ducote sisters occupied the sofa opposite us, and they were already involved in conversation.

"Done." Ernie gave Diesel a couple more pats on the head. "I do indeed know Jack and his lovely wife, Wanda Nell. Both fine people that I am pleased to call friends."

"Are you aware of Mr. Pemberton's interest in me?" I said.

"Yes, he told me about the project," Ernie replied.

"I read one of his books last night. It was excellent."

"He's an accomplished writer," Ernie said. "I've never been much of a true crime reader myself, but I make an exception for his books."

"I think I will, too," I said. "Though generally I prefer my murders to be fictional."

Ernie chuckled. "Well, not completely fictional, you must admit, Charlie."

It took me a moment to catch on to what she meant, and then I had to laugh. Before I could respond, however, she continued.

"Actually, that's something you and I have in common, along with Wanda Nell and Jack. Murder as a hobby, so to speak."

SEVEN

Murder as a hobby? Those words took me aback. I wasn't quite sure how to respond to Ernie's comment. Apparently my expression revealed my confusion.

"Sorry, Charlie." Ernie frowned. "I didn't mean that to be as crass as it probably sounded. I'm afraid I tend to have a rather dark sense of humor, and it doesn't always translate well."

I nodded to acknowledge that I understood.

She continued, "Like you, I have a few times found myself involved in murder investigations, but not by choice."

I smiled. "I didn't choose to be associated with any of the murders, but generally I didn't see much of an alternative."

"Exactly," Ernie replied, looking relieved. "That's what happened to Wanda Nell and Jack, too, and I tell you this because I think it will help you see that Jack understands your experiences much better than another writer might."

"I see your point," I said. "My main concern is privacy. I prefer to remain out of the limelight. The credit really goes to our local sheriff's department, namely the chief deputy, Kanesha Berry. She's a remarkable woman."

Ernie gazed at me, her expression skeptical. "I suspect you're being far too modest, Charlie, but let's leave it at that. I imagine Jack will want to interview Chief Deputy Berry, but his interest is more in the amateurs who find themselves involved in these cases."

"I'm willing to talk to him to explore the possibility," I said. "I have to be honest, though. On the whole, I think I'm still inclined to keep my accidental sleuthing activities out of the public eye." I decided not to mention to Ernie that the local newspaper had thus far been circumspect about not including my name in articles about homicides in Athena the past several years. That was thanks to the reporter Ray Appleby. He had managed to enhance his own reputation, thanks to me, because Kanesha gave him exclusives on the cases. They both won acclaim, and I got to stay behind the scenes—exactly as I preferred. And now I was considering stepping into the public eye. Was I really ready for that?

Ernie regarded me, her eyes narrowed, and I began to feel uncomfortable. She didn't appear pleased with me.

"Frankly, I think you aren't quite ready to talk to Jack yet, Charlie." Her expression softened. "Even though you just said you are willing, I don't think you're comfortable with that decision. Am I right?"

She had read me well. I nodded. "You're right. I'm still uneasy at the thought of being in the public eye suddenly."

Ernie chuckled, and that surprised me. "We're back to the beginning, then. When I get back to Tullahoma, I can tell Jack that I met you and explain how you feel. He will probably try again, however, to persuade you."

"That's okay," I said. "In the meantime I'll think about it, and I might come to feel differently."

"No harm done either way," Ernie said.

"Thanks."

"Don't worry." Ernie flashed a smile before she focused her attention on the conversation going on across the coffee table.

I leaned back and let the conversation flow around me. I soon became engrossed in my own thoughts. I felt relieved that Ernie understood my hesitation, but underneath I felt foolish. Surely I was old enough by now to know my own mind? Why was I having trouble making a firm decision?

Perhaps subconsciously I wanted the attention that would come if the public knew more about my role in the investigations in which I had assisted. Had I been hoping for that all along? Had I been suppressing a desire for acclaim?

Much of this indecision had to do with my upbringing. My parents had always been proud of my achievements. I had made good grades in school and had graduated second in my high school class. I had even acquitted myself well in sports, though I never had the talent to play beyond high school. My parents had taught me that a gentleman, a man of honor, doesn't push himself forward in order to get attention. His behavior and his deeds should speak for themselves. A man who goes around calling attention to himself, seeking glory, is no gentleman. And to my parents, not being a gentleman was a bad thing indeed.

I had instilled the same beliefs in my children, and I found it somewhat ironic that my daughter had chosen to be an actress. Laura hadn't performed simply for the sake of attention, I knew. She loved the art and the craft of assuming a role and bringing that character to life. If she had valued empty attention and accolades beyond other things, she never would have decided to become a teacher and stay in Athena with her husband to raise a family.

Sean was thriving as a small-town lawyer. He had quickly come to hate practicing corporate law in Houston. Here in Athena he knew he was helping people who needed honest legal counsel, not a huge corporation, and that brought him great satisfaction. I was proud of him for his dedication to his work and to his family.

Helen Louise called me out of my reverie, and I became aware that Clementine, the Ducotes' housekeeper, stood by me with a tray of cake and cookies.

"I'm sorry, Clementine." I picked up a dessert plate from the tray and helped myself to a small slice of cheesecake and two chocolate chip cookies. "I was off in my own little world." *That is an understatement*, I thought. The way my mind meandered these days surprised me, hopping from one thought to the next like a frog in a jumping contest.

Clementine chuckled. "Not to worry. You just enjoy." She set the dessert tray down on the coffee table and picked up the tea tray. "I'll be back with more tea in a minute."

"Thank you, Clementine," Miss An'gel said. "Now, Charlie, what had you looking so perturbed? I wish you could have seen the frown you were giving us."

"Looked awful serious to me," Miss Dickce said. "Whatever it was."

"My apologies, ladies." I glanced at Helen Louise and could see she was holding back a smile. I figured she knew what I had been fretting over. "I hope I didn't alarm you. I was simply thinking about, well . . ." I paused for a moment as I sought the best way to express myself without being overly personal. "About having been raised by my parents to be reticent about certain things."

"Behaving like a gentleman, in other words, and not putting yourself forward unnecessarily," Ernie said.

She was a bit unnerving, I decided, the way she could read my thoughts, not to mention the way she cut right to the heart of things. I nodded. "More or less."

"Nothing wrong with that." Miss An'gel sniffed. "Far too many people these days have no concept of manners or decent behavior."

"And far too many other people think it's their business what everyone else is doing," Miss Dickce said.

"That's how small towns work and probably always have." Helen Louise smiled as she reached for a cookie from the dessert tray.

Diesel, who had been extraordinarily quiet for several minutes now, must have decided to add his thoughts to the conversation right then. He sat up and emitted a couple of loud meows, followed by a trill. Then he went back to his relaxed position on the rug, having had his say.

Miss An'gel and Miss Dickce exchanged amused looks, while Ernie Carpenter laughed aloud. "I don't think I've ever heard a cat talk like that before. I'm sure he was agreeing with y'all."

"He usually has to put in his two meows' worth." I grinned and shook my head.

Miss An'gel, perhaps sensing my discomfort at having the conversation focused on me, changed the subject. "Speaking of gentlemen, Ernie, didn't you tell us that young cousin of yours, Andy, I believe, has recently published a book?"

"He certainly has," Ernie said. "His dissertation has been published." She glanced at me, then at Helen Louise.

"He has a doctorate in medieval history, and he and his partner live in Houston where they both teach. I don't have a copy of the book yet, but I'm heading to Houston soon for a visit and will get one while I'm there."

Helen Louise and I both said the appropriate things, and Ernie and the Ducotes talked about cousin Andy and his book for a few minutes. I noticed Helen Louise glance at her watch a couple of times, and I got the signal. Time for us to be going.

When a lull came in the conversation, I explained that we must be heading out. I thanked the sisters, as did Helen Louise, and expressed delight again at having met Ernie Carpenter. A few minutes later, after Diesel had been appropriately noticed and petted, the three of us headed for the car and drove back home.

We had barely reached the end of the long driveway at Riverhill before Helen Louise brought up the subject that had been exercising my mind most of the afternoon.

"You've been having second thoughts about being a part of this book," she said.

"Second, third, fourth, and so on," I said. "I thought that talking to Miss Carpenter and hearing more about the writer would help me make up my mind to go ahead with it, but I keep shying away from it."

"Because of the way you were raised," Helen Louise said. "I understand that, believe me. My parents were the same way."

"So what should I do?"

"I think you should go ahead and talk to the writer," she replied. "If you don't, you'll always wonder. Besides, he could go ahead with the project without your permission. If he really wants to, he can find a way around it."

"And then I would find myself in the invidious position of being damned if I do *or* don't," I said. "Take legal action to stop him, thereby bringing the attention upon myself that I didn't want in the first place."

"Yes, I'm afraid so." Helen Louise's tone expressed her sympathy for my position.

I sighed. "I guess I'll e-mail him and tell him I'm willing to meet with him, then."

"It will all work out okay," Helen Louise said. "Ernie Carpenter seems to think a lot of him, and Miss An'gel and Miss Dickce obviously have great affection and respect for Ernie. We both have tremendous respect for the Ducote sisters and their intelligence. So, if you follow my chain of reasoning, Jack Pemberton ought to be a stand-up kind of guy."

"I don't think that reasoning would hold up in court," I said. "But for now I guess I'm going to have to believe that you're right."

My parents would have understood that reasoning, and for the most part I did, too. I had to hope that Jack Pemberton, via Ernie, via the Ducote sisters, didn't put the lie to it.

EIGHT

I e-mailed Jack Pemberton before I went to bed that night, and the next morning I had a response. He explained that he was teaching summer school at the community college and that it would be difficult for him to come to Athena during most of the week. He was free on Friday, if that suited me. I e-mailed back to say that Friday was fine. He could come to the public library, and we could talk during the time I usually took my lunch hour. That worked for him, and so our meeting was set.

During the week I had plenty to occupy my time and thoughts besides the upcoming meeting with Jack Pemberton. I worked my three days in the archives at Athena College. There were two graduate students in the history department using materials from the archives for their dissertations, and they took up some of my time because I had to supervise their use of documents. Diesel, when he wasn't sleeping in the window behind my desk, visited them to check their progress and to offer encouraging chirps and trills. Luckily they were both amenable to that, and I didn't have to leave Diesel at home while they worked or try to keep him away from them. He had learned as a younger kitty not to jump on the tables where they were working, and I was thankful to have a well-behaved feline.

The college library's new director, Andrea Thomas, had a warm and ebullient personality. She had been on the job since the first of June, and thus far all the staff seemed to have taken to her well. I liked her, not least because she made no fuss about Diesel's continuing to accompany me to work. She quickly earned the official seal of approval from my friend, Melba Gilley, who had been the Athena director's administrative assistant for more than a decade.

"She's smart," Melba told me after Andrea's first week. "Plus she's even better organized than I am." That was saying a lot, because Melba had always been the best organized person I ever knew.

With Andrea at the helm the library had now settled back into a happy, efficient rhythm after seven months of uncertainty and turmoil. I had no regrets at turning down the offer to be the director. Now with baby Charlie on the scene and another grandchild soon to appear, I had other ways to spend my time. I would keep working at the archive as long as I continued to enjoy what I was doing, and then I would happily retire. One of these days.

By Thursday evening, with my workweek at the college library complete, I began once more to let my thoughts focus on tomorrow's meeting with the writer. I had not made a final decision, but I was leaning toward declining to participate.

When Diesel and I left home the next morning for our day at the public library, Laura and baby Charlie were in the kitchen with Azalea. I hated to leave the house while my grandson was there, but I would see him over the weekend. Diesel stayed by Charlie's side until it was time to go.

Teresa Farmer greeted us at the door and let us inside. A few minutes later, we opened the front doors, and several patrons entered. Among them was Bill Delaney. He nodded in my direction after I caught his eye, but he made a beeline for the chair in a far corner, the same chair he had used every time I had worked at the library during his visits.

This morning, instead of working at the reference desk, I was cataloging and processing new books purchased from funds raised by the Friends of Athena Public Library. Their generosity and tireless efforts made a huge difference in the amount and variety of resources the library had to offer. The state library commission did its best, but lack of proper funding meant limited resources for the many public libraries across the state.

Diesel stayed with me for a few minutes before he evidently decided that he would get more attention if he assisted Teresa at the reference desk. I knew Teresa would keep an eye on him and not let him get into mischief or let him be mishandled by anyone.

I worked steadily until eleven fifteen. Jack Pemberton was due to meet me at eleven thirty. I had e-mailed Teresa last night to tell her I was expecting a visitor to discuss a project. I hadn't told her what the project was, and she didn't press me for details even though I knew she was curious.

I joined Teresa and Diesel at the reference desk.

"He's been a good boy," Teresa said.

Diesel meowed to agree, and both Teresa and I smiled. We chatted for a couple of minutes, until a patron came to the desk for help with a database. I remained there while

Teresa followed the patron back to the computer she was using.

At eleven twenty-five, a tall, lean, bespectacled man entered the library. He appeared to be in his midforties, roughly a decade younger than I. I recognized him from the author photo in the book I had read. He approached the reference desk.

"Good morning, Mr. Pemberton," I said. "I'm Charlie Harris."

"Good morning, Mr. Harris," he replied as he extended a hand. "It's a pleasure to meet you. I appreciate you agreeing to meet with me to discuss my proposal."

"Glad to do it," I said. "If you'll follow me, we can talk about it in the back, in the staff-only area." I moved from behind the desk, and Diesel came with me.

Jack Pemberton smiled. "So this is your famous sidekick. He's a beautiful animal. I'm afraid I've forgotten his name, though."

"Diesel," I replied.

Diesel sniffed Pemberton's extended fingers, then butted his head against the man's hand. He warbled, which was his sign of approval. Pemberton had passed one important test without knowing it. Diesel appeared to like him.

"Nice to meet you, too, Diesel," Pemberton said as we continued into the staff area. I pointed the writer to a seat by the desk where I worked. Diesel remained near him while I made myself comfortable behind the desk.

I offered my guest a bottle of water, and he accepted. After he had a drink, he capped the bottle and set it on the floor by his chair.

"Thanks," Pemberton said. "I know you have questions for me, but I thought I would start by giving you a more detailed description of the project I have in mind."

I nodded. "Yes, please do."

Diesel meowed, and the writer chuckled. "I guess your assistant is ready to hear more about it, too. I know you met a good friend of my wife's and mine on Sunday, Ernie Carpenter." After I nodded again, he continued, "I'm sure Ernie mentioned that Wanda Nell, my wife, and I also have some experience as amateurs involved in murder investigations. Wanda Nell and I haven't sought publicity for our part in these cases before now, and we're still not. I believe you said you had read one of my books?"

"Yes, *Hell Has No Fury*," I replied. "I thoroughly enjoyed it. I have to say that it was the first true crime book I've ever read. You write well, and I liked the fact that you didn't sensationalize the truly tragic aspects of the case the way other writers might have done."

"Thank you." Pemberton smiled. "I think the facts in these cases are dramatic enough in themselves, and reporting them is enough to make the point. My approach is the same in each of the books I've written so far, and I don't plan to deviate from that. Based on my research into some of the cases here in Athena, I'd say the facts of them are pretty dramatic, so they don't need embellishment. The same is true of the cases Wanda Nell and I have been involved with."

My take thus far on Jake Pemberton was that he was a forthright, down-to-earth person. A *stand-up guy*, to use Helen Louise's term. I thought him sincere in what he said about his work and his approach toward it. Because of this, I felt more relaxed with him. My reservations about participating in the project had begun to waver.

Pemberton reached for his bottle and drank more water. "What I propose to do—and, of course, my publisher would have to approve, or I won't be doing the book—is write about these cases and bring in the aspects of how amateur sleuths assisted the police. I'd like to write about two or three of them per book."

"So you're thinking of a series of books, then," I said.

"Yes," Pemberton said. "All these cases are interesting, but they're not the long, drawn-out kind that I've written about before. I don't think they need the full-length-book treatment."

"That makes sense," I said. "I have to say that I find your approach to this interesting. My only real concern in this is that I don't want to find myself in the spotlight afterward. I don't want the attention this could bring."

"Understood," Pemberton replied. "Wanda Nell and I don't want that kind of attention, either. For that reason I am not intending to use real names. I would give you a pseudonym, just like I will be giving myself and my wife."

"That's fine, up to a point," I said. "But there will be people who read the books who will recognize the cases, of course. They might also know enough to recognize the real identities of the amateurs involved."

"That's true," Pemberton said. "I can't do anything about that, so there is still a risk involved. There is another issue, though, that could affect this project. I don't know about the attitude of local law enforcement in Athena, but in Tullahoma I know they're not going to be eager to acknowledge the roles that Wanda Nell or I might have played in bringing the killers to justice. They want the credit for that, and for the most part, I think they deserve it."

"I agree with you on that," I said. "Chief Deputy Berry, who is the chief homicide investigator here, is a smart, capable officer. We haven't always gotten along well, but we managed to work out our differences. I wouldn't want her to think that I suddenly decided I wanted all the credit for the work she and her officers have done in the past."

"I understand," Pemberton replied. "And the same for

me and my wife. This project has a number of hurdles, and I have to see if I can get over them before it can go forward. I haven't broached the idea with my agent and my editor yet, and they could very well tell me not to go forward with it."

Until now I'd had the impression that Pemberton was ready to get started, once he had my permission. Frankly I was relieved to hear that not everything was settled yet.

"What do you think?" the writer asked. "Will you co-operate with me, if I get the go-ahead on this?"

I hesitated before I replied. "I have to be honest with you. I'm still uneasy over the situation, but if you can get the go-ahead from Chief Deputy Berry, then I will participate, too."

Pemberton smiled. "Thank you, Mr. Harris. I'm delighted to have you on board. Luckily I was able to arrange a meeting with the chief deputy for this afternoon. I have some time to kill. Could I treat you to lunch?"

"Thank you, that's kind of you, but I brought my lunch today," I said. "I'll be working here until three. If you need a recommendation for a place to eat, I can recommend the French bistro on the square." I rose from my chair.

Pemberton stood. "I've eaten there before. Great food. Thanks for reminding me." He extended his hand again, and we shook.

"Let me walk out with you," I said. Diesel accompanied us.

"I'll be in touch," Pemberton said when we neared the door. He gave Diesel a couple of pats on the head before he exited.

"Nice guy," I said, and Diesel warbled. "Come on, time for lunch." I turned back toward the staff area, but we had moved only a few steps before Bill Delaney approached me.

"Sorry to bother you," he said. "Can we talk somewhere private for a few minutes?" He looked away, then his gaze focused on me again. He had his hands shoved into his pants pockets.

I wondered what was making him so uneasy. "Sure, come on back with me." Diesel trotted ahead, and I guided Delaney to the work area. "Have a seat, and tell me what's on your mind." I indicated the chair that Jack Pemberton had vacated only a few minutes ago.

Delaney nodded and removed his hands from his pockets. He perched on the edge of the chair, and I could see he was still uneasy about something. Diesel came to sit by my legs behind the desk. I think he had picked up on Delaney's emotional state, and it was making him a little uneasy, too.

Delaney looked at me for a moment, then stared down at his hands. He didn't look up when he began to speak.

"I found out that you live in that house," he said. "The one I asked about that used to belong to Delbert Collins." He raised his head, and I could see that he was confused.

"Yes, I do," I said. "My aunt was married to Delbert Collins, and that was their home. When she died, she left it to me."

Delaney nodded. "Figured you might be kin some kind of way to one of them."

"I didn't tell you before," I said, "because frankly I wasn't sure what your reason was for being so interested in the house."

"I understand," Delaney replied. "I'll tell you why now. Delbert Collins was my father."

NINE

||||||||||||||||||||||||||||||||

Bill Delaney's revelation surprised me. He had originally said his mother and Uncle Del were friends, and I had seen no reason to doubt that. I could understand why he hadn't told me the full story before. Until he knew of my connection to Uncle Del, his past really was none of my business.

"I wasn't aware that Uncle Del had any children," I said. "I can't remember my aunt ever mentioning a son or a daughter." I knew she would have loved to have had a child, even a stepchild, to lavish love and attention on after the loss they suffered.

"I'm pretty sure he never knew about me," Delaney said.

That was even more surprising. How could Uncle Del not know he had a son? Another thought followed swiftly on that one. Maybe he never had a son, and Bill Delaney was trying to deceive me for some reason.

"How could he not know?" I asked in a neutral tone.

"He and my mother were married for about six months," Delaney said. "Guess they found out they couldn't stand each other, though according to what my mama told me, they were desperate to get married. But he walked out on her, and she didn't find out she was pregnant until a month later."

"Surely she would have let him know," I said. "Are you sure she didn't?"

Delaney shrugged. "You'd'a had to know my mama. The Lord never created anybody stubborner than her. The way she told it, she wasn't going to go running after him and try to get him back just because she was going to have a baby. Far as I know she never saw him again."

"When you were old enough, did you try to find him?"

"Didn't know his name," Delaney said. "Mama wouldn't tell me. That's why my last name is Delaney. She went back to her maiden name right away. Wouldn't talk about him. Threw away anything that had to do with him. Every picture she had except one. That's what she told me."

"How did you find out who he was?" This story sounded like something out of a melodrama.

"Mama only died three months ago," Delaney said. "She was ninety-two. I found their marriage license in an old shoe box with some other papers. There was his name, Delbert Collins."

"You originally told me that Uncle Del and your mother had once been friends," I said.

Delaney nodded. "I had to think of something to explain why I was interested in where he lived. I didn't want to go around telling strangers I was his son. At least not until I knew whether he was still living or not."

I had watched him closely as he told me his story, and he came across as completely sincere. I have always fancied myself as a good judge of character, but I have been fooled before. I thought he was probably telling me the truth, at least as he knew it, but I wasn't going to accept his story without concrete proof.

I thought about how to phrase the question I intended to ask, but I couldn't come up with a tactful way to do it. If he was telling me the truth, he shouldn't be offended, I realized.

"Do you have the birth certificate with you?" I asked.

"In my bag," Delaney said. "I left it by the chair I've been sitting in." He rose. "I'll go get it and be right back."

After he left the room I looked down at Diesel and found him regarding me with what I called his serious expression.

"What do you think, boy?" I asked in a low tone. "Is he telling us the truth?"

Diesel meowed, and I interpreted that as a yes.

"I think he probably is, too," I said, "but until I know for sure, and know exactly what it is he's after, I think *caution* is the watchword."

Diesel meowed again, and I rubbed his head.

While we waited for Delaney to return, I realized I felt hungry and ready to have my lunch. I was such a creature of habit. I had my routine, and I liked to stick to it. My lunch hour was nearly over, and I might have to skip eating, though I would give Diesel his tidbits. I couldn't sit and have a meal in front of Bill Delaney when he didn't have anything to eat himself. I decided, however, that missing a meal would do me no harm.

Delaney returned and handed me a folded document before he resumed his seat. He set his bag down beside him. I accepted the paper and opened it gently. The paper looked new. The birth certificate must have been kept in the shoe box and rarely ever removed all these years.

According to the date on it, Bill Delaney would be sixty-six this coming December.

"I see you were born in Tullahoma County," I said. The county and its county seat, both named Tullahoma, lay only about a two-hour drive southwest of Athena. He had lived so close to his father yet had never met him. There was a sad irony in that.

"Lived there most of my life," Delaney said. "Except for the time I spent in the service. Marine Corps. Eight years."

I heard the note of pride in his voice when he mentioned his branch of the service. My father had served in the Marines in World War II, and he, too, had always been proud of that.

I nodded before I turned my attention back to the birth certificate. I found the parents' names and ages. Sylvia Delaney, age twenty-five, and Delbert Collins, age thirty. I had no idea when Uncle Del was born, though I knew he was a few years older than Aunt Dottie. She would have been eighty-eight this year.

The certificate looked legitimate. At the moment I had to accept it at face value. "Thank you for showing it to me." I handed the paper back to Delaney.

Delaney nodded. He folded his certificate and placed it in a pocket in his bag. "Can you tell me anything about him? I haven't been able to find out much in the newspapers here."

"I'm afraid I don't have a lot to tell you," I said, "but I'm happy to share what I can. You see, he died when I was about nine or ten. My memories of him are pretty hazy."

"Whatever you can remember is surely more than I know now," Delaney said.

I could feel the sadness in him, and I suddenly imagined

myself in his place. How would I feel if I had never known my father? I figured I, too, would want to know as much as I could, especially if he weren't around for me to meet and talk to in person.

"He was an invalid," I said. "Frankly, I don't know exactly what the problem was, other than supposedly a weak heart. I remember that when I went to visit them, Uncle Del was usually in his room resting. I wasn't supposed to make any loud noises that might startle or upset him." I smiled briefly. "For me that wasn't a problem, because my aunt had lots of books. I spent most of my visits with her reading."

"He didn't have a job?" Delaney frowned.

I shook my head. "Not that I ever knew. I was always told he was too sick to work. Aunt Dottie worked, though, and took care of him. She had help, of course. They always had a housekeeper who would look after him while my aunt was at work."

In the back of my mind I was having cynical thoughts. I wondered whether Delaney was angling to find out if Uncle Del had had any money. Was he hoping for an inheritance of some kind? If he was, he was bound to be disappointed. Aunt Dottie earned all the money and paid all the expenses, including the mortgage. The house was in her name, which was unusual for the time. After Uncle Del died, she invested money and invested wisely. She became moderately wealthy because of her own hard work and good business sense. She left everything to me. Bill Delaney had no viable claim on her estate.

Even if he wasn't angling for money, I knew he did want to know more about his father. That I could do something about. Aunt Dottie had kept photograph albums over the years, and there were probably numerous pictures of Uncle Del. There might also be some mementos of him that she had kept. I had several boxes of her things stowed away in a closet. Azalea could help me go through them to see whether there was anything that belonged to Uncle Del. I would be happy for Bill Delaney to have such things.

"How would you like to come to my house for dinner tomorrow evening? I imagine there are pictures of your father in my aunt's photo albums, and you're welcome to some of them, if you'd like to have them." I decided not to mention the possibility of personal items because I didn't want him to end up disappointed should there prove to be none.

Delaney's face lit briefly with a smile. "That's mighty kind of you. I'll take you up on the offer of dinner, too. It'll be real nice to have a meal with someone for a change."

"I'm glad you can come," I said. "How about six? Will that time work for you?"

"That'll be fine," Delaney replied. "I have the address."

"Do you need a ride?" I asked. "I'd be happy to pick you up and take you home again afterward."

"I thank you, but I'll find my way there," Delaney said. "No need to put you to any extra trouble." He picked up his bag and stood.

"Okay, but the offer's still on the table if you change your mind." I got to my feet since it was evident he was ready to go.

Delaney smiled briefly. "See you tomorrow evening."

Diesel came from behind the desk and warbled loudly as if he were adding his invitation to mine. Delaney reached out with a hesitant hand and touched the cat's head. When Diesel warbled again, he stroked the cat briefly. Then Delaney ducked his head in a gesture of farewell and walked out of the office.

"We don't have much time left for lunch, boy," I told the cat. "We'd better eat. Is that okay with you?"

Diesel answered with two loud, assertive meows. I laughed as I retrieved our lunch from the fridge in the staff kitchen. Diesel accompanied me there and back again to the desk. I fed him bites of boiled chicken while I ate my sandwich and a banana.

My thoughts turned to Bill Delaney again. The first thing I wanted to do when I got home was dig out one of those photo albums and look at pictures of Uncle Del. To save my life, I couldn't recall his face clearly at the moment. If Bill Delaney looked like Uncle Del, then that would be a clincher as far as I was concerned.

I felt sorry for the man. My father had been a good, hardworking man who sometimes had difficulty showing his emotions, but I knew he loved me and was proud of me. As an adult and a father myself, I appreciated him even more for all the things he taught me about fatherhood without my ever having realized it.

I hoped there would be some things of Uncle Del's that my aunt kept. It would be nice if there were something concrete for Delaney to have as a physical connection to his father. But if there were no mementos, he would at least be able to see where his father had lived.

Where his father had lived. The words resonated in my mind. I recalled that, according to the information in our patron database, Delaney lived in a small apartment in a shabby area of town. As my uncle's son—my step-first-cousin, I supposed—should I do more for him?

I thought then about what Aunt Dottie would have done in this situation.

She would have opened her door and welcomed him in to stay. That's what she would have done.

Could I do any less?

TEN

‖‖‖‖‖‖‖‖‖‖‖‖‖

The afternoon passed quickly. I helped patrons with their questions and also spent another couple of hours cataloging. All the while I concentrated on the task at hand, in the back of my mind I kept coming back to that one thought: Should I really consider inviting a stranger into my home? I felt sorry for the man because I figured his living conditions were probably not comfortable, perhaps even unsafe. Over and above that, though, I felt a sense of obligation to my aunt and her principles of charity and inclusiveness.

My parents had reared me to do what I could for those who needed help, and my aunt had reinforced those lessons by her actions. She was a tireless worker through her church, slowing down only when the cancer that took her life made her too weak to leave her bed. I had no doubt what my aunt would do in this situation.

The question was, did I have the courage—and the spirit of charity—to do the same?

By the time Diesel and I were in the car and on our way home, I had made my decision. I would offer Bill Delaney one of the vacant bedrooms on the second floor. Now that both Sean and Laura had vacated their rooms, I had plenty of space for another person. There was the possibility, of course, that Delaney would decline my offer. I would simply have to wait and see what transpired tomorrow evening.

Once we were home, I left Diesel to visit the utility room and headed for the den. I wanted to look through Aunt Dottie's old photograph albums and find pictures of Uncle Del. Would Bill Delaney bear any resemblance to him? If he did, that would explain the niggling sense of familiarity about him that I had felt from the first time I saw him.

I opened the cabinet and pulled out one of the albums from more than fifty years ago when Aunt Dottie and Uncle Del were first married. I sat at the desk, turned on the desk lamp, and opened the album. I thumbed through several pages until I found a photo from the time right after they were married and settling into life together in this house.

I stared at it. Aunt Dottie and Uncle Del, both in their early thirties, stared back at me. Aunt Dottie was smiling while Uncle Del looked somber. I recalled him as a quiet man who hadn't had much to do with me because of his invalid status, and he died when I was nine or ten. My memories of him had been dimmed by time, but I got a shock as I examined his face more closely.

No wonder Bill Delaney had seemed familiar. He looked like an older version of Uncle Del. I went back to the cabinet and found an album from the year I was eight years old. It took me only a minute to find a picture of an older Uncle Del, worn down by his poor health. The likeness between Bill Delaney and my uncle was even more striking.

I closed the albums and put them away, my mind buzzing the whole time. The implication seemed clear. Bill Delaney was definitely related to Uncle Del. With a likeness that striking he probably was my uncle's son. With my aunt and my parents gone, there was no one else I knew who knew Uncle Del or might know more about his past before he married my aunt.

No, that wasn't correct, I realized. There was one person who might know. Azalea Berry had worked for my aunt for many years before Aunt Dottie died and after she became a widow. Azalea knew more about Aunt Dottie than anyone else. I wouldn't see Azalea again until Monday, but could I wait that long to talk to her? I didn't like calling and disturbing her on her days off unless it was an emergency. I couldn't really call this an emergency, could I?

After dithering over it for over a minute, I decided I had to call. Otherwise I would have to wait until Monday morning, spending the weekend fretting over all this. I had better things to do with my time, not to mention my mental energy. Laura and Frank were bringing my grandson over tomorrow for me to look after while they went out to lunch and a movie. I didn't want to be distracted while he was in my care. I pulled out my cell phone, found Azalea's name in my contacts, and called her.

The call went to voice mail, and I left a brief message asking her to return my call at her convenience. I stressed there was no urgency, that I simply had a question I wanted to ask about my aunt's husband.

That done, I realized I was hungry and ready for my dinner. I found Diesel in the kitchen, waiting by the refrigerator. He knew what time it was, and he was hopeful that there was more chicken lurking inside the big white box. He meowed three times to let me know how near starvation he was, then threw in a few sad chirps to emphasize his dire state.

"You really are a fraud, you know." I shook my head. "I know if I went into the utility room right now and checked your bowl there will probably be plenty of dry food in it."

Diesel regarded me with what I would label a solemn expression. He meowed loudly, and I understood that to mean that dry food was not adequate—as it so often wasn't, because someone had become spoiled by being given too many tidbits from the table.

I had to laugh. The cat knew how to work me, and pretty much everyone else around him, to get what he wanted. I did keep an eye on his weight because I didn't want to have Diesel's veterinarian fussing at me for letting him get fat. The problem was that I couldn't always resist these little performances of his.

According to the note I found on the refrigerator door, Stewart and Haskell were out again this evening. "Looks like it's just you and me tonight, boy," I told the cat. I opened the door and took out the pot of meat sauce Azalea had prepared. I set it on the stove to warm up, then found the pot I needed to cook the pasta.

While the pasta cooked, I made myself a small salad. Diesel chirped at frequent intervals to remind me that his situation remained serious since I had yet to provide anything for him. He couldn't have any of the meat sauce because of the garlic and onions in it, but there was more of the boiled chicken for him.

The pasta was ready before my cat expired from hunger. I enjoyed my meal thoroughly while I doled out bites of chicken to Diesel. All the while, in the back of my mind, I was urging Azalea to return my call. My curiosity was going to get the better of me.

My cell phone rang when I was nearly through cleaning up after my dinner. I put my plate in the dishwasher, shut the door, and then retrieved my phone. I was happy to see that the caller was Azalea.

After a quick exchange of greetings, and my repeated assurance that everything was fine, I told Azalea a little about Bill Delaney and his relationship to Uncle Del. I also mentioned the strong resemblance between the two men.

"Did he have any relatives that you know of?" I asked.

"Not that I can recall," Azalea said. "Miss Dottie talked about him sometimes, but I can't say she ever mentioned he had any family. She sure didn't ever mention he had a son. You say he looks like Mr. Del?"

"Yes, he does. They're obviously related."

"Miss Dottie did tell me one thing about Mr. Del," Azalea said. "She did tell me he had been married before, but he and his first wife couldn't get along. So they got divorced. Your grandparents weren't happy about her marrying a divorced man."

I remembered my grandmother, who died when I was fifteen. She had been old-fashioned about many things, divorce included.

"Your grandmama had conniptions, Miss Dottie said, but she and your granddaddy finally gave in."

"That fits in with what Bill Delaney told me," I said. "He said Uncle Del walked out after about six months and never knew his wife was pregnant."

"Miss Dottie never knew a thing about a son, I can tell you that," Azalea said. "She would have loved having a child, even a stepchild, to take care of."

"Yes, I'm sure she would have." I hesitated a moment, not sure whether I was ready to confide my plan to Azalea.

Then I realized that she had the right to know that there could potentially be another person living in the house. "I think she would want me to do what I can for him, don't you?" I told her about where he lived and my concern that his living conditions weren't good.

"She would," Azalea said. "Miss Dottie was a saint walking on this earth, sure enough. I won't mind a bit having another man in the house, but I reckon Miss Dottie wouldn't want you to do it if you don't feel like it would be safe."

"I've invited him for dinner tomorrow evening," I said. "That will give me a chance to get to know him a little better." A thought occurred to me, and I shared it with Azalea. "I haven't asked him whether he intends to stay in Athena. He's from Tullahoma originally, and for all I know he might have a home there that he's planning to go back to."

"That's true," Azalea said. "He might not be looking to stay here for long, just till he finds out what he wants to know about his daddy."

"I can't tell him much more myself," I said. "I can show him Aunt Dottie's photograph albums and let him have some of those photos, if he likes. I don't really know much at all about Uncle Del because he died when I was so young."

"I didn't know him myself," Azalea said. "Miss Dottie'd been widowed for several years before I came to work for her." She fell silent for a moment. "I'll be thinking on it, see if I can come up with somebody who might have known him."

"I should have thought of that myself," I said. "I wonder, do you think Miss An'gel and Miss Dickce might have known him?"

"They might have," Azalea said.

"I'll talk to them," I said. "Thank you, Azalea. I appreciate your help with this."

"Can't say I helped all that much, but you're mighty welcome."

I ended the call and set the phone aside. I thought about calling Miss An'gel to ask her about Uncle Del, but I decided it could wait until tomorrow.

Before I went any further with this idea of mine, I wanted to discuss it with Helen Louise. The problem was that by the time I could talk to her tonight, she would be exhausted from a long day at the bistro. She would also be up pretty early tomorrow morning to go in for another long day.

This was one of the frustrations in our relationship. I valued Helen Louise's opinion, particularly on a decision this important, but I wouldn't have time to discuss it thoroughly with her before Bill Delaney showed up for dinner tomorrow evening.

I could always postpone the dinner until Sunday evening, I reckoned. But other than going to his apartment and knocking on his door, I had no way of getting in touch with Delaney. I doubted he had a landline phone. Then I realized he would most likely be at the library tomorrow. I could talk to him there and see if he was amenable to changing the date.

With that settled, I decided I was ready for some quiet time with a book. Diesel followed me upstairs, and we settled in for the night. It took some effort, but I pushed all thoughts of Bill Delaney out of my mind. There would be time enough tomorrow to think about him and any potential repercussions of inviting him to stay here.

ELEVEN

||||||||||||||||||||||||||||||||||||||||||||||

All night long I dreamed of having strange people in the house. Nothing terrible happened, at least nothing that I could recall when I awoke briefly after one of the dreams. Yet when I finally woke, ready to start the day, I felt uneasy, and it took me a while to shake that off. During my nightly call with Helen Louise, I forbore to mention Bill Delaney because I didn't want to keep Helen Louise on the phone when she needed rest. Perhaps if I had been able to discuss the matter thoroughly with her, though, I wouldn't have gone to sleep with subconscious doubts eating away at me.

One point hit me when I woke up. I had recently met two people from Tullahoma who might have knowledge of Bill Delaney. Ernie Carpenter and Jack Pemberton had lived there all their lives, and they might know him or know something about him. Tullahoma wasn't a big town, not as big as Athena, anyway.

I decided I would e-mail Jack Pemberton this morning

and inquire whether he knew anything about my prospective houseguest and alleged step-cousin. Later on I might call Ernie Carpenter. Since she and my aunt had been good friends, she might know something about my uncle Del as well. He might have been from Tullahoma himself for all I knew.

Diesel ran downstairs ahead of me, no doubt eager to get to his litter box. I retrieved the newspaper from the front yard before I headed into the kitchen to make the coffee. To my delight I discovered the coffee already made, thanks to Stewart. He had his head in the fridge, and I called out a "Good morning" to let him know I was there. He started slightly, almost banging his head as he withdrew it. He pivoted to return my greeting before delving into the fridge again.

I poured myself some coffee and, paper in hand, seated myself in my usual spot at the table. I glanced at the main headlines on the front page of the paper. All pertained to local matters, none of which sounded particularly intriguing.

Stewart emerged from his foray into the fridge with the egg carton, a bag of shredded cheese, and a pint of milk. He set everything on the counter. "How are you this morning, Charlie?" he asked when he turned to face me.

"Doing fine," I said. "And you?"

"The same," Stewart replied. "I'm about to scramble eggs for breakfast for Haskell and me. Can I throw a couple more in for you?"

"Yes, thanks," I said. "What can I do to help?" Stewart sometimes allowed me to assist him but most of the time he preferred to do everything himself.

"How about making the toast?" he said. "Two pieces of buttered wheat toast each for Haskell and me."

"I can do that." I waited until he had whipped up the

eggs and poured them into the skillet before I started on the toast.

Diesel ambled in from the utility room and meowed loudly. He halted his progress near Stewart and looked up at him adoringly. He warbled to let Stewart know he was hungry and in desperate need of scrambled eggs with cheese.

Stewart laughed. "They'll be ready soon, I promise. I'll let you have a couple of bites, never fear."

Diesel chirped his thanks. He remained near Stewart until the eggs were done.

By the time Stewart had the eggs plated, I was finished with the toast. I set it on the table. "Do you need to call Haskell down?" I asked.

"No," Stewart said. "He's in the backyard with Dante letting him do his business and run around a bit. If you wouldn't mind getting out the jam and utensils, I'll go let him know the food is ready." He headed out of the kitchen, Diesel right on his heels, despite the fact that there was food on the table.

I retrieved two kinds of jam from the fridge, Azalea's homemade blackberry and a store brand of grape. I knew Haskell always wanted the latter, while Stewart and I usually went for the homemade. By the time I had utensils and napkins on the table, the two men and the two pets returned.

"Good morning," Haskell said. I returned the greeting.

Dante, Stewart's toy poodle, barked and ran to me to be petted, and as soon as I had patted his head a couple of times, he dashed back to his best friend, Diesel. The cat outweighed the dog by at least twenty-five pounds and towered over him. Dante adored Diesel, and while Diesel seemed fond enough of the dog, he occasionally got tired of the slobbering affection.

Right now both pets knew there was food to be had,

and they settled down as we three humans took our seats at the table. Diesel and Dante took up positions on either side of Stewart's chair, aware that he was the easiest touch. Stewart laughed and gave each of them a bit of cheesy scrambled egg.

"When will Justin be back?" Stewart asked. He referred to my other boarder, Justin Wardlaw, who was a student at Athena College. He was currently vacationing in the Caribbean with his father and half siblings.

"Not for another week," I said. "Classes don't start until the third week of August. When he gets back from the cruise he's going to stay with his family until a couple of days before classes start."

"He's a senior now, isn't he?" Haskell asked.

"Yes," I replied. "Hard to believe, for me, anyway. Doesn't seem that long ago that he started college."

"Do you have any idea what his plans are after he graduates?" Stewart gave Dante and Diesel another bite of egg.

"The last time he talked about it to me," I said, "he was thinking about either law school or graduate school."

"He could stay at Athena for either," Stewart said. "Of course, he might be ready to get away from here and study elsewhere."

"He hasn't said anything about where he plans to apply," I said. "Where he applies will depend on which career path he decides to take." I paused for another bite of egg and toast before I turned the conversation in a slightly different direction.

"Speaking of boarders," I said, "we might have someone joining us here, at least for a while."

"Really?" Stewart said, one eyebrow raised. "What new lame duck are you planning to take in now? As one of your previous lame ducks, I'm curious." He grinned, and Haskell rolled his eyes.

"Interesting that you should put it like that," I replied. "The person who might move in here is a man who I believe does need some help. His name is Bill Delaney, and he is the son of my uncle Del, my aunt Dottie's husband."

"Not a blood relation?" Stewart asked.

"No, only a step. I only found out yesterday about Uncle Del's first marriage and the son he never knew he had."

"'Never knew he had'?" Haskell frowned. "How did that come about?"

I shared the basics of Bill Delaney's story with them. Diesel chirped a couple of times for no apparent reason, although he probably thought he was helping me explain things. When Diesel chirped, Dante barked. We had quite the conversation going until the pets stopped chiming in.

"What do you really know about this Bill Delaney?" Haskell leaned back in his chair and folded his arms over his chest. He had gone straight into deputy sheriff mode.

"So far only what he's told me," I said. Haskell started to speak, and I held up my hand to stem the flow. "I know what you're going to say, that it's not a smart thing to do, bringing a stranger into the house."

Haskell nodded. "You're one of the good guys, Charlie. I can understand why you feel like you have to help this man, and I certainly can't tell you not to do it. I do think you ought to find out more about him, though, before you bring him into your home."

"Charlie took me in," Stewart said. "I came to him and begged him to let me move in because I was afraid for my own safety in my uncle's house." His expression turned grim. "For all he knew, I was the one who killed my uncle. But he trusted his instincts, and here I've been for several years now."

I could feel my face redden even as I wanted to squirm in my seat. I had never felt comfortable in such situations.

"I know the story." Haskell's expression softened as he looked at his partner. "You've told it to me several times."

Stewart nodded. "I can see your point, too, of course." He grinned suddenly. "I knew I wasn't a murderer when I moved in here, but we don't know that this Bill Delaney isn't."

"We don't," Haskell replied. "That's why I plan to check him out." He turned to me. "You said he was from Tullahoma, right?"

I nodded. "He told me he's lived there most of his life, except for a stint in the Marine Corps."

"I've got a buddy in the sheriff's department there," Haskell said. "I'll call him up and find out if there's anything you ought to know about this guy Delaney."

"I appreciate it," I said. "I was planning to do some checking on him myself, actually, but I didn't get a chance to mention that before." I told them briefly about Jack Pemberton and Ernie Carpenter. "I figured one or both of them might actually know Delaney."

"Glad to hear you had a plan." Haskell flashed a rare smile. "Go on ahead and talk to them, and I'll talk to my buddy. He's been there for twenty years, so if there's anything to know, he'll know it."

"One way or another," Stewart said, "you ought to be able to find out whether this guy is safe to bring into the house."

"I'll text him now." Haskell felt for his phone in the pocket of his gym shorts. He stood. "Left it upstairs. I'll run and get it."

When Haskell said *run*, he meant it. Moments later I heard him running up the stairs to the third floor. Not long after that I could hear him running down again. He arrived back in the kitchen less than two minutes after he'd left it. And, I noted with envy, he wasn't even breathing hard. I supposed that if I went to the gym as religiously as he and Stewart did, I might be able to run like that.

I might also become emperor of China. Oh, well, I could dream, anyway.

Haskell texted a message right after he resumed his place at the table. Then he laid his phone aside and picked up his coffee cup. Stewart stood and began clearing the table. I still had a few bites of scrambled egg, and I finished them quickly.

By the time Haskell finished his coffee and got up to take the cup to the sink where Stewart was busy rinsing the dishes, his cell phone started ringing.

"It's Steve, my buddy in Tullahoma," Haskell said when he looked at the caller ID. He answered the call and greeted his friend.

"Yeah, that's right," Haskell said. "Guy named Bill Delaney." He turned to me. "How old is he?"

"Sixty-six," I replied.

Haskell relayed the information and then fell silent while his friend talked. His expression changed from intent to grim after a couple of minutes. Finally he thanked his friend and ended the call. He laid the phone aside.

"Something tells me the news isn't good." I felt suddenly tense because Haskell's grim expression hadn't changed. Diesel, sensing my unease, laid a large paw on my thigh and warbled. I patted his head to calm him while I waited for Haskell's reply.

"No, it isn't good," Haskell said. "Steve says Bill Delaney got away with murder. Multiple murders, in fact."

TWELVE

‖‖‖‖‖‖‖‖‖‖‖‖‖‖‖‖‖‖‖‖‖‖‖‖‖‖‖‖‖‖‖‖‖‖‖‖‖

For a moment I couldn't take in what Haskell had said. Then, as the import of his words finally sank in, I collected myself and was able to respond.

"Multiple murders?" I asked. "If he committed multiple murders, why is he not in prison?"

"Exactly," Stewart said. "Something about that doesn't add up."

Haskell nodded. "I know. Thing is, according to Steve, Delaney was never convicted. Never even brought to trial, but Steve reckons Delaney was guilty all right. They just couldn't prove it."

"He seems like such a quiet, unassuming man," I said, still shocked by the revelation.

"That's no proof against someone being a killer, Charlie," Haskell said. "You ought to know that by now."

I nodded. "I do. But, I don't know, somehow it just doesn't seem right to think of my uncle's son as a multiple murderer."

"They were sure he was the killer," Stewart said, "but they didn't have the evidence to bring him to trial, you said."

"Yes," Haskell replied. "That happens. Police can be certain who did it, but for whatever reason, there's no evidence that will stand up in court."

"Are you at all familiar with the case?" I asked.

"Yes," Haskell replied. "I remembered it when Steve told me the basic facts."

"What are they?" Stewart asked.

"Four members of a family were shot to death," Haskell said. "Parents and two young children. One child, an older girl, survived because she wasn't home at the time. I think she was spending the night at a friend's house."

"How horrible," I said, my imagination only too easily conjuring up a mental version of the crime scene. "What connection did Bill Delaney have with the family?"

"Father was a farmer. Delaney worked for him," Haskell said. "They lived out in the county about fifteen miles from Tullahoma." He frowned. "I think their name was Barber."

"What motive did he have for killing the family?" Stewart asked.

"He'd had a big blowout with Mr. Barber over something, can't recall what it was now," Haskell said. "All this was according to a neighbor. Barber fired Delaney, but he kept coming around. Don't know why. Maybe he thought Barber owed him money. Then about a week after Delaney got fired, he allegedly went to the house one night and killed four people."

"They couldn't prove any of this?" I asked.

"No, Delaney had some sort of alibi. Even though the cops thought it was fishy, they couldn't break it," Haskell said. "Trouble was, they couldn't find anyone else with a strong enough motive."

"Couldn't it have been a murder-suicide thing?" Stewart asked. "Surely that's the obvious answer."

Haskell frowned. "Of course they thought of that. With any murder you always look at the domestic angle first. Thing was the evidence of the wounds didn't bear that out. None of them was self-inflicted. So that ruled out murder-suicide."

"What about the possibility of a stranger?" I asked.

"Delaney kept saying that it was probably a stranger. Claimed to have seen a guy lurking around one of the outbuildings on the farm," Haskell said. "Apparently Barber was in the habit of keeping a pretty good bit of cash on hand. That was missing. I don't think it ever turned up."

"So the case has never been solved," Stewart said. "I'd hate to have that kind of thing hanging over me."

Dante yipped twice suddenly, and Stewart picked the dog up and put him in his lap. "What was all that about, you silly dog?"

"Attention," Haskell said in a tone of irritation. "You've been ignoring him, and he hates that."

Stewart did not respond to that remark. Instead, he said, "Charlie, I think you should get the writer interested in this case. Maybe the two of you together might be able to solve it. You might find out things the police never did."

I shook my head. "No, I don't think so."

"I wouldn't get involved in it if I were you," Haskell said. "They might reopen the case, now that they know Delaney is back. He disappeared about a year after the murders, and they hadn't known where he was until now."

"What are you going to do about him?" Stewart asked me. "Are you still thinking about letting him live here? Supposing he wants to, that is."

"I don't know," I said. "This really complicates everything. I'm going to have to find out more about the case and the fact that he was, or perhaps still is, a murder suspect. In the meantime, I'm going to see if I can find Delaney at the library today and put off the dinner until tomorrow evening. I was planning to do that anyway so that I'd have time to talk it over with Helen Louise, but now I think it's even more important to postpone having him here."

"I agree," Haskell said. Stewart nodded.

"I also want to see what more I can find out about him, from a source other than the law," I said, with a quick look at Haskell. He didn't appear insulted by my statement, so I continued, "I'll see what my two new contacts from Tullahoma know and go from there."

"Sounds like a reasonable plan to me," Stewart said.

Diesel evidently agreed because he meowed twice. Either that, or he—like Dante—was tired of being ignored. I scratched his head until he purred. That done, I said, "If you'll excuse me now, I'm going to e-mail Jack Pemberton and Miss An'gel." Seeing both men frown, I added, "For Ernie Carpenter's phone number, or her e-mail address, whichever Miss An'gel feels comfortable sharing with me. I forgot to ask Ernie herself last weekend."

"Go right ahead," Stewart said. "We're going out in a little while, unless you need us to hang around here for any reason."

I knew what he meant—for protection, in case Bill Delaney should show up here uninvited. I hadn't told them that I had seen him walking down the sidewalk in front of the house last week.

"No, I'll be fine. Once I've finished with e-mails, I'm going to shower and get ready to run by the library. Thank you, though."

Diesel and I left them in the kitchen. The cat followed me to the den and stretched out on the sofa while I turned on the laptop and waited for it to boot up. Once that was accomplished, I opened my e-mail program to compose my messages. First, to Miss An'gel, asking for contact information for Ernie. I didn't tell her anything about Bill Delaney. They would find out eventually. Then I sent a message to Jack. I did give him some basic information about Bill Delaney and why I was interested. I didn't mention the murders, however. I wanted to see what Jack might have to tell me about the man first.

Those tasks complete, I set the laptop aside. Time now to head upstairs to shower and get dressed for the day.

"I'm going upstairs now," I told Diesel. He eyed me sleepily for about three seconds, yawned, and closed his eyes again. Evidently the sofa was too comfortable because Diesel remained there when I left the room.

By the time I finished getting ready to leave the house, however, Diesel had joined me in my bedroom. I came out of the bathroom after a last quick combing of my hair to find him sitting in the middle of the bed. I picked up my watch from my bedside table, buckled it on my wrist, and looked down at the cat.

"I'm ready to go. Are you?" I asked.

Diesel chirped to let me know that he was indeed ready.

"Come on, then," I said, and he followed me downstairs. I gave him time to visit the utility room before we left. Finally, at about a quarter past nine, we were ready to walk out the door to the garage and be on our way. Until, that is, my cell phone rang.

I pulled it out of my pocket. I didn't recognize the number, but the exchange looked familiar. I thought it was a Tullahoma number, and so it proved to be.

"Hi, Charlie," Jack Pemberton said. "Got your e-mail, started to reply, but then I figured it would be a lot easier just to call you and tell you what I know. This a good time to talk?"

"Yes, it is. What can you tell me about Bill Delaney?" I walked over to the table and took my usual seat. Might as well sit down, I thought, because this could be a long conversation.

"All right, here goes," Jack replied. "First off, I recognized the name right away. I didn't know Delaney myself, but he was known around town. I hate to tell you this, since he might be related to you, sort of, but he was a suspect in a multiple murders case about twenty years ago."

"I've heard about that," I said. "What do you know about the murders?"

"Quite a lot, actually," Jack replied. "I've been interested in it for years. I was out of college and back here in Tullahoma teaching eighth-grade English when the murders happened. They were all anybody talked about for months. The girl I was dating at the time taught one of the Barber children. She was horribly upset, like everyone else. The children were popular, unlike their father."

"Why didn't people like the father?" I asked.

"I never dealt with him myself, you understand," Jack replied, "but my girlfriend at the time did. So did a couple other people I knew. They all said he was rude and always convinced someone was trying to cheat him. Had a hard time getting along with anyone."

"What about his wife?" I asked.

"Everyone felt sorry for her is what I heard," Jack said. "She was supposed to be a really nice woman, and one person I knew said she was a saint for putting up with her husband all those years." He paused. "In fact, some people thought she might have finally snapped and killed him."

"Would she have murdered two of her children?"

"No, I don't think so. Everyone said she lived for her

kids," Jack said. "I was more inclined to think that Barber suddenly snapped for some reason and did it himself."

"But the police must have thought otherwise," I said.

"The evidence didn't support a suicide. Someone murdered all four of them." Jack paused. "The only real suspect was Bill Delaney."

"What was his motive?" I asked, curious to hear Jack's take on the subject. He had revealed a couple of interesting bits that Haskell had not shared, if he knew them, that is.

"Allegedly because he was angry at old man Barber for firing him and not paying him the money he was owed for all the work he'd done," Jack said. "Delaney was a hard drinker back then. Maybe he still is. He also was known to have a quick temper. Folks figured he got lit and went out and confronted Barber. Barber pulled a gun on Delaney, Delaney got it away from him and killed him. Then Delaney killed Mrs. Barber and the two kids because they saw it happen."

"Nasty." I could picture it all too easily.

"Yes, it was," Jack said. "Problem was, well, there were two problems. First, they never found the weapon. Second, Delaney had an alibi they couldn't shake."

"What was the alibi?" I asked.

"Delaney swore up and down he was dead drunk that day. He'd been on a bender, stumbled home, and his mother locked him in his room until he sobered up."

"And all this took place at the same time the murders occurred?"

"His mother said it did. The cops tried to break her down, but she was apparently a tough old lady. Regular pillar of her church, known to be a good woman, all that kind of thing. People respected her, and when she stood by her son, that had a lot of weight."

"I heard a version of the story a little while ago from one of my boarders, who's a deputy in the sheriff's department here," I said. "The cops were convinced Delaney was the killer, weren't they?"

"Yes, they were," Jack said. "Now, you remember I said people thought Barber might have threatened Delaney with a gun?"

"Yes, I remember," I replied.

"Even though they never found the weapon, as I also told you, they were sure the killer used Barber's shotgun," Jack said. "A friend of his swore one was missing."

THIRTEEN

"The killer used Barber's shotgun," I said. "But the shotgun disappeared. Sounds to me like the killer was someone who knew about Barber's habit of keeping a lot of cash on hand and seized the opportunity to make off with the cash and the gun."

"That's what I think," Jack said. "The Barber farm was about five hundred acres, if I remember correctly. There aren't any other houses close to the Barber house by a couple of miles."

"So no one who lived in the area observed anything out of the ordinary the day of the murder?" I asked.

"Not that I recall," Jack replied. "I'm not sure how much effort the sheriff's department put into searching the area around the house and the farm. There's a wooded area behind the house running between a couple of pastures. The woods extend about half a mile to an old logging road that isn't much traveled. The killer could have approached the house through those woods."

"That sounds like a strong possibility to me," I said. "Besides Bill Delaney, though, wasn't there anyone else who might have had a grudge against Barber? If he was always sure he was being cheated, he could have made quite a few enemies."

"True," Jack said. "I'm sure the sheriff's department investigated a number of possible suspects. Barber had a reputation as a hothead. He had three or four field hands who worked the farm, and they were all known to have complaints about how he treated them. Also I think he had a long-running dispute with the man who owned a neighboring property."

"With all that you've told me, I have to wonder why the authorities were so sure Bill Delaney was the killer," I said.

"Because he already had a record and had served time in jail for assault," Jack said. "He beat up one guy pretty bad, but that happened ten years or more before the Barber murders. He kept clean once he was out of jail, or so I understand."

I felt overwhelmed by all the information about the Barber murders and Bill Delaney's connection with the case. And now his conviction for assault. Was this a man I really wanted living in my house?

I expressed as much to Jack.

"That's a tough call," he replied. "All of that happened a long time ago, and for all we know, Delaney has turned his life around."

"I suppose," I said. "At the library he's always quiet, almost self-effacing. His demeanor is always respectful, and I haven't noticed any signs of him being hungover."

"I don't know how much experience you have with hard-core alcoholics," Jack said. "I've dealt with a couple, and I have to tell you that they can cover up their drinking to the point you'd swear they were teetotalers."

"I'll have to take your word for that," I said. "I never had any close dealings with an alcoholic that I can recall. A few times over the years in Houston I had to call the cops to remove someone for being drunk and disorderly in the library, but that was it."

"For your sake, if you decide to take him in, I hope he's quit drinking," Jack said. "I promise you that you don't want to have to deal with a drunk in the house."

"No, I certainly don't," I said. "Thanks for all the information, Jack, I really appreciate it. You've given me a lot to consider. Right now I need to get over to the library and see if Delaney is there. I need to reschedule the invitation to dinner until I've had time to talk to my family about this crazy idea of mine."

"Good luck," Jack said. "I don't envy you. But I have to say you've gotten me interested in the Barber case again. I'm going to see what I have in my files about it."

"If you find anything else that pertains to Bill Delaney, I wish you'd let me know," I said.

"I will," Jack said. "Talk to you later."

"Thanks." I ended the call and briefly stared at the phone in my hands. I wondered whether Miss An'gel had responded to my e-mail yet. If she had I thought I would go ahead and get in touch with Ernie Carpenter. After hearing what Jack had to say about Delaney and the Barber murders, I wondered what Ernie's take on it all would be.

I tapped the mail icon on my phone and waited for the inbox to update. The last time I remembered looking at mail on the phone was about three days ago, so I had to wait a minute or so before I could see any new messages.

Nothing from Miss An'gel, although I had a couple of spam messages. I deleted those quickly and put my phone away.

"Come on, Diesel, this time we're going to the library."

The cat meowed loudly at me as if to say *It's about time*. I knew I had confused him by getting ready to leave the house and then stopping to have a conversation.

Less than ten minutes later we arrived in the library parking lot. All the spots on the one side that claimed any shade from the trees already had cars in them, so I had to park in the full sun. Today was going to be a scorcher, too, with temps in the high nineties. With the humidity, the *feels-like* temperature would be over a hundred degrees. At least I could accomplish what I needed to do and get home again before the worst heat of the day. I intended to stay home the rest of the day once I had spoken with Bill Delaney.

I spotted Teresa Farmer at the reference desk the moment Diesel and I stepped inside the front door. She looked our way and smiled, though she also appeared a bit surprised. I rarely came to the library on a Saturday, especially after I had worked there the day before.

Diesel chirped when he saw Teresa, and he ran around the counter so he could properly visit with the head of the library. There was no one standing in front of the desk waiting to be helped, so I walked up to the counter. Teresa was busy patting Diesel and talking to him in a low voice.

After a moment Teresa turned her attention to me, and we exchanged greetings. "What are you doing here on a Saturday morning?" she asked. "Not that I'm not glad to see you, of course."

"I need to talk to one of the patrons if he's here," I said. "An older gentleman named Bill Delaney. Do you know who I mean?" I looked toward the area where Delaney usually sat, but the chair stood empty.

"Yes, I know him." Teresa frowned. "I haven't seen him this morning, and that's rather odd, come to think of it. He's usually here, waiting for the door to open every day. At least, he has been for the past several weeks since he first came in and got his library card. I hope he's not ill."

"Maybe he had errands to take care of this morning." I didn't want to alarm Teresa about Delaney's welfare. Given what I now knew about his history, I wondered whether he had fallen off the wagon and was in his apartment, passed out. Or he could have had a heart attack or a stroke. I was beginning to make myself uneasy over him. My imagination could conjure up numerous scenarios, none of them pleasant.

"Don't worry about him," I said, my tone as nonchalant as I could make it. "Diesel and I will go check on him. I know where he lives."

"That's kind of you to take an interest in his welfare," Teresa said. "I got the impression that he doesn't know anyone in Athena."

"I'm not sure whether he does or not." I hesitated to tell her about Delaney's connection to my family. Now really was not the time to go into personal history. I realized belatedly that a patron stood behind me waiting to talk to Teresa. "We'll go now and see if he's okay. Come on, Diesel."

I stepped aside to let the woman behind me approach the desk. Diesel sauntered out from behind the counter and joined me. He meowed to let me know he hadn't had quite enough attention from Teresa yet. "Tough luck," I told him softly. "We need to get going. Let's go to the car."

He knew what that meant, and I carried him to the car without further protest.

Ten minutes later I pulled up in front of the seedy-looking apartment building that Bill Delaney had listed as his home address for his library card. The squat brick building, two stories tall, needed cleaning to remove spiderwebs and other visible dirt stains. Each window on the front had decorative shutters on either side. Several were slightly askew, and they all needed a fresh coat of paint. The small area of landscaped yard in front had been let to run to seed. Overall the place exuded shabbiness and desperation, to my mind, anyway.

I put Diesel in his harness and attached the leash. The neighborhood ambience made me uneasy, and I wanted to be sure the cat stayed next to me at all times while we were here. I opened the door and picked up Diesel. I locked the car, and we proceeded up the walk to the front arched entrance to the inner courtyard of the building.

A row of battered metal letter boxes adorned the short passageway to our right. Ahead I could see an overgrown common area with a couple of wrought iron tables and several rickety chairs. I turned my attention back to the letter boxes, hoping that one of them bore Delaney's name. I couldn't remember the number of his apartment. I wasn't sure if he had even included it on his application. I didn't want to have to go knocking on doors to find him. I preferred not to disturb any of the other residents of the building if I didn't have to.

I found Delaney's name on the box for apartment ten. I glanced around the courtyard to make a swift count of doors. There were sixteen, so eight up and eight down. I figured that number ten was upstairs, and I led Diesel to one of the four sets of stairs—one in each corner—that climbed to the second story. On the way I kept an eye out for broken glass or other objects that could injure feline paws.

We climbed the stairs to our right and found ourselves in front of apartment sixteen when we stepped onto the landing. I set Diesel down since the landing was shaded from the sun, as was the gallery around the courtyard. I turned to the right, and the next apartment was number nine. A few steps farther on, I stopped in front of the door to number ten. There was a large window near it, but the blinds were drawn, and I couldn't see inside.

I listened for a moment. The complex was quiet, except for the faint noise of a television set emanating from somewhere on the bottom level. I rapped three times on Delaney's door and waited.

I estimated thirty seconds had passed, and I knocked again, louder this time. After a few seconds I heard what sounded like a moan coming from inside the apartment. I listened intently, and then I heard it again.

I put my head close to the door and spoke. "Mr. Delaney, it's Charlie Harris. Are you okay?"

I heard what sounded like mumbling. What I didn't hear were footsteps approaching the door. I was worried now that he was injured or incapacitated and couldn't get up. I tried the knob, and it twisted in my hand. I pushed, and the door opened.

The first thing I noticed was that the room was sparsely furnished, but clean. The second thing I noticed was the odor of beer. The room was dark, and the only light was the sunshine coming through the open door. I pushed the door open wider to let in more light.

Now that I could see better, I noticed a daybed against the wall to my left. Numerous empty beer cans littered the floor around the daybed. Bill Delaney was lying on the bed on his back, his right arm over his face. He was mumbling, but I couldn't make out the words.

I wondered what had set off this binge drinking. Maybe he did it every weekend and stayed sober during the week. I had no idea. I took a few steps closer to the daybed. I wanted to assess his condition to decide whether I needed to call an ambulance.

The mumbling continued as I moved near. He startled me by removing his arm from his face and squinting at me.

"Who're you?"

"Charlie Harris, Mr. Delaney. From the library."

He closed his eyes. "Go 'way. Don't wanna talk. Leave me alone."

I hesitated. He was probably just sleeping off all the beer he had consumed and would be okay later on. While I stood there, Delaney rolled on his side, face toward the wall. His breathing seemed normal, and I reckoned he had gone to sleep.

I backed away, and for the first time I realized Diesel wasn't beside me. I felt the leash go taut, and I looked around the room. Diesel was in the corner on the other side of the room batting something around.

"What on earth have you found?" I said in an undertone. "Stop that, and let's go."

Diesel looked up at me and then batted the object toward my feet. I looked down. A tube of lipstick.

I left it where it was and urged the cat out of the room. I pulled the door shut. I stood on the landing, wondering why Delaney had a tube of lipstick in his apartment. Who had been visiting him?

FOURTEEN

My head had begun to throb, a sure sign that my stress level was inching up. Finding Bill Delaney passed out drunk had complicated things in a way I definitely hadn't expected. I wasn't eager for him to show up at the house for dinner tonight, should he recover enough from his binge. The only thing I could do now was leave a note for him. I had to hope that he would see it and stay home.

"Come on, Diesel," I said. "Let's go back to the car. I need to find paper and a pen so I can leave a note."

The cat warbled in response, and back down the stairs we went. I usually had a small notebook in the glove compartment of the car, though I had been known to take it out and forget to replace it. Today it was where it should be, but I had to search for a moment to find a pen. Finally, under the car user's manual and assorted paperwork, I found one.

I scribbled a quick note to Delaney that I needed to reschedule, but I didn't explain. I gave him my phone number and asked him to call me when he could. I had decided not to invite him to dinner tomorrow night, either. In light of all I had learned about him and the Barber murders, I wanted time to discuss the situation with not only Helen Louise, but with Sean as well. I appreciated the legal point of view my son provided. He always had my best interests at heart, although we occasionally disagreed over exactly what those best interests entailed.

I signed the note and tore the page out. After I restored the notebook to the glove compartment, I told the cat we were going back upstairs. He meowed loudly, and I couldn't decide whether he was complaining or commenting. Either way, he followed me back to Delaney's door. I folded the note and wedged it into the crack between the door and the frame beside the knob. I hoped no one would come along and remove it, but there wasn't much I could do about it if that happened.

"Okay, Diesel, we're going back to the car, and this time we're leaving." I received a quick trill in response.

I would be happy to get home again and stay out of the heat for the rest of the day. The older I got, the less I liked the high heat and humidity of a Mississippi summer. I had given thought recently to the idea of buying or renting a property in a cooler climate for the summer months. I hadn't done any in-depth research yet, nor had I discussed it with Helen Louise. There would be no point in my buying or renting if she wasn't willing to come with me. In a couple of years, perhaps, she might consider it if she could actually bring herself to step back from micromanagement of the bistro.

Back at home, I gave Diesel fresh water and added dry food to his bowl while he supervised. He rewarded me with a couple of happy warbles when I finished. Now it was my turn for refreshment.

Nothing appealed more to me at the moment than a tall glass of ice water. I downed a third of it in one gulp, re-filled it, and took my place at the kitchen table. I pulled out my phone to check e-mail. If Miss An'gel had responded to my request for contact information for Ernie Carpenter, I planned to get in touch with her.

Once my new e-mail messages appeared, I scrolled through them. Three obvious spam messages, and two legitimate ones. The latter came from Miss An'gel and Jack Pemberton. I was a bit surprised to hear again from Jack so soon after the phone call that morning, but I supposed he might have further information.

I read Miss An'gel's message first. To my surprise, she informed me that Ernie was once again at Riverhill for the weekend. Miss An'gel extended an invitation to Diesel and me to come to lunch, if we were available. Should we not be, however, she provided Ernie's cell number and suggested I call her around eleven. I checked the time at the top of the screen. Less than five minutes until ten thirty. I wouldn't have to wait long to call Ernie.

In the meantime I replied to Miss An'gel's invitation. The thought of a meal at Riverhill always enticed me, be-cause Clementine was as talented a cook as Azalea—though I would never have told the latter that. I thanked Miss An'gel but declined with the always-useful-but-vague statement that I had a prior engagement. I ended by saying that I would call Ernie around eleven.

I drank more water before I opened Jack's message, the subject of which read: *Great idea*. The message was brief, only three sentences. I skimmed the words, shaking my head in disbelief. Jack's *great idea* was for the two of us to work together to solve the Barber murders.

I started to respond with *no thanks*, but, after a mo-mentary hesitation, I instead laid the phone on the table.

Sean and Laura would no doubt tell me that I should keep my nose out of this cold case, and I agreed. Sort of. I couldn't help thinking that I would never be certain about Bill Delaney until I knew whether he was a cold-blooded killer. Didn't I owe it to Aunt Dottie to do what I could for her husband's only living offspring?

Some might tell me I was foolish to think about doing anything for a man to whom I had no blood ties. But Aunt Dottie had served as a profound influence in my life, and I knew without the least bit of doubt that she would encourage me to do what I could to help. Even if that included delving into a twenty-year-old unsolved murder case. Because if Delaney did kill that family, he should be brought to justice.

From time to time I hated my conscience because I ended up in uncomfortable situations like the current one. Doing the right thing was often inconvenient. I simply had to pray that, in this case, it didn't turn out to be life-threatening as well.

I decided I wasn't ready to say yes to Jack. I'd have to let my subconscious stew over it a while longer. I had to be absolutely certain that assisting Jack was the right thing to do.

The sound of the doorbell interrupted my reverie. I rose from the table and headed for the front door. Diesel scampered past me. He always wanted to see who was on the other side of the door. I remembered that Laura and Frank planned to leave baby Charlie with me while they had a respite from childcare. I opened the door, ready to see my grandson and his parents.

Instead I found Helen Louise, bearing a picnic basket in one hand and a bottle of wine in the other.

"Surprise." She grinned at me and stepped into the front hall.

I shut the door behind her and took the basket from her hand. We exchanged a kiss, and all the while Diesel rubbed against her legs and chirped for attention.

"A wonderful surprise," I said. "I thought you'd be at the bistro until late tonight."

Her free arm linked through mine, we strolled into the kitchen while she explained.

"Clever Henry found a wonderful young man who needs part-time work, but he can only work on Saturdays. He has excellent experience, and he hit the ground running this morning. So I decided that the boss lady was going to have lunch with her fella and also get to spend some time with the infant version of said fella." She set the bottle of wine on the table beside the basket.

"Marvelous," I said. "I have to remember to thank Henry, often and fervently."

Helen Louise laughed. "He's quite pleased with himself, let me tell you. He was desperate to get me out of his hair so he could take over."

"I'm proud of you for letting him." Frankly I was amazed that she appeared to be happy with the situation and not merely tolerating it.

"The upside to this is I get to spend more time with you and Diesel." She was busy scratching the cat's head as she talked. "And also the most perfect baby boy I've ever seen."

"He is amazing, isn't he?" I knew I was infatuated with the baby, but I didn't care. Being a grandfather was the best thing there was.

"Little acorns don't fall far from the old trees," Helen Louise said. "When are Laura and Frank dropping him by?" She ceased her attentions to Diesel, and he meowed loudly. "You've had enough for the moment, you greedy boy."

Diesel responded with a sad warble, but he didn't pester her again.

"Around eleven thirty," I said. "Shall we wait until after they're gone to open up the basket?"

Helen Louise nodded. "Yes, a couple of things need reheating, but that won't take long. How about a glass of wine now? I think it should still be chilled enough. I had it in a cooler on the way over."

"Sounds fine, even though it's before noon." I found the corkscrew while Helen Louise retrieved wineglasses from the cabinet. "Only one glass for me, though, since we'll have the baby here."

I opened the wine and poured it. Helen Louise took a seat at the table to my right. We toasted each other and sipped at the wine.

"I have a lot to discuss with you," I said. "I didn't think I'd be able to until tomorrow. Another reason this is such a lovely surprise."

"What's going on?" Helen Louise asked.

I started to launch into an explanation but I caught a glimpse of the kitchen clock. The time was now seventeen minutes to eleven. That didn't give me much time before I needed to call Ernie Carpenter. I explained to Helen Louise that I would have to interrupt our talk at eleven in order to make an important call. She nodded, and I started to fill her in.

By two minutes to eleven, I think I had managed to give her the salient facts of the situation with Bill Delaney and the Barber murders as well.

"So now you're going to get Ernie's take on the situation?" Helen Louise asked.

"If she knows who Delaney is," I said. "I'm sure she'll be familiar with the murder case even if she isn't acquainted with him personally."

I waited until a couple minutes past the hour before I made the call. Ernie answered almost immediately.

"Good morning," I said. "How are you?"

"Doing fine," Ernie replied. "And you?"

"The same," I said. "I hope you don't mind my interrupting your visit to ask you a few questions."

"Not at all," Ernie said. "Though I have one for you first, if you don't mind."

"Ask away."

Ernie chuckled. "I wondered if you had made a decision yet about Jack's project. Are you going to take part in it?"

"We're still discussing it," I said. "Though I suppose I'm leaning toward doing it."

"Excellent," she said. "I think it has every potential to be a big success."

I wasn't so sure about that, or whether I even wanted it to be. The bigger the success, the more notoriety that could result.

"That's possible, certainly," I said. "Now, the reason I wanted to talk to you is to find out whether you know a man called Bill Delaney. He grew up in Tullahoma, and he's sixty-six. Do you know anything about him?"

"Yes, I know who he is, and if I were you I wouldn't have anything to do with him."

FIFTEEN

The import of Ernie's words surprised me. "Why do you say that?"

"He's a drinker, a heavy one, more often drunk than not in my experience," Ernie replied, her tone harsh. "I have no use for men who waste their lives like that."

"I see. How well do you know him?"

"We are not friends, though I have known him for over fifty years. He was several years behind me in school," Ernie said. "How do you know him?"

I explained that he was now living in Athena and that he frequented the public library. "He told me that Uncle Del is his father but that Uncle Del never knew about him."

"Good heavens," Ernie said. "Why didn't he ever try to make contact with Del?"

"He, Delaney that is, only found out about it when his mother died a few months ago," I said. "He somehow tracked Uncle Del to Athena, and he came here to find out more about him."

"I knew Sylvia Delaney," Ernie said. "I thought Delaney was her married name. When did she and Del get divorced?"

"According to their son, six months after they married. His mother didn't know she was pregnant until after Uncle Del left her, or so she told Bill Delaney. Apparently she wanted nothing more to do with her ex-husband so she never bothered to tell him he had a son."

"In this case the sins of the father have truly been visited upon the child," Ernie said grimly.

I wasn't sure what she meant by that. "Could you explain that? I don't follow you?"

"Delbert Collins was a heavy drinker," Ernie said. "He kept it hidden from Dottie for the first year or so of their marriage, but he came home roaring drunk one night and she discovered the truth."

"I had no idea," I said. "Aunt Dottie never said a word about it. I suppose she might have told my parents."

"I imagine they knew," Ernie replied, "but, of course, it wasn't something they would have talked about in front of you."

"No, I guess not," I said. "Poor Aunt Dottie, having to deal with that."

Ernie chuckled, surprising me again. "You, of course, didn't know your aunt in her younger days. I have to tell you, Dottie had enough steel in her spine to withstand just about anything. She put her foot down, as they say. Told Del Collins that he had two choices. He could continue drinking and going his own way or he could stay married to her and give it up. She wasn't going to put up with his coming home drunk all the time."

As Ernie talked, I remembered occasions when I had experienced that steel. Aunt Dottie was the sweetest, most loving aunt I could have wished for, but when I misbehaved at her house, I soon realized the error of my ways.

"Was the drinking the reason for Uncle Del's health problems?" I asked.

"To a degree, I expect it was," Ernie said. "He had a couple of heart attacks before you were born, I'd say, and later on a stroke that left him considerably diminished."

"Mostly what I remember about him is that he spent just about all of his time in his room," I said. "I actually didn't see him much except at mealtimes when I stayed with them."

"He was in pretty bad shape," Ernie said. "If he had been on his own, he probably would have died long before he did, frankly. Dottie took exceptionally good care of him. On top of working and earning a living for both of them. A good living, I have to say."

"Thank you for telling me all this," I said. "As I said, I never knew any of it."

"You're certainly welcome. I don't think Dottie would mind your knowing. Now tell me, other than being a drunk like Del, what kind of proof does Bill Delaney have to back up his claim that he's Del's son?" Ernie asked.

"A birth certificate from Tullahoma County that lists Uncle Del as the father. It appears authentic to me."

"I suppose that could be faked," Ernie said, "but it's probably authentic. I know someone in the county clerk's office in Tullahoma. I'll get her to check it out on Monday." She paused for a moment. "This really isn't any of my business, but I'm a nosy old woman so you'll have to bear with me. Has he hit you up for money? He isn't entitled to any of Dottie's money, and he certainly has no claim to her house."

"I don't mind your being nosy." I chuckled. "He hasn't asked for anything from me, except for information. My impression so far is that he simply wants to know about his father, and I can understand that. The problem is that I don't have much to tell him."

"No, you really wouldn't have," Ernie said. "If Dottie had known about the relationship, she would have taken him in. That was her way."

"Yes, she would have," I said. "And that is my dilemma. Knowing what Aunt Dottie would do, how can I not try to help him? It's what she would want."

"Yes, she would," Ernie said. "I would counsel against it, frankly, but then I have never been as bighearted and accepting as Dottie was. I would have told her the same thing. You'll have to follow your conscience on this."

"Yes," I said. "What else can you tell me about Bill Delaney?"

"Let me see," Ernie replied. "Now, I know he spent some time in the Marine Corps. Probably should have made a career of it, but he didn't. He came back to Tullahoma and did mostly manual labor. I think he was smart enough to have gone to college and would have done well, except for the drinking. He started that as a teenager, and that ruined him. He had a hard time keeping a job for long because sooner or later he went on a bender and disappeared for days, even a week or two, at a time."

"That's sad," I said. "You mentioned that you knew his mother, I believe."

"Yes, I did. Sylvia Delaney was a good woman. Worked hard all her life, was a devoted member of her church. A good woman in every respect. She was no plaster saint, mind you. She had a temper, and you didn't want to get her angry, believe you me." Ernie paused. "I didn't get to know her, mind you, until Bill was in high school. By that time I myself was fresh out of college and in my first or second year teaching at the high school in Tullahoma."

"Was Bill one of your students?" I asked.

"I had him for sophomore English," Ernie replied. "He had potential, but even then he was slipping around drinking. I had to send him to the principal's office on several occasions because he came to class high as a kite. I met Sylvia for the first time when she came to school to talk to his teachers and the principal about his escapades. The principal threatened to expel him more than once."

"But he did manage to finish high school?"

"Yes, he did. By some miracle he managed to stay sober through his junior and senior years, and after that he joined the Marines," Ernie said. "I suspect, but I don't know this for sure, that he was dishonorably discharged."

"Then he came back to Tullahoma?"

"He did," Ernie replied. "Stayed there until about twenty years ago, then he disappeared. If Sylvia knew where he was, she never said."

"That was after the Barber murders," I said.

"I wondered if you knew about that."

"Jack told me about the case," I said. "Bill's mother was his alibi, Jack said."

"Yes, and that was what saved him. They tried hard, the sheriff's department did, but they could never shake Sylvia," Ernie said. "Some people still believe to this day he killed the Barbers, despite Sylvia's swearing up and down Bill was with her all that night and never left the house."

"What do you think?" I asked. "Did she lie to protect her son? Or was she telling the truth?"

"Let me put it this way," Ernie said. "The Sylvia Delaney I knew wouldn't tell a lie to save her own life, and I don't believe she would lie to save her son's, either."

I thought I detected a note of doubt in Ernie's voice. "But?" I asked.

"But Bill was her son, and she had done everything she could all her life to take care of him. She was like a tigress where he was concerned," Ernie replied. "But, in the end, I can't be sure she didn't lie."

"I have learned over the years that, no matter how well you think you know someone, you can never really know everything about them. They always have the capacity to surprise you."

"True," Ernie said. "We would all do well to remember that."

I had been so absorbed in my conversation with Ernie that I had shut out everything else. Now, however, I came out of my fog of concentration to hear Helen Louise speaking to me and Diesel meowing at the same time.

"Excuse me a moment," I said into the phone. "Yes, sweetheart, what is it?"

"I've been trying to get your attention for two minutes, I swear," Helen Louise said. "I want you to ask her a question." She rubbed Diesel's head to quiet him down.

"What is it?"

"Ask her what happened to the daughter," Helen Louise replied. "The one child who survived the murders. I've been wondering about her."

"Good point," I said. "Ernie, Helen Louise, who is here with me, has a question. What happened to the one Barber child who wasn't home when the murders took place? What was her name?"

"Elizabeth Barber," Ernie said. "She was sixteen or seventeen at the time. A junior in high school, and a girl with a bit of a reputation. Too beautiful for her own good, if you ask me. She was spending the night with a friend. She's still in Tullahoma, married now with several young children of her own. She's Elizabeth Campbell now, and her husband is a prominent businessman in town."

"I didn't realize she was that old," I said. "For some reason I thought all the children were younger."

"Elizabeth was about ten years older than her brothers, who were twins," Ernie said.

"Were you acquainted with their parents?"

"To my regret, yes," Ernie said. "At least in Hiram Barber's case. He was a petty, disagreeable man who thought the whole world was against him. His wife was a quiet, sweet woman, and I never could figure out what she saw in Hiram. Perhaps when he was younger and they were first married, he was a nicer man. Somehow I doubt that, though."

I loved the way Ernie didn't mince words when it came to assessing someone's character. Miss An'gel didn't hold back, either, though in typical Southern grande dame fashion she could deliver a devastating set-down in such a polite way that the person involved was never quite sure he or she had been snubbed.

"Sounds like you had personal experience of him," I said.

"I had Elizabeth for junior English," Ernie said. "A beautiful, headstrong girl, bright, but lazy. If she didn't want to do an assignment, she wouldn't no matter what I did. The result was that, by the end of the first six weeks, she was failing the class. The next thing I knew, Hiram Barber was in my face, chewing me out for being unfair to his precious baby." Suddenly Ernie chuckled. "At least he tried to chew me out. I don't think he'd ever had a woman talk back to him the way I did. By the time I was finished with him, he couldn't apologize enough. Evidently he went home and had a good talk with Miss Elizabeth. After that she made more of an effort. Never to her full potential, in my opinion, but enough to make more than passing grades."

"I had a similar problem with my son," I said. "Because he was mooning after a girl in his class who wouldn't have anything to do with him."

"That was part of Elizabeth's problem," Ernie said. "She was too beautiful for her own good, and she loved male attention." She paused for a moment, and when she continued she sounded sad. "The horrible thing was, it wasn't long after the incident with her father that her family was murdered."

SIXTEEN

||||||||||||||||||||||||||||||||||||||||||||

"That poor girl," I said. "I can't begin to imagine how she felt, losing her whole family like that. Did she have any other kin?"

"As I recall," Ernie replied, "she had an aunt on either side. Her mother's unmarried, younger sister lived in Tullahoma at the time, though I believe she has since passed away. The father's sister lived in Alabama. Elizabeth wanted to stay in Tullahoma and finish high school there, and her maiden aunt agreed to take her in."

"With everything that happened," I said, "I think I would have wanted to get as far away from it all as I could have. For a while, anyway."

"I was frankly surprised myself by her decision," Ernie said. "And the murders seemed to have changed her. When she came back to school, she was like a different girl. She paid attention in class, did all the assigned work, and her grades improved dramatically."

"An event like those murders probably had a profound

psychological effect on her, I suppose," I said. "Sometimes great shocks can really change a person."

"That definitely happened with Elizabeth Barber," Ernie said. "She even went to college. Started out at the local community college and then finished up at Mississippi State. I believe someone told me she wanted to be a veterinarian, but she met her future husband while they were both students at State. They married when he started working on an advanced business degree, and she never went on to vet school."

"I hope she has a happy life now after such a horrible tragedy," I said. "What happened to the farm? Do you know?"

"Yes, I do," Ernie replied. "Barber left a will. I don't know the terms, but the end result was that Elizabeth inherited everything. She didn't want to go back there to live, though, and one certainly can't blame her for that."

"No, I can understand that," I said. What terrible memories there would be in a house where four people had been murdered, I thought. If any place was ever haunted, surely that house would be.

"Elizabeth sold the farm to one of those farm corporations," Ernie said. "They razed the house and turned the area into a field. I think that was the right thing to do because I don't think anyone else would have wanted to live there, either."

"I certainly wouldn't," I said. "You're a gold mine of information, Ernie, and I appreciate all you've told me."

"I'm glad I could answer your questions," Ernie said. "Is there anything else you want to know?"

"I can't think of anything else right now," I said.

"Feel free to call me if you do," Ernie said.

"I will." I thanked her again, and we ended the call.

"You look a little dazed," Helen Louise said. "Overwhelmed by everything Ernie told you?"

"A little, I guess." Diesel had come over and put a large paw on my thigh. I scratched his head, and he chirped. "I'll fill you in once Laura and Frank have gone. They should be here any minute with the baby."

Right on cue, the doorbell rang, and Diesel took off for the front door. I think he knew that Laura and Frank would be there with little Charlie. "Be back in a minute," I said to Helen Louise before I left the room.

Diesel was pawing at the door when I reached it. He was anxious to see the baby, I guessed. "Stand back and let me open the door," I told him. He meowed at me once before he complied with my request.

When the door swung open I beheld Laura with the baby in her arms. Behind her stood her husband, Frank, laden with bags. "Hi, Dad," Laura said. "Here we are, right on time."

"Yes, you are. Come in. Diesel is having a fit to see the baby." I moved aside and they entered.

"Isn't that Helen Louise's car in the driveway?" Frank asked. "I figured she would be at the bistro all day."

"I decided to follow the advice of a very sensible and quite attractive man I know," Helen Louise said as she came toward us from the kitchen. "I'm learning to delegate and let my capable staff take care of things."

"Good for you," Laura said as she gave me baby Charlie to hold. "He finished a meal right before we left the house, so he should be content to sleep for a while." She kissed my cheek.

"Thanks for looking after the baby while we have some time to ourselves," Frank said. "I'll go put the bags in the living room."

"You know I'm always happy to see this little guy." I gazed adoringly down at my sleeping grandson. I felt like my bones would melt every time I looked at this small miracle in my arms. The same way I had felt with my children when they were infants.

Diesel warbled loudly to let everyone know how happy he was to see the baby. Frank, returning from the living room, laughed at the sight of the cat reared up on his back legs, his front legs braced against my side, as he tried to get a look at little Charlie.

"That cat just about kills me," he said. "If I didn't know better, I'd swear he was a little person in a fur suit. I don't think I've ever seen an animal so in love with a baby before."

"Diesel is a cat with extraordinarily good taste," Laura said. "Aren't you, boy?"

The cat meowed and reached out a paw to tap my arm.

"All right, come on," I said to Diesel. "Let's go put Charlie in his crib, and you can keep an eye on him, okay?"

That question elicited happy chirps, and Diesel followed me into the living room. I got the baby situated comfortably in the crib. I gazed down at him a moment, drinking in those perfect tiny features. Then I somehow managed to tear myself away, though I could have stood there for an hour or more to watch him

When I left the room, Diesel was up on his back legs, looking into the crib. Since the cat was a bit over four feet long from the tip of his nose to the tip of his tail, he could easily see the baby. I knew he wouldn't try to get into the crib. He would be content to watch the baby sleep, and the moment the baby stirred, he would let us know.

". . . lunch at the bistro," Frank was telling Helen Louise when I walked back into the front hall. "Then a movie. One of Laura's friends has a small part in it, and Laura has been wanting to see it."

Laura cast a longing glance in the direction of the living room.

"Have a good time," I said. "Now, go and enjoy yourselves." I put my hands on my daughter's shoulders and turned her toward the front door. "Go."

Laura laughed and gave me another quick kiss. "Thanks, Dad." She gave Helen Louise a hug. "I promise we'll call and let you know if the bistro is in a shambles because you aren't there."

Helen Louise made a shooing motion with her hands. "Get out of here before I call Henry and tell him to charge you triple for whatever you order."

Frank grinned and took hold of Laura's arm. "We poor academics can't afford that, so we'd better leave. Come on, honey." He opened the door and ushered his wife out.

I closed the door behind them. Helen Louise headed for the living room, and I followed.

We stood in the doorway. Diesel hadn't moved since I'd left him and the baby. The cat's gaze seemed to be focused intently on the sleeping infant. Helen Louise and I looked at each other and smiled. I pulled my cell phone from my pocket and took a picture of the scene to share with Laura and Frank later.

Then Helen Louise and I returned to the kitchen. I was hungry, more than ready for the lunch she had brought.

I refreshed our wine while Helen Louise retrieved the hamper and began to unpack it. I felt my mouth begin to water as I watched. First came the brie, followed by grapes. Next she uncovered a bowl of vichyssoise, the only cold soup I liked. After that, a plate of baked chicken. Finally, a container of French bean salad.

Flourishing the latter, Helen Louise said, "Let me warm this, and lunch will be ready." She took the container to the microwave. "Ordinarily I wouldn't do this, but this is best served warm."

While she attended to the bean salad, I set the table.

We started with the cold soup, then moved on to the chicken and the bean salad. Our final course consisted of brie and grapes. During the meal I shared with Helen Louise all that Ernie Carpenter had told me about Bill Delaney, his mother, and the Barber family.

"Horrible," Helen Louise said when I finished. "Just horrible. I wish they had found the killer. I'd hate to think that person is still walking around free and unpunished."

"Yes, me too," I said.

Diesel came into the kitchen, meowing. Over that I heard baby Charlie crying. "Probably needs his diaper changed." I pushed back my chair and moved toward the hallway. "I'll go check on him. He can't be hungry already." I stopped suddenly as something occurred to me. "What would we feed him if he is hungry? Surely Laura and Frank brought milk."

Helen Louise said, "Yes, they did. Frank put it in the fridge while you were in the living room with the baby."

"Thank goodness." I hurried to the living room as my grandson's volume began to increase. Diesel trotted right along with me to supervise.

The bawling ceased when I touched the baby. He looked up at me with such trusting eyes, and I smiled, my face now only about twelve inches from his. "It's okay, Charlie. Grandpa's here, and so is your nursemaid." Diesel warbled loudly, and the baby smiled.

He had really smiled. It wasn't just the reflexive smile all babies have in their first month or two. He smiled in response to my smile. He was also making eye contact with me. Two milestones in a baby's life, and today of all days. Laura hadn't mentioned to me that Charlie could do either one of these things.

"We'll have big news for your mama and daddy when they come to pick you up." I examined the diaper, and my nose wrinkled at the smell. "You definitely need a change, mister."

Diesel meowed loudly, no doubt intrigued by the smell. He watched as I cleaned the baby and put him in a fresh diaper. I talked to Charlie the whole time, using every chance I had to get him accustomed to my voice. It shouldn't be long now before he started cooing.

Helen Louise joined Diesel and me beside the crib. "He is the most perfectly beautiful child I've ever seen," she said.

I heard the wistful note in her voice. We had talked once about having children, and she admitted during that conversation that she would have loved to be a mother. Trying to establish her law career and working the long hours that entailed gave her no opportunity for motherhood. Then when she decided she'd had enough of the legal career and moved to France to pursue her culinary dream, she'd been too busy learning. Back in Athena again, she was working hard to establish a new business. By the time she thought about having a child, she was over forty with no good prospect for a father in sight. Now that I was in the picture, with us both in our early fifties, we were too old to have a child. Nor did either of us any longer have the energy to adopt and rear one.

"Yes, he is." I put my arm around her and drew her close. We stood that way for a minute or two, Diesel as entranced by the baby as we were. He smiled again as we both talked to him. Then he yawned, ready to go back to sleep. I wrapped him up again, and Helen Louise and I returned to the kitchen. The ever-vigilant feline nursemaid remained on duty.

"There's a bit of brie left." Helen Louise gestured toward the cheese as she resumed her seat. "I know it's your favorite, so it's up to you to finish it off." She picked up a grape and popped it in her mouth.

I sighed. "Yes, it is. I've already eaten too much, but I can't resist that lonely piece." I picked it up and was enjoying it when the house phone rang. I hurriedly swallowed so that I could speak clearly into the phone. I grabbed the receiver and greeted the caller. "This is Charlie Harris."

A woman's voice sounded in my ear. "Good afternoon, Mr. Harris. I'm calling from the emergency room at Athena Medical Center."

SEVENTEEN

||||||||||||||||||||||||||||||||||||||||||||||||||||||||||||||||||

My heart rate increased dramatically as my mind conjured up terrible images of family members in distress.

Before I could speak, she gave me her name, which I promptly forgot. She continued, "We have a Mr. William Delaney here who's been badly injured in an apparent hit-and-run. He is asking for you. He says you're his cousin."

"Yes, I am." There was no point in arguing over the technicalities of the relationship. "I'll be on the way in a minute. How badly is he hurt?"

"It would be better to talk about it here," the woman said. "Please come as soon as you can." She ended the call.

I hung up the phone and turned to Helen Louise. Noting her expression of concern, I quickly relayed the gist of the call.

"You go," she said. "I'll stay here and keep an eye on things. Call me and let me know how he is when you know more."

I made sure I had my cell phone in my pocket. I gave

her a quick kiss, grabbed my keys, and headed into the garage. The last thing I wanted to do today was spend time in a hospital. I had spent more time than I ever cared to remember in hospitals, thanks to my parents' health issues in their later years, though they both died relatively young, in their sixties. I clocked many an hour in Houston hospitals because of my late wife Jackie's diagnosis of pancreatic cancer.

By the time I found out, a few months after Jackie died, that Aunt Dottie had been diagnosed with the same cancer, Aunt Dottie had only a week to live. She hadn't wanted to worry me, she said, because she knew I was grieving the loss of my wife. Because Azalea thought I should know my aunt was dying, I managed to see her the last day of her life, in this same hospital, long enough to say good-bye to her.

No, I wasn't fond of hospitals, but I felt I had no choice. I couldn't ignore Bill Delaney's request.

The hospital wasn't all that far from my house, but with traffic and stoplights it took me almost twenty minutes to get there. Once I parked and locked the car, it took me several more minutes to get to the emergency room. By the time I reached the desk, I reckoned half an hour had passed since the call. I feared the worst when I inquired about the status of Bill Delaney.

"I'm his cousin, Charlie Harris," I said. "Someone called and told me he has been asking for me."

The woman at the desk nodded. "I called you. He's in room six. You can go on back. The doc wants to talk to you. I think she's with him now." She pointed the way.

I hurried to Delaney's room, surrounded by the sounds of people talking in quiet tones along with the hums and beeps of machines. A baby cried nearby, and my heart constricted. I hoped the child wasn't the patient.

I found room six and knocked on the door. A woman's voice called for me to come in, and I did. The first thing I saw was Bill Delaney, his head bandaged, lying on the bed. On either side of him stood a woman and a man in scrubs. The woman wore a white jacket. Once I closed the door behind me, I also noticed another person in the room, a police officer who was standing in the corner. The chill air of the room made me all too conscious of my thin-cotton short-sleeved shirt.

"I'm Charlie Harris, Mr. Delaney's cousin. How is he?"

"Stable." The doctor, whom I recognized from a previous visit here a few years ago, introduced herself as Leann Finch. "I remember you, Mr. Harris. You've been here before."

I nodded. "Yes, I remember you, too, Dr. Finch. Will he be all right? The woman who called said he'd been injured in a hit-and-run."

"We've checked for internal injuries, and I'm thankful to tell you that there don't seem to be any. Just external wounds. Badly scraped head and arms. The real problem is his legs. He has broken both of them. The officer here can tell you more."

The policeman stepped forward. "I spoke to a couple of witnesses who said they saw him a few seconds before the car hit him. He was walking down the sidewalk about twenty feet away. Husband said Mr. Delaney seemed unsteady on his feet and stepped into the street. Into the path of the car."

"I see," I replied. "Thank you."

The policeman nodded and moved back to the corner. I turned to the doctor again.

"Does your cousin have a history of alcohol abuse?" Dr. Finch asked.

"From what I know of him," I said, "yes, he does." I

explained quickly that I had only recently met my so-called cousin and only knew a little about his history.

"His blood alcohol level indicates that he's inebriated, well over the limit," Dr. Finch said. "That accounts for him being unsteady on his feet."

"No doubt." I shook my head as I regarded the unconscious man. "I went by to see him this morning and found him passed out. He roused for a moment but then went back to sleep." I turned to the policeman. "Did anyone catch a glimpse of the driver who hit him?"

"The two witnesses who saw it happen said they thought the driver was a woman, but it might have been a man with long hair, too." He shrugged. "They're actually in the waiting room if you want to talk to them. Young couple just finished eating at that place on the square, you know, the French café."

"I know it well," I said. "I would like to talk to them. Thank you, Officer."

"We need to set the patient's broken legs, Mr. Harris," Dr. Finch said. "There's nothing else you can do at the moment." She glanced at Bill Delaney, sound asleep on the bed. "The pain medication knocked him out. He'll be able to talk to you later this afternoon when we have moved him to a regular bed."

"Thank you, Doctor," I said. "I'll be in the waiting room if you need me."

Dr. Finch nodded, already turning back to tend to Delaney. I left the room and made my way back to the waiting room. I was anxious to speak to the young couple who had witnessed the accident. I felt compelled to know everything I could about what had happened.

I passed the desk and walked into the large waiting area. I hadn't gone more than three steps when I heard my daughter's voice. Shocked, I turned to see her and Frank in the far corner of the room to my left. I walked over to them, and they rose from their seats to greet me.

"Dad, what on earth are you doing here?" Laura laid a hand on my arm and regarded me closely, her expression anxious. "Is it Charlie?"

"Is everything okay with Charlie? You didn't bring him here, did you?" Frank asked at the same time.

"Everything is fine. Helen Louise is at home with little Charlie." I watched them both relax, the worry draining from them. They sank back into their seats and looked up at me. I took an empty seat next to Laura. "Let me ask you two a question. Are you here because you were witnesses to a hit-and-run outside Helen Louise's place?"

"How on earth did you know that?" Frank stared at me and shook his head. "You're not psychic, are you?"

"I know because the man who was hit is Bill Delaney," I said. When they continued to look blank, I realized they had no idea who I was talking about. "Sorry, I need to tell you a few things."

I gave them the short version about Bill and his parentage. The rest of the story that included the Barber murders could wait till later.

"So he told the staff he's your cousin, sort of?" Laura's nose wrinkled, an habitual sign of confusion with her.

"By marriage only," I said. "I'm the only person he knows here, I guess, and I'm certainly the closest thing to family he has left. At least that I know about."

"The poor man," Laura said. "He was stumbling along, and I told Frank I was afraid he was going to end up in the street. Sure enough, he did, and that car hit him."

"Rotten break for him, though I can't say I'm surprised. He reeked of beer," Frank said. "Is he going to be okay?"

I relayed what the doctor had told me, and they both looked relieved. "The broken legs will be problematic, once they release him from the hospital. He has a second-floor apartment, and I don't think he'll be able to get up and down the stairs in his condition."

"No, he won't," Laura said. "What about one of those skilled nursing facilities? Frank's grandmother went to one after she fell at home and broke both arms. They took good care of her until she was able to go home again."

"That's an excellent idea." I had been envisioning bringing Delaney to my house and looking after him with Azalea's assistance. A skilled nursing facility was obviously the better option.

"If he has Medicare," Frank said, "I believe they'll cover it, depending on how long he needs to stay."

"He's sixty-six," I said. "I assume he has it. That takes a load off my mind, I can tell you."

"Why? Were you thinking you'd have to look after him?" Frank asked.

I nodded. "I couldn't in all conscience let them send him back to that apartment on his own."

Laura patted my arm. "No, *you* wouldn't, Dad, but most people wouldn't go that far out of their way for a stranger."

I smiled my thanks for her sweet words. "There's something else I have to tell you about him, I'm afraid."

"This doesn't sound good, judging by your tone," Frank said.

"It's not." I told them about the Barber murders, and while I talked, I caught an odd expression on my son-in-law's face. I supposed he must recall the case since he grew up in the delta not far from Tullahoma.

"How horrible," Laura said. "People really thought he did it?"

I nodded. "His mother was his alibi. According to her he came home drunk that afternoon, and he stayed in his room all night and never left the house. The police tried to shake her, but she never wavered. That's what I was told, anyway." I glanced at Frank. "You obviously know something about this case."

"Yes, I do," Frank said. "I was twelve years old when the murders occurred. I've never brought this up before, not even to Laura, because it's not exactly the kind of thing you casually introduce into a conversation."

"What are you talking about, honey?" Laura asked, obviously puzzled.

"Elizabeth Barber is a cousin of mine," Frank said. "My second cousin, actually. We share a great-grandmother through my father and her mother. We never had much to do with the family, though, because my dad couldn't stand Hiram Barber. I wouldn't have recognized him if I'd met him on the street."

"Talk about a weird coincidence," Laura said. "Your cousin is the only survivor of a multiple homicide." She shook her head. "Creepy *and* weird."

This turn of events fascinated me, and I wanted to talk to Frank more about the Barber family and his family's take on the case. Before we got into that, however, I wanted to bring the subject back to Bill Delaney and his accident.

"I want to talk to you more about it, if you don't mind," I said. Frank nodded. "At the moment, though, I want you to tell me about the hit-and-run. How much did you see?"

Frank and Laura looked at each other. Then Frank nodded again, and Laura turned to me and began, "We had barely walked out of the bistro's door and onto the sidewalk when I glanced to my right and noticed this elderly man kind of tottering along. I told Frank to look at him because I was afraid the man was going to fall any second."

Frank took up the account. "Laura's right. He was

stumbling badly, and I moved around her so I could get to him quickly if he started to fall."

"How far away from him were you?" I asked.

"Maybe twenty feet," Frank said.

"About," Laura said. "Maybe a little farther away."

"What happened next?" I asked.

"He suddenly stumbled sideways," Frank replied. "Two seconds, and he was in the street. Well, in the parking spots, actually. I started after him, and he kept moving, still mostly sideways. He cleared the parking spots and was almost two feet, I'd say, into the street. I lunged after him, but before I could get to him a car sideswiped him and knocked him to the ground. The car kept going. I tried to see the license but the sun was in my eyes. I recognized the make and model, though."

"You saw all this, too," I said to Laura.

"Yes, and more than Frank because I was looking at the street." She paused, frowning. "I know this might sound crazy, but I think that car swerved deliberately to hit the man."

EIGHTEEN

||||||||||||||||||||||||||||||||||||||||||||||||

Laura's statement disturbed me. If she was interpreting what she saw correctly, that meant someone had deliberately tried to kill or injure Bill Delaney. Why on earth would someone want him dead?

"Think about it carefully," I said. "Close your eyes and replay the scene in your mind. Tell us what you see."

"All right, Dad." Laura closed her eyes.

Frank and I watched her. She didn't speak right away. She leaned back in her seat. I could see her relaxing her body, bit by bit. "Okay," she said. "Frank and I are coming out of the bistro. He's holding the door like he always does. Such a Southern gentleman." She smiled briefly, then resumed her narrative. "I step out first and glance to my right because I don't want to walk into anyone. I see an elderly man weaving his way toward us. He's about thirty feet away, maybe." She paused.

"That's excellent," I said in a low tone. "Go on."

Laura nodded. "I'm worried the poor man might fall and hurt himself, so I tell Frank to look at him. Frank does and then he moves around me to walk toward the man to help him in case he does start to fall. Then the man kind of shambles sideways a few steps, and he's off the curb now into an empty parking space."

Laura paused for a deep, steadying breath. "I see that Frank is moving toward him quickly to try to catch him before he falls into the street. I'm afraid a car might hit him, so I glance toward the street. A car is coming kind of fast, a big, dark SUV of some kind. I want to shout and wave at the car, but I can't. I'm too horrified. I watch as the car gets near the poor man who is now a little bit into the street. Frank is almost there."

She frowned. "The car seems to jerk, hard to the right, as it nears the man. It hits him, and Frank reaches for him but he falls to the pavement. The car accelerated and disappeared down a side street." She opened her eyes.

"Have you told this to the policeman?" I asked.

"I wasn't sure I really saw it," Laura said. "Now, though, I know I did."

I believed her. She had an excellent visual memory.

"You know, I saw it, too." Frank frowned. "I was visualizing it while Laura talked, and now I remember seeing the car come close and hitting the man. There was a kind of jerky motion to it. So I think Laura's right. Whoever did it meant to do it."

"Did either of you get a look at the driver?" I asked.

"Sort of," Laura said. "The windows were lightly tinted, but I could see someone in profile. Whoever it was had longish hair, but I didn't see them long enough to get an impression of gender."

"I didn't see that much," Frank said. "I was focused on the victim."

"Anything else about the car, other than that it was a large, dark SUV?" I asked.

"Yes." Frank told me the make and model. "An expensive vehicle, probably less than two years old."

"It's not much to go on," I said, "but there could be other witnesses. That's up to the police, though."

Laura nudged me. "Here's the cop now," she said in an undertone.

I stood to greet the officer. "Bizarre coincidence, as it turns out. This young couple who saw the accident are my daughter and son-in-law. My daughter has more information for you."

"What would that be, ma'am?" the policeman asked.

"Excuse me." I saw the woman from the front desk in the doorway to the waiting room waving at me. "I think I'm needed."

I approached the woman. "What can I do for you, ma'am?"

"We're hoping you can help us with more information about the patient," she said. "Would you mind coming back to the desk with me?"

"Of course," I said as I followed her. "I have to tell you, though, I may not be much help. I barely know Mr. Delaney despite the fact that we are somewhat related."

"Anything you can tell us is helpful," she said. "The person with the questions is at the end of the desk there." She pointed toward a young black man with a clipboard.

I walked over. The young man stood and indicated a chair by the desk. I took it while he resumed his seat. "What can I help you with?"

"You're related to Mr. Delaney?" the young man asked.

I nodded. "By marriage. His father was married to my aunt. Both of them are deceased. I didn't meet Mr. Delaney until recently, and I don't know many details of his life. I'm willing to answer whatever I can."

"Thank you." The young man had his eyes on his

clipboard. "He has his driver's license and his Medicare card with him. According to the license he lives in Tullahoma. Is that correct?"

"As far as I know," I said, "that is his permanent residence. He has been staying in an apartment in Athena, however, for the past few weeks." I gave him the address, and he added it to the form.

"Are you his next of kin?"

I shrugged. "In a way, I suppose I am. I don't know whether he has any other family. Whether he's married, divorced, has children of his own, anything like that."

"For our purposes, you'll do, if you consent to that."

"That's fine," I said. "Do you have any other questions?"

"No, sir. Thank you for your help."

I stood and nodded, smiling, then I walked back to the waiting room. The policeman was still with Laura and Frank.

Laura looked unhappy, and Frank looked aggravated. I gathered that perhaps telling the officer they thought the hit-and-run was deliberate hadn't gone over well.

"What's the matter?" I asked when I reached them.

"I don't think he believes us," Laura said, confirming my suspicion.

I stared hard at the policeman. "Officer, if my daughter tells you she saw that car swerve toward Mr. Delaney, then that car swerved toward Mr. Delaney."

The policeman put up a hand as if to ward off a blow or to get me to be quiet. "Okay, whatever you say. Now, since you're the only one here who seems to know the victim, what can you tell me about him? Other family? He seems to be from Tullahoma, according to his driver's license."

Once again I went through the bare list of facts I knew about Bill Delaney, omitting, of course, anything about his connection to the Barber case. If the police wanted to delve into his past, it wouldn't take them long to find it out for themselves.

"So you don't think he knows anyone here?" the policeman said. "Do you know where he's staying here in town?"

"I can answer the latter question." I gave him the address. "As to whether he knows anyone, I don't know. I've only encountered him at the library." While I was speaking, a memory surfaced. That lipstick Diesel found in the apartment. That must belong to someone Delaney knew.

"I went to see him earlier today, I believe you will remember my telling y'all that in his room a little while ago."

The officer nodded, and I continued. "While we—my cat and I, that is—were there, my cat found a lipstick on the floor and was playing with it. So someone else had been in the apartment, presumably, besides us and Mr. Delaney."

"You had your cat with you?" The policeman frowned. "Hey, wait a minute, I know who you are now. You've got that ginormous cat, and you take it around all over town with you."

"Yes, I do. His name is Diesel, and he's a Maine Coon." I didn't feel like giving the man the rest of the spiel about the breed that I usually shared. The size of my cat had nothing to do with the present situation. I was getting irked by this man and his attitude. I glanced at his badge and noted his name. *Kernodle*. I would remember it.

The policeman must have sensed my annoyance. He turned back to Laura and Frank. "We don't have much to go on with the description you gave me of the car, but we'll have to see if anyone else in the area saw what happened. If we're lucky, maybe someone got the license number, or one of the businesses might have a surveillance camera."

We'll be in touch if we need to talk to you again." He nodded before he turned and strode out of the waiting room.

"What now?" Frank looked at Laura. "I guess we'd better give up on the movie for today."

"I'm not in the mood for it anymore," Laura said. "Maybe next weekend?"

Frank looked at me. "That okay with you, Charlie?"

"Of course," I said. "At the moment, I don't have any plans for next Saturday. If anything comes up, I'll let you know."

"Thanks, Dad." Laura hugged me. "You're the best."

"Are you going to stick around here?" Frank asked as they prepared to leave.

"I was planning to, but I'm having second thoughts about that," I said. "It could be a couple of hours or more before I can see Delaney and talk to him. I'm thinking of going home. They can call me if I'm needed. It's not like I live an hour away."

"No, there's nothing in Athena that's more than about thirty minutes from anything else." Frank smiled. "One of the perks of living in a small town."

"Yes," I said. "After living in Houston all those years, it's a pleasure not to have to spend an hour in the car to get to a place not that far away." I did miss a few things about Houston, chiefly its variety of restaurants and bookstores, but not its size or its traffic. "Y'all go ahead. I'm going to stop by the desk and let them know I'm going home."

Laura and Frank headed for the parking lot. I spoke briefly to the woman at the desk, and I finally noticed her name tag. *Rosalie McAlister.* I felt bad about not having remembered her name earlier. I thanked her, using her name, after I gave her my home phone number.

"Someone will call you when he's able to have visitors," she said.

With that assurance, I left the hospital. On the drive home I thought about the hit-and-run. Why had someone hit Bill Delaney on purpose? A random act of violence? Sadly there were people in the world who would do things like that, I knew. I suspected, however, that there was a personal motive behind this attack.

I didn't know what Delaney's personality was like when he was drinking heavily. Was he combative? Aggressive? Or was he the quiet type of drunk who didn't bother anyone and kept to himself?

If he was the nasty, bellicose sort of drunk, he could easily have made a number of enemies over the years, I reckoned. Maybe one of them had seen him lumbering toward the street and seized the opportunity when he moved within striking distance.

I suddenly remembered something Haskell had told me. Not long after the initial investigation into the Barber murders failed to produce a viable suspect, Delaney had disappeared from Tullahoma. No one, perhaps other than his mother, knew where he had been since then. He suddenly resurfaced in Athena after his mother's death. In Tullahoma, I presumed. I ought to check on that and find out where she died. Ernie Carpenter might know. I figured there would have been something in the Tullahoma newspaper about Sylvia Delaney's passing.

I had the uneasy feeling that the hit-and-run was connected to the events of twenty years ago—the Barber case. There was that lipstick in Delaney's apartment to account for. It could have been left there by the previous tenant, I supposed, but somehow I didn't think it had. Surely Delaney would have noticed it and disposed of it before Diesel found it this morning.

Delaney's life could be in danger. If the person who struck him down found out Delaney was still alive, he or she might try again. The man seemed to have no friends, and we were connected by the fact of his father's marriage to my aunt. My step-cousin.

I knew what Aunt Dottie would want me to do.

By now I had reached home. I turned into the driveway and pulled into the garage. I left the car's motor and air-conditioning running while I dug my phone out of my pocket. I found Jack Pemberton's number in my list of calls and tapped the call button. I waited long enough for an answer that I thought the call was going to voice mail, but Jack finally answered.

He must have recognized my number because he greeted me by name. "Have you thought it over?" he asked. "About us working on the Barber case?"

"Yes," I said. "I'm in."

NINETEEN

‖‖‖

I regretted those last two words the moment they were out of my mouth because I foresaw nothing but difficulties in involving myself in a twenty-year-old quadruple homicide case. I also knew that I couldn't back out now, not with Aunt Dottie's voice in my head urging me to do whatever I could to help Uncle Del's son.

"That's great, Charlie," Jack said. "How about we get together tomorrow and talk about it? That is, if you've got time. I can come to Athena or, if you'd rather, you can come here. My wife knows all about this and is really looking forward to meeting you."

"I'll have to call you back later today about getting together," I said. "I need to discuss this with my family first. I made the decision only a minute ago, and they need to know about it. There's also more to tell you from this end, but I can't go into it right now."

"Okay, whatever works. Call me when you're ready," Jack said.

"Will do." I ended the call.

I sat in the car, trying to plan how I was going to present my decision to Helen Louise and my children. I didn't think any of them would be really happy with me about this. Sean would be more upset than anyone else. He was the one who usually nagged me the most about my knack for getting involved in murder cases.

I switched off the air conditioner and the ignition. *Time to go in and get it over with*, I told myself.

Diesel greeted me at the door with a loud recital of things he had to tell me. A couple of the meows sounded like complaints because no matter whom I left him with, he was always aggravated that I left him behind when I went anywhere. I rubbed his head several times, which had the desired effect. I seemed to be forgiven.

"He was perfectly happy with me and baby Charlie until he heard you pull into the garage." Helen Louise gave me a kiss. "I guess that's when he remembered that you abandoned him."

I laughed. "He's the nagging wife I never had, or at least it feels that way sometimes." I kissed Helen Louise back. "Are Laura and Frank still here? I didn't notice whether their car was parked on the street."

"They're in the living room getting Charlie ready to go home," Helen Louise said. "They haven't said much of anything about Bill Delaney because Laura couldn't wait to see the baby. How is he?"

"Two broken legs and skinned up in various places, including his head," I said. "My impression was that he would be okay. They didn't find any signs of internal injuries."

"Thank goodness. That poor man," Helen Louise said. "I hope they catch the driver."

"I do, too." I helped myself to a can of diet soda from

the fridge before I joined Helen Louise at the table. Diesel had evidently gone back to check on the baby after he finished chastising me and being petted.

Frank stepped into the kitchen. "Thanks for looking after Charlie." He smiled. "My only regret is that you didn't get to do it a bit longer today."

Helen Louise and I smiled. "Next weekend," I said. "Hopefully things will be calmer then." Seeing Frank start to turn away, I said, "If y'all can stay a few more minutes, there's something I really need to talk to you about."

"Sure," Frank said. "Let me get Laura." He disappeared into the hallway.

"I need to remind Laura about the milk she brought over. I gave Charlie one bottle a little while ago, but there's another one in the fridge," Helen Louise said.

I nodded. Moments later Laura and Frank came into the kitchen. Laura held my sleeping grandson. Diesel kept pace beside her. "What is it you want to talk about, Dad?" Frank pulled out a chair for her, and once she was settled he took the vacant chair across from her. Diesel stretched out on the floor beside Laura's chair.

"Before I forget it, there's one bottle of milk left," Helen Louise said. "I forgot to tell you earlier."

"Thanks," Frank said. "I'll grab it before we leave."

"Go ahead, Dad," Laura said. "We're listening."

Here goes, I thought. "You all already know that I feel a sense of responsibility for Bill Delaney's welfare, thanks to his connection to Aunt Dottie, tenuous as it is after all these years."

They all nodded. Helen Louise's eyes narrowed as she regarded me intently. I had a feeling she had figured out what I was going to say to them.

"Jack Pemberton wants to investigate the Barber murders to see if he can solve them," I said. "He wants me to help him, and I called him a few minutes ago and said I would. And here's one reason why. Someone attempted to kill Bill Delaney today. I don't believe it was a random thing. I believe that his life could be in danger as long as the Barber case remains unsolved."

Helen Louise's expression of shock reminded me belatedly that she hadn't heard Laura's version of the hit-and-run. I hastily explained, and the shock faded, to be replaced by calculation. I knew that meant she had her legal mindset engaged and was assessing the facts. I loved her ability to analyze and draw reasonable conclusions.

"Seems to me there are two plausible motives for the hit-and-run," Helen Louise said. "The first is revenge. Someone believes Bill Delaney got away with murder and decided to see justice done. The second is fear. The murderer believes Bill Delaney knows something that could incriminate him."

"Exactly what I've been thinking," I said.

"Sounds reasonable to me," Frank said.

"Me, too," Laura said. "But, Dad, whoever the killer is, he isn't going to be happy to find out you and Jack Pemberton are digging into the case. You could both be putting your lives at risk. I don't like that."

Diesel sat up and warbled. He came to stand beside me and placed a paw on my leg. The tension level in the room had risen suddenly, and he was worried. I scratched his head. "It's really okay, boy," I told him.

"I don't like it much myself," I said. "I suppose the police might reopen the case now, or rather the sheriff's department in Tullahoma. I believe they ran the first investigation. If it were the Athena County Sheriff's Department, Kanesha would be in charge of it, and I'd be happy not to get any more involved. I have faith in her intelligence and her abilities. I know nothing about her counterpart in Tullahoma."

"Unless they've turned up compelling new evidence," Frank said, "I doubt they're going to reopen the case. I don't think they'll consider the hit-and-run reason enough. Reopening the case will cost money, and budgets are tight. They might not be able to afford it."

"You realize what you just said will only encourage him." Laura's voice had taken on an acid tone. I had never heard her speak like that to her husband.

"I know that, honey," Frank said, his tone sharp. "But I don't think I said anything your father hasn't probably already figured out for himself."

Laura sighed. "You're right. Sorry I got huffy."

Frank grinned. "You know you can't stay mad at me."

Laura rolled her eyes in response.

I glanced at Helen Louise, and I could see immediately that she was not happy with me. "Your turn," I said.

She continued to regard me in silence, and I thought perhaps she was too angry to speak. Then she said, "One of the things I love about you, Charlie, is your caring heart. This man, this stranger, has no real claim to your time or your concern, despite the fact that his biological father happened to be married to your aunt. But you think helping him is the right thing to do to honor your aunt's love for her husband and the gratitude you feel for all she gave you. I'm not talking about the house and the money, though they're part of it. She was one of the most wonderful, bighearted, generous women I've ever known, and she helped make you who you are. I bless her for that. I'm not happy about your putting yourself at risk over this situation, but I understand your sense of obligation."

As she talked, her expression softened, and I not only

heard but felt the love in those words. I wasn't sure I deserved a partner as understanding and supportive, but I was thankful every day that she had come back into my life.

"Frank, get that bottle out of the fridge, please." Laura stood, baby Charlie in her arms. "I think it's time we went home." She looked from me to Helen Louise and back. "I think there's nothing more that needs to be said other than: I love you, Dad, so please be careful." She smiled.

I felt too overwhelmed by my jumbled emotions at the moment to speak. Diesel rubbed his head against my leg and, as if by reflex, my hand began to stroke his back.

I managed to pull myself together enough to walk to the front door with my departing daughter and son-in-law and baby Charlie. I kissed the baby's forehead. He opened his eyes and smiled. Then he yawned and went back to sleep.

After I saw them out the door, I watched, Diesel at my side, until they drove away. When I closed and locked the door, I turned to see Helen Louise waiting at the foot of the stairs. She held out a hand to me as I walked over. I grasped her hand, and we walked slowly upstairs.

Two hours later my ringing phone roused me from sleep. I felt Helen Louise stirring beside me. I watched her for a moment, reluctant to let the outside world intrude. She yawned and pushed strands of dark hair away from her eyes.

"Hadn't you better answer that?" she asked.

Diesel, who must have walked in while we were sleeping, meowed.

"Unfortunately, yes," I said as I reached for the receiver. I knew it must be the hospital. "Hello, Charlie Harris speaking."

"Good afternoon, Mr. Harris," a male voice said. "I'm a nurse at Athena Medical Center, and I'm calling you on behalf of one of our patients, a Mr. William Delaney. He is awake and resting comfortably. He would like to talk to you when you have time to come see him."

"Thank you for calling," I said. "Please let him know that I'll be there in about thirty or forty minutes."

"Sure thing."

I replaced the receiver and turned to Helen Louise and Diesel. "The hospital," I said. "Bill Delaney would like me to visit. He's awake and resting comfortably."

"What time is it?" Helen Louise asked. She yawned again, and that made me yawn.

I checked the bedside clock. "Three forty-seven." I turned back to her. She placed a hand on my chest, and I covered it with my own hand. Then I grasped her hand, pulled it to my lips, and kissed it.

Helen Louise smiled. "Are you going?"

I sighed. "Yes, though I'd much rather stay right here with you."

Diesel warbled.

"And with you, too, silly boy," I said. The cat chirped and looked smug. "I need to shower first."

"Go ahead," Helen Louise said. "Diesel and I will be right here." She stroked the cat's head, and he began to purr.

I threw back the covers and slipped out of bed. I turned for a moment to look at my beloved, and I wanted to climb right back into bed and pull her into my arms again. But duty called.

Forty minutes later I arrived at the hospital. I checked at the front desk to find out Delaney's room number. He was on the third floor. I headed to the elevator.

The door was ajar. I knocked, and a hoarse voice called out, "Come in."

I left the door halfway open after I entered the room. I approached the bed, shocked by Delaney's appearance even though I had seen him earlier in the emergency room. His head was still bandaged, but he seemed alert. His legs had casts, and they protruded from the covers on the bed. Both arms had bandages, and his face appeared haggard. I noticed two scraped places on his face, one on his chin and the other on his left cheek. His eyes were sunken, and he looked much older than his sixty-six years.

"Thanks for coming."

"I'm sorry you were injured so badly." I moved closer to the bed. "I hope you're getting pain medication because I'm sure you're hurting." I pulled up a chair, positioned it close to the bed so he could see me, and sat.

"Don't feel much of anything right now," he said.

"Do you remember what happened?"

"No." He looked away as if embarrassed. "Too drunk. I don't remember leaving the apartment." He frowned as he turned his head to face me again. "Don't know how I got downtown. I was so lit I don't see how I made it down the stairs without killing myself."

I had wondered about that myself. His apartment was several miles from the town square. How *had* he managed to walk that far in his condition? *Probably took the bus*, I thought. He couldn't have walked that distance.

"You must have got on the bus somewhere near your apartment," I said.

"Maybe," Delaney replied. "Got a bus pass."

"The police will find out," I said. "I'm sure the driver would remember."

"Probably so."

"My daughter and son-in-law happened to be there when it happened," I said. "They saw the whole thing."

Delaney frowned. "I don't remember anything. Can you tell me what they saw?"

"Sure." I related the story to him. "Now, my daughter is sure that driver deliberately hit you. Do you know anyone who would have a reason to do that?"

Delaney looked startled, and for a moment he also looked afraid. Then his expression turned bland. "No."

He was lying. I knew by his reaction he had an idea who had run him down. Why wouldn't he give me a name? Who was he protecting?

TWENTY

‖‖‖‖‖‖‖‖‖‖‖‖‖‖‖‖‖‖‖‖‖‖‖‖‖‖‖‖‖‖‖‖‖‖‖‖

"Are you sure about that?" I asked.

"Yeah," Delaney replied. "I appreciate you coming to the hospital, but I really got no claim on you. You've been kind, but I can't impose on you anymore."

He wanted to get rid of me, and that convinced me he was lying about the hit-and-run driver. I didn't think now was the time to press him on the subject, however. He looked beaten down and vulnerable due to his condition, and I couldn't force myself to play a bad-cop routine when he was like this. I would give him a day or two to think about it, because he had obviously had no idea someone tried to kill him until I told him. After he thought about that nasty fact he might change his mind about talking to me.

I rose. "I've been glad to help, although I really haven't done much. Is there anything you need?"

He shook his head, then winced. "No, thanks. Like I

said, you've done more than enough. Right now I just need to rest."

"All right," I said. "But if you change your mind, I'm only a phone call away."

He nodded, then closed his eyes. I stood there a moment longer, but he didn't move or open his eyes. I turned and left the room, pulling the door halfway closed as it had been when I arrived.

As I approached my car in the parking lot a few minutes later, I remembered I needed to call Jack Pemberton and fill him in on today's events. I didn't like talking on the phone while I was driving, even though I now had a car—purchased last month—that allowed me to sync my cell phone to its audio system and talk hands-free. I had used the feature only twice, but, while it was convenient, I was still concerned that I might get distracted. Even though I had conversations when there were people in the car with me and managed not to have accidents, a phone conversation didn't feel the same.

When I arrived home, Helen Louise and Diesel greeted me at the back door. I kissed Helen Louise before I gave Diesel a scratch on the head, and he didn't seem to mind.

"You're back sooner than I expected," Helen Louise said.

"Sooner than I expected also," I replied. "He says he doesn't really remember anything, other than that he thinks he took the bus to get downtown from his apartment. After that he's pretty blank."

"Did you tell him what Laura saw?"

I nodded. "Right after that he suddenly didn't want to impose on me anymore. Thanked me for my help but pretty much told me to buzz off. Not rudely, though."

"Maybe he didn't believe you about the deliberate hit," Helen Louise said.

"I'm pretty sure he did, although he denied knowledge

of anyone who would want to injure or kill him. I decided there was no point in arguing with him today. He looks pretty pitiful." I described his appearance to Helen Louise.

She grimaced. "Poor man, I hope he's going to be able to recover from this."

"He'll get excellent care at the hospital," I said, "but I have no idea how long they'll keep him there. When I go back to see him in a day or two, he might know more about what the plan is for his rehab."

"I hope he's sensible and confides in you, or at least in the police," Helen Louise said.

"We'll see," I replied. "What are your plans for the rest of the afternoon and this evening?"

"Depends on what you have in mind," Helen Louise said.

"I need to call Jack Pemberton and bring him up-to-date on the latest events," I said. "Plus arrange to get together to plan our investigation. That shouldn't take more than an hour. I'd say we might go out for dinner, but Diesel would have to be on his own. Unless Stewart and Haskell are going to be here."

Hearing his name, the cat meowed loudly. I always suspected he understood the word *alone*. He wouldn't be happy left in the house by himself. I wouldn't be happy, either. I knew I spoiled him terribly, but he was a member of the family.

"I'd just as soon stay at home for dinner," Helen Louise said. "I thought I might run home, have a quick shower and change. I have the ingredients for what I'd like to cook, and I'll bring them back with me."

"Wouldn't you rather cook at your house?" I said. "Diesel and I can come to your place if you'd prefer."

"I'd rather come back here." Helen Louise gave me a

kiss before she picked up her purse from the counter. "I'll be back in an hour."

The muffled sounds of a cell phone ringtone emanated from her purse. Helen Louise dug the phone out and frowned when she saw who was calling. "The bistro," she said to me before she answered.

I heard only her side of the conversation, and it didn't take long to figure out that one of her employees had injured himself and was out of commission for the rest of the day. Helen Louise ended the call after promising to be there in about half an hour. She put the phone away.

"Sorry, love." She grimaced.

"Who's hurt?"

"Henry cut his left hand pretty badly, and a friend who was in the bistro when it happened has taken him to the emergency room. They're shorthanded now, so I'm going to have to go in and work. Probably tomorrow, too, because I don't imagine Henry will be able to do much."

"You get going. I'm sorry your day away ended like this, but even sorrier for poor Henry." I slid my arm around her and pulled her to me for another kiss. After several highly satisfying seconds she pulled away.

"Talk to you later," she said. Diesel followed her to the door, warbling all the way. She rubbed his head quickly before she walked out the door. He stood there for at least thirty seconds, but when she didn't come back through the door he returned to my side.

Time to call Jack Pemberton. I poured myself a glass of ice water before I settled at the table. Diesel stretched out by my chair.

Jack answered right away. "Hi, Charlie. What's been going on?"

"Hey, Jack," I said. "Interesting developments involving Bill Delaney. I'm curious to get your take on everything." He listened while I told him what had happened today and didn't comment until I finished. That pleased me because I really hated having my train of thought interrupted while I was trying to make sure I didn't leave out any details. "So what do you think?"

"First off, I think you're right. He has some idea of who might want to put him out of the way permanently. Now, whether it's an old enemy with a score to settle, or the killer in the Barber case trying to get rid of him before he tells what he knows . . ." He paused. "Could be either situation."

"True," I said. "It could also be a vigilante type who thinks he got away with murder and decided to see justice done. I'm inclined to think it's got to be related to the murders in some way."

"Hadn't thought of the vigilante angle," Jack said. "I agree that it's related to the Barber case. That's what my gut instinct tells me, and it's hardly ever wrong."

"So we're agreed on that," I said. "Now, about getting together. I'm available all day tomorrow. If you don't mind, why don't you come here? In the afternoon we can go to the hospital to talk to Bill Delaney." My children would be visiting their respective in-laws with their spouses tomorrow, so my usual Sunday family dinner was canceled. With Helen Louise busy at the bistro, Diesel and I would be on our own.

"That sounds good. I'd like to meet Delaney. Maybe between the two of us we can encourage him to trust us," Jack said.

"Yes, whether he's guilty or innocent, we need to get him talking to us," I said.

"Would ten o'clock work for you?" Jack asked.

"That's fine." I gave him the address.

"I'll e-mail you the files I have on the Barber case,"

Jack said. "If you have time to look them over before tomorrow morning, that would be great."

"No problem," I said. "I've nothing else to do this evening."

"Great," Jack replied. "See you in the morning." He ended the call.

I put my phone aside and gazed down at the dozing cat by my chair. "We're going to have company tomorrow, Diesel. It's going to be a busy day." He roused long enough to offer a sleepy meow in acknowledgment before going back to his nap.

"Uh-oh," I said as I suddenly realized something. With most of my usual cat-sitters otherwise occupied tomorrow, I had no one to keep an eye on Diesel while Jack and I went to the hospital. I couldn't remember what Stewart might have told me about his and Haskell's plans for tomorrow. If they weren't going to be at home, I'd have to send Jack to the hospital by himself.

I picked up my phone to send a text to Stewart.

Hey there. Hope you're enjoying your day. Are you and Haskell going to be home tomorrow morning?

I set the phone aside for the moment and got up to refill my water glass. That done, I looked through the fridge to see what my options were for dinner. Sandwich, salad, some hard-boiled eggs. No, I wanted a more substantial meal, although I probably should have gone with a couple hard-boiled eggs and salad. I opened the freezer to find one of Azalea's casseroles and discovered only one left. Chicken and rice. I took it out and set it on the counter to thaw for an hour or so before I put it in the oven. Casserole plus salad would make a satisfying meal.

In the meantime I decided a small snack wouldn't hurt, so I peeled a banana. Diesel knew I was eating so he perked up and became interested in my snack. I pinched off a piece of banana and gave it to him. Cats can't taste sweet so fruit generally doesn't interest them. Diesel sniffed at the banana for a moment, then he gulped it down. He looked up at me, obviously wanting more. I gave him one more small piece and ate the rest of the banana myself. I sometimes thought the fact that I shared my food with him was more important than the taste of the food itself.

I discarded the banana peel and washed my hands. I had barely finished drying my hands when my phone emitted the new text alert sound. I read Stewart's response to my message. Evidently Haskell was on duty tomorrow, so Stewart was planning to spend the day at home. I texted back to ask if he would mind babysitting Diesel for a while, and he quickly responded that he'd be happy to. After a quick *Thanks* back, I put the phone in my pocket.

"Come on, Diesel, let's go to the den," I said. "Time to check e-mail." He ambled along beside me as we left the kitchen.

A few minutes later we were comfortably settled on the sofa in the den. Diesel lay stretched out beside me, his head against my leg. I had the laptop open, waiting for my e-mail to finish loading. The process was taking a little longer than usual because Jack had evidently sent me several large files.

Finally the last of them loaded, and I opened the one that had arrived first. Jack had written a brief explanation of the contents of the file, in this case scans of all the newspaper articles he had been able to find about the Barber case. I opened the file and discovered that there were nearly sixty pages of scans. If the other files were this big, I would do well to read them all and digest the information before our meeting tomorrow.

I heard a beep that alerted me to a new incoming message. From Jack again, this time marked with a red exclamation point, denoting that it was sent with high importance. I opened it to find out what was so urgent.

Managed to track down Elizabeth Barber's best friend from high school. Girl she spent the night with the night her parents and siblings were murdered. Turns out she's a doctor and lives in Athena. Leann Finch. Know her?

TWENTY-ONE

<hr>

The ER doctor, Leann Finch, was Elizabeth Barber's best friend in high school. What an odd coincidence, I thought, like my son-in-law turning out to be related to the Barber family. Frankly, it wasn't all that unusual in Mississippi to stumble over connections like these. At least, I thought so, after all those years in Houston where the population of the metropolitan area was more than twice as large as that of the whole state of Mississippi. Since I'd moved back to Athena, I had encountered this phenomenon more than once.

My thoughts focused on Leann Finch. If she and Elizabeth Barber had been such good friends, would Leann have known the Barbers' hired man, Bill Delaney? In light of this new information, I considered the scene in the emergency room. I never saw any sign that the doctor was acquainted with her patient, but that didn't mean she wasn't aware of his connection to the Barbers.

The connection might mean nothing at all, at least in

terms of solving the murders. Jack and I couldn't ignore the possibility that it did, however. We would have to talk to Dr. Finch about the case. We definitely had to go to the hospital tomorrow afternoon, and if Dr. Finch wasn't there, we would have to track her down somehow.

I fashioned a quick reply to Jack's e-mail to explain how I knew Dr. Finch and share the rest of my thoughts about the connection. Jack responded a few minutes later, saying that he agreed with me.

With that out of the way I could focus on all the reading material Jack sent. I was tempted to print it all because my eyes tired more quickly from staring at a computer screen than from reading hard-copy printout. I decided, after considering the advantages of having a more portable paper copy as opposed to having to use the laptop, I would go ahead and print.

The process took twelve minutes to complete. One file was sixty pages, another ten, and the final one eight. I put the laptop away and settled down with the pages. I decided to start with the largest one first, all the scans of the newspaper coverage.

Jack had them organized in chronological order, and his sources ranged from the Tullahoma paper to those of other towns and cities, including Jackson and Memphis. The early headlines were lurid, especially one from the Tullahoma paper: *Barber Family Butchered in Their Sleep.* I snorted as I read it. I wasn't sure how anyone could be butchered with a shotgun, but I reckoned the editor had wanted to grab everyone's attention and sell more papers. Despite the headline, however, the article itself was not sensational in tone.

After reading the early accounts of the crime, I had a fairly clear picture of the opening stages of the investigation. Elizabeth Barber had come home around nine in the morning after spending the night with an unnamed friend, who turned out to be Leann Finch. She discovered the bodies and started screaming the place down. One of the hired men heard her and came running. He got her out of the house and called the sheriff's department to report the discovery. He then took Elizabeth back to the Finch home, where Leann's mother ministered to the girl.

Suspicion quickly focused on Bill Delaney, who was known to be a heavy drinker with a sometimes violent temper. One of the other hired men, a man named Sonny Willis, had overheard a loud argument between Delaney and Hiram Barber two days before the murders. During the altercation, according to Willis, Delaney threatened Barber's life if Barber didn't pay Delaney his back wages.

The investigation limped along after Sylvia Delaney gave her son an alibi for the night of the murders. She could not be shaken, and the sheriff's department reluctantly (my interpretation) had to start looking for other suspects. The fact that the murder weapon belonged to Hiram Barber but had disappeared wasn't mentioned until several weeks after the first account in the Tullahoma paper. The sheriff's department, assisted by volunteers, did an extensive search in the area around the Barber farm but without result. The murderer had apparently taken great pains to make sure the weapon would never be found. If it had turned up at some point in the past twenty years, Jack hadn't mentioned it.

Reporters had talked to residents in the community where the Barber farm was located. No one had any information to offer on potential suspects but several allowed as how Hiram Barber was extremely difficult to deal with and not highly regarded in the community. The locals liked his wife, however, and generally felt sorry for her and the children. One person, a Mrs. Mitzi Gillon, told the reporter from the Jackson paper that poor Mrs. Barber was always embarrassed about how worn and out-of-style her clothes were. Barber begrudged his family any money spent on fancy things, with the exception of his teenage daughter. Elizabeth, Mrs. Gillon concluded, got most anything she wanted as long as it wasn't too extravagant, while her mother and brothers had to make do with very little. "They didn't even have a TV," Mrs. Gillon said at the end of the interview.

Hiram Barber sounded like a thoroughly unpleasant man, a skinflint of the worst kind. The other farmers in the area who spoke with reporters said Barber's farm was prosperous enough that the family didn't need to go without. Barber simply hated to let loose of money.

Such a sad story, I thought. A miserable man who deprived his family—except for the daughter—of ordinary things like decent clothing and a television set. It sounded to me like Hiram Barber was stuck in the 1930s, the Depression era. I wondered if his parents had been like that. He must have learned that behavior somewhere.

His daughter had done well for herself, despite the loss of her family. She had sold the farmland and ended up marrying a man who became a prominent businessman in Tullahoma. She had children of her own and no doubt a nice house with as many amenities and luxuries as they could afford. A far cry from her early life, certainly.

Eventually the press revealed the name of Elizabeth's friend. Leann Finch and her family provided Elizabeth Barber's alibi, though it didn't seem to me that the sheriff's department had seriously considered her a suspect. According to Leann, the two girls were up most of the night, talking in her bedroom. Leann was home for the weekend from her first semester of college, and the girls hadn't seen each other in several weeks. Elizabeth wanted to know all about college life, and college men in particular.

The case languished due to the lack of new leads or viable suspects, and the press coverage dwindled away. Jack had found a few articles across the intervening years, all of which mentioned the main facts of the case but offered no fresh insights as to who might have been behind the killings. It seemed like an impossible case to solve, and I had momentary doubts about my involvement in the whole thing.

Then I remembered my daughter's conviction that the car deliberately swerved to hit Bill Delancy. Things like that hadn't happened before in Athena, to my knowledge. It might be a regular occurrence in big cities, but unless we had a crazed psychopath on the loose, targeting victims with his vehicle for some twisted reason of his own, this was no random event.

I wondered whether the sheriff's department had investigated neighbors from the surrounding farms at all. Given what people had to say about Hiram Barber, one of the other farmers could have had a grudge against the man. Perhaps some kind of property dispute? An argument over a boundary line, or cattle straying from one property to another because of inadequate fencing?

Most of these ideas sprang from old television shows I had seen growing up—my father watched just about any Western that came on—because I had no real experience of farm life other than what I had seen on television. I knew from things I'd read that farming was a hard way to earn a living, especially on a small farm, nothing like the big plantations in the Mississippi delta, for example, which were enormously profitable.

I set aside the printed-out newspaper scans and picked up another one. This was the ten-page document, which I had not even examined before printing. The contents turned out to be photographs with captions. I had an excellent laser printer that could handle color, so the photographs had turned out pretty well. Five of the pages contained photographs of the Barber farmhouse from various angles along with the different outbuildings: a barn, a tool shed, and a much larger shed for tractors and other farm equipment.

The single-story house had been built of wood, probably at least fifty years ago or more, or so I judged from the style and the condition. The boards appeared weathered in the photograph, worn to a dull gray. The steeply pitched metal roof would have ensured that rain didn't collect on it. The house appeared to be large in size, and a porch extended across the front and down one side. Judging by the number of windows on the front of the house, I guessed that there was either a large front room, perhaps a parlor, and two smaller rooms, or else there were four rooms at the front of the house, two on either side of the front door. There were four windows on the side of the house with the porch, spaced well apart. I wondered if there were surviving photographs of the interior of the house. Elizabeth Barber might have some, of course, but I wasn't about to ask her simply to satisfy my curiosity.

The other five pages consisted of photographs of the Barber family. One was a family portrait, and I wondered, based on what I'd learned of Hiram Barber's skinflint ways, how he'd been persuaded to pay for it. I could see in the photograph that Mrs. Barber and the twins wore noticeably worn clothes, while Mr. Barber looked even shabbier in old overalls and a plaid work shirt. Elizabeth, a striking girl with flame-red hair, was the only one wearing decent clothing.

I thought I could detect signs of strain and unhappiness in Mrs. Barber's expression in the picture, and the two boys seemed to peer at the camera as if they were frightened of it—or perhaps by something else. Elizabeth faced the camera with confidence. She actually looked a little flirty, offering a saucy, knowing smile. Her father, on the other hand, glowered. He was probably thinking of the money this was costing him, I figured.

The rest of the Barber photos were some of the children's school pictures. The photos of the twins were basic head shots, and the boys were hard to tell apart. There were three of Elizabeth engaged in various school activities, two of which were cheerleading and playing basketball. An interesting combination, I thought. The third showed her in the school beauty pageant standing next to a girl with a crown. I deduced from this that Elizabeth was probably the first runner-up.

Having finished perusing the pictures, I picked up the final printout. Eight pages of information on other people with some potential connection to the Barbers and to Sylvia and Bill Delaney. Occasional statements in quotation marks popped out at me as I skimmed through.

Sylvia would do anything to protect that boy of hers.
    Bill was a spitfire from the time he was fifteen, always getting into trouble with somebody.

Spent time in jail on assault charges. This also referred to Bill Delaney.

Mean as a snake, Hiram was. Didn't want nobody setting foot on his property if he didn't know they was planning to come.

I always felt sorry for Betty Barber. Never could figure out what she saw in a man like Hiram.

I laid the pages aside. I would go back to them later. All these terrible things people had to say depressed me. Now that I knew more about Bill Delaney's past—and his reputation for drunken violence—I began to believe Sylvia had forsworn her very soul to keep her son from being convicted of four murders.

Would Jack and I be able to prove or disprove that after all this time?

TWENTY-TWO

By nine thirty the next morning my impatience hit peak levels. I should have asked if Jack could arrive earlier than ten. I was eager to brainstorm with him, and I planned to suggest that we head to the hospital by noon instead of waiting until the afternoon. Thinking about the week ahead, I had realized that I wouldn't have much time to assist Jack if I stuck to my usual schedule. With that in mind, I had e-mailed my boss last night to let her know I wouldn't be in this coming week. I apologized for the short notice, but within a few minutes she responded, "No problem. Have a good week."

Now I was free to focus on the Barber murders without the distractions of work. Helen Louise was back to a full schedule at the bistro because of Henry's accident. He wouldn't be back up to full speed for a week, perhaps longer. I felt bad for Henry, but I supposed accidents like his occurred even with professionals in the kitchen.

The doorbell rang, and Diesel meowed to make sure

I'd heard. Then he darted out of the kitchen. One of these days I was afraid he would figure out how to unlock the front door. He already knew how to open the door onto the back porch, as long as it was already unlocked, of course. I glanced at the clock on my way to the front door. Jack had come early after all, nearly twenty-five minutes early.

Except that it wasn't Jack at the door. "Sean, this is a nice surprise. I didn't think I'd see you today. Come in." I stood aside to let him enter.

He rubbed Diesel's head, and the cat meowed in appreciation. "Morning, Dad," he said. "I hadn't planned on it, but after I had a talk with Laura last night, I decided I needed to talk to you."

I knew that tone. Lawyer Sean had decided I needed a lecture. I rolled my eyes at his back as he preceded me into the kitchen. Diesel ambled along beside me. He stretched out on the floor by my chair when I resumed my place at the table.

Sean stood behind the chair across from mine. Any moment now he was going to fold his arms across his chest, fix me with a stern gaze, and lecture me. I settled back in my chair and awaited the inevitable.

"Now, Dad, about this Bill Delaney," Sean began, his hands on the back of the chair. "As I understand it, he has no legal claim on Aunt Dottie's estate. Has he been asking you for money?"

"He has not," I said. "All he wants is information."

"So far." Sean frowned. "Are you sure he's who he claims to be?"

"He has a birth certificate that looks legitimate," I said. "He also looks just like Uncle Del. I'm sure."

"Nothing I say is going to stop you from getting further

involved in this, I suppose." I saw his hands tighten their grip on the chair back.

"There are things you could say to stop me," I replied. "But they wouldn't be worthy of the man I know you to be."

He smiled at that. "You don't always play fair, you know." He shook his head. "I would never, I hope, say those kinds of things to you. As always, I'm concerned about your welfare. Keep this in mind, if nothing else: Whoever killed those people twenty years ago may still be around, and they're not going to be happy to discover you're trying to find them, whoever it is. You need to be really careful."

"I know that," I said. "I'm not going to be working on this alone. Jack Pemberton is actually taking the lead in this."

"I've read his books," Sean said. "He's good at what he does, so he must be pretty smart." He laughed suddenly. "Maybe the two of you can keep each other out of trouble."

Diesel warbled, and Sean laughed again. "Make that the three of you. I know Diesel will help, too."

That last statement elicited another warble and a couple of chirps. "Diesel agrees," I said. "Now, the really important thing is: How is Alex?"

Sean grinned and let go of the chair back. "Ready to be done with it and have the baby, but she's got another five or six weeks to go. I'm ready, too. I want to hold my baby in my arms."

"Same here," I said. "Have you settled on any names yet?" So far neither Sean nor Alex would reveal their choices.

"Not yet," Sean replied. "We've got it narrowed down

to about five. We'll know when the time comes, I hope."
He checked his watch. "I'd better get going."

I got up from the table to escort him to the front door
with Diesel's assistance. Right before I opened the door
Sean gave me a hug. "Be safe, Dad."

I knew he worried about me. His mother's death had
hit him particularly hard, and after some difficulties in
our relationship, he and I were closer than ever. I didn't
like having him upset or concerned, but I couldn't stop
living my life the way I saw fit. He understood that, and
he was always ready to help me in any way he could.

The doorbell rang again five minutes after Sean left,
and once more Diesel reached the door ahead of me. This
time my expected guest stood on the doorstep. I invited
him in and suggested we talk in the kitchen. He had a
backpack with him, no doubt containing his files on the
Barber case. I wondered if there was any material he
hadn't already shared with me.

"Would you care for something to drink?" I asked.

Jack looked up from scratching Diesel's head and chin.
"Ice tea if you have it, otherwise water, thanks." Diesel
stretched out by Jack's chair. He often did that, stayed
near a new person, once he decided that person was okay.

"Ice tea coming up," I said. "I'm ready for some myself. It's unsweetened, though."

"No problem." Jacked smiled. "As long as you have
some kind of sweetener, I'm good to go."

"I have several kinds." I reeled off their names, and
Jack chose the natural sugar substitute that I myself preferred.

Once I served the tea, I was ready to focus on plans for
our investigation. I told Jack I had the coming week free,
with the exception of Friday, my usual day at the public
library.

"That's great," Jack said. "We can get a lot done over the next few days. Now, I've been thinking about our strategy. Let me outline it to you, and you tell me if you agree."

I nodded. "Go ahead."

"We obviously will talk to Bill Delaney today," Jack said. "We need him to open up and talk to us about the case, and about the hit-and-run. I feel sure it's connected. If possible, we also need to talk to Leann Finch today. She was Elizabeth Barber's best friend, and she might know things about the family that didn't surface during the investigation. Or at least things that didn't make it into the newspaper." He paused for a sip of tea. "Depending on what we find out from Delaney and Leann Finch, we can move on from there. I think we need to talk to people in the community around the Barber farm. I've done some research, and most of them are still there."

"I agree. We need to find out everything we can from the neighbors. I feel sure there's something that got overlooked," I said. "Some incident, some piece of information that people at the time may not have realized was significant."

"Definitely," Jack said. "We have to do the same with Sylvia and Bill Delaney's neighbors. Several of the families closest to the house are no longer there, but there is one woman, a widow, who still lives next door."

"What about the Delaney house?" I asked. "Does Bill own it?"

Jack shook his head. "No, from what I gather, it had to be sold to help pay for his mother's care. Another family lives there now."

"I wonder where Delaney's been living in Tullahoma then," I said. "I never asked him because I sort of assumed he had inherited his mother's house."

"I don't know where he was," Jack said. "Apparently he turned up out of the blue a week or so before his mother died. Nobody except maybe his mother had heard from him in years. That's what a friend at the sheriff's department told me."

"How did he find out that his mother was dying?" I asked.

Jack shrugged. "That I don't know. Could be that his mother knew how to get in touch with him, and the nursing home called or wrote to him." He reached for his backpack and extracted a notebook and a pen. "That's a great question." He flipped the notebook open and began writing. "It might not be important in the long run, but we don't know that it won't be."

"I agree," I said. "I also wonder where he's been all these years and what he's been doing? Did he maintain contact with anyone in Tullahoma besides maybe his mother?"

Jack scribbled in his notebook. "More good questions." He looked over at me. "Would you consider him our chief suspect?"

"After reading all the newspaper articles and other things you sent," I said, "frankly, I find it hard to believe that anyone else did it, based on what I've recently learned. He had a history of drunkenness and violence, he was overheard having a blowout with Hiram Barber not long before the murders, he felt he had a grievance against Barber." I shrugged. "Add to that Barber's reputation for being cheap, and I can see him refusing to pay Delaney his back wages and Delaney snapping."

"I agree," Jack said. "I can see Delaney killing Barber without much problem. What really gets me, though, is killing the wife and the two boys."

"Yes, that part is hard for me, too," I said. "But if they

witnessed Barber's death, then Delaney might have felt he had to kill them in order to protect himself."

"I know," Jack said, "but killing those two boys . . . Well, it makes me sick to think about." He grimaced.

"The murders of children are beyond comprehension," I said. "I don't know whether you have children yourself, but I have two, with one grandchild recently born and another one on the way. A parent's worst nightmare is violence against their child."

"I don't have any children of my own," Jack said. "My wife has three, a son and two daughters, and two grandchildren. I understand how you feel, though."

"All the more reason that the monster responsible should be identified and made to pay the price for what he did."

"What monster are you talking about?"

Stewart walked into the kitchen, and I hastily introduced him to Jack. Diesel let Stewart know that he was available for attention, and Stewart took a chair and began scratching Diesel's back.

"The monster who killed the Barbers," I said. "Particularly the deaths of those two boys."

"Horrible," Stewart said. "I've been doing some reading about the case. I found a fair number of newspaper articles on the Internet. It's a fascinating case. The chief suspect had an unshakable, but unprovable, alibi. Evidently Mrs. Delaney was fiercely protective."

"She had to have been," Jack said, "to stand up to the kind of pressure the sheriff's department would have exerted. They wanted Bill Delaney for the murders."

"Interesting thing about alibis." Stewart glanced first at me, then Jack, then back to me again. "They work both ways. Mrs. Delaney gave her son an alibi. Said he was passed out drunk all night."

"Yes, that's right." I suddenly saw where Stewart was going with this, and I was angry with myself for not realizing it before now. I let Stewart have his moment, however.

Jack started to speak, but Stewart got in first. "Sylvia Delaney's only alibi was her dead-to-the-world son. That's no alibi at all."

TWENTY-THREE

"I should have thought of that before now," I said, feeling chagrined.

"You beat me to it." Jack shared a rueful grin. "You're right. I was so focused on Bill Delaney's alibi that I hadn't really thought seriously about his mother as a suspect."

"Who we know was protective of her son from what people said about her." I finished my tea and got up to refill my glass from the fridge. "Stewart, would you like tea?"

"No, thanks," Stewart replied. "What do you know about Sylvia Delaney's character? For example, was she hot-tempered like her son? Did she drink?"

"My friend Ernie Carpenter—Charlie met her recently—told me she knew Sylvia Delaney a little," Jack said. "According to Ernie, Mrs. Delaney was a pillar of her church, known to be a fine, upstanding woman, although she had a temper. Not as bad as her son's, though."

"That doesn't sound like a woman who had a problem

with alcohol," Stewart said. "She sounds too straitlaced to have killed anyone."

"She might sound that way." I resumed my place at the table. "But don't ever underestimate what a parent might do to protect a child. Even if that child was in his midforties, as Bill Delaney would have been at the time. He was her only child, remember."

"Pillars of the church have murdered before," Jack said. "I don't know if you've read my books, but one of them was about a preacher in a small town in Texas who murdered three people who had left everything in their wills to his church. He needed the money to pay off his gambling debts."

"I haven't read it, but now I want to. Sounds absolutely fascinating," Stewart said. "What's the title?" He pulled out his phone in preparation for making a note. He kept all kinds of information on his phone, I had observed. Mine could probably do those things, too, but I had never explored all the apps to find out.

"*Past Praying For*," Jack replied. "I hope you'll enjoy it."

"I'm sure I will," Stewart said as he tapped on his phone's keyboard.

"Obviously we need to dig deeper into Sylvia Delaney," I said. "Besides Ernie and the one neighbor who still lives next to the old Delaney house, do you know anyone else who might have known her back then?"

"I'm sure there are people from her church we could talk to," Jack replied. "How well they knew her is anybody's guess. In my experience many people are careful about what they share with people in their church, especially in a small church."

"There are always too many people who want to gossip in churches, just like everywhere else," Stewart said. "The minute they grab on to a juicy tidbit, they fall all over themselves finding people to tell."

"True," I said. "But if it weren't for people willing to share gossip, then we might never find out what we need in order to solve a murder. Jack, do you know what church Sylvia Delaney attended?"

"No," he replied. "I'll check with Ernie later."

"Now you have another suspect," Stewart said. "My work is done. When are you leaving for the hospital?"

"What do you think?" I looked at Jack. "Shall we go now, or are there other things you want to discuss first?"

"We can go now, if you're ready." Jack shoved his notebook and pen back in his backpack.

"Let's go, then," I said. "Stewart is going to look after Diesel while we're gone. We can grab lunch after the hospital."

"Sounds good," Jack said. "Stewart, thanks for your help."

"My pleasure." Stewart pushed back from the table and stood. "Come on, Diesel, let's go upstairs. Dante wants to play with you." He explained to Jack that Dante was his dog before he walked over to the door into the hall. "Come on, boy."

Diesel looked at me as if to ask permission. He uttered a plaintive meow.

"Go with Stewart," I said. "I have to go out now, and you can't come with me." The cat stared at me for a moment. Then he turned and followed Stewart out of the room.

Jack chuckled. "That cat of yours is quite a character. Does he understand everything you say to him?"

"I don't know," I said. "Much of the time he seems to, but I'm never completely sure. He is very smart, I do know that." I rose from the table. "Would you like me to drive?"

"If you don't mind, that would be good," Jack said. "The AC in my car is acting up, and I can't count on it working half the time."

"I know how that is," I said as I led the way to the garage. "I went through a Houston summer once without a working AC in the car."

"Brutal."

Once we both had our seat belts fastened and Jack's backpack stowed securely in the backseat, we drove to the hospital. On the way we discussed the approach we wanted to take with both Bill Delaney and Leann Finch, should the latter be at the hospital and available for a meeting.

"Bill Delaney first, though," Jack said, and I agreed.

"I want to find out whether he knew Leann Finch back in Tullahoma," I said.

"Speaking of Tullahoma," Jack said, "tomorrow we need to talk to Elizabeth Barber. I know where she lives, but talking to her at home might not be a good idea. I found out she has a part-time job as a vet tech with one of the veterinarians in Tullahoma. A friend of mine takes her dogs to that vet. I thought we should try there."

"Why there?" I asked. "Surely it would be better to talk to her at home."

"Catch her off guard at work and rattle her a little," Jack said. "But if she isn't working tomorrow, we'll have to try her at home."

"Okay." Since Jack was the one who suggested we work together, I had no problem with him taking the lead and directing the investigation. I would speak up, though, if I disagreed with him on what I considered an important point.

I pulled into a parking space, and we left the car. Jack shrugged his backpack onto his shoulders as we walked.

"I hope Delaney is in his room and not off having some

kind of test," I said. "I'm not fond of hospitals, and I don't want to have to sit around waiting."

"I don't care for them, either," Jack said. "But if he isn't in his room, we can go see if Dr. Finch is on duty today."

A couple of minutes later we stood at the closed door of Bill Delaney's room. I tapped on the door, and a voice bade us enter.

Delaney looked slightly better today, I thought, despite the fact that he was still heavily bandaged. His color had improved, and he appeared more alert than when I saw him yesterday. He was reclined at a comfortable-looking angle in bed, and the television set mounted on the wall was on with the volume set at a low level.

I approached the bed. "Good morning, Mr. Delaney. How are you feeling today?"

Delaney regarded me warily. "About the same, I guess. They've given me pain pills so I don't feel much of anything. Who's that?" He indicated Jack with a movement of his head.

I introduced Jack. "He's a friend of mine from Tullahoma, and he and I are working on something together. He wanted to come with me to see how you are and to talk to you, if you feel up to it."

"Talk about what?" Delaney asked, still wary.

"We'll come back to that in a minute." Jack and I had agreed that we would try to get him to talk about the hit-and-run first, then move into talking about the Barber case. "Jack was shocked when I told him that somebody hit you deliberately and drove off."

"That could be considered attempted murder, you know," Jack said. "Charlie is worried about you, and I can't say I blame him. If whoever hit you finds out you're still alive, he might try again."

Delaney's expression changed from wary to blank. I

figured he planned to stonewall us as he had done with me yesterday. I had to get through to him somehow, though. Jack remained near my side, ready to step in on the right cue.

"I think you're wrong." Delaney shifted his gaze toward the television screen. "Nobody tried to run me down. Just an accident."

"I'm sorry, Bill, I simply don't believe that." I used his given name deliberately to try to establish a more personal connection. "My daughter is a bright, observant young woman, and I believe what she tells me."

"I told you, I got no claim on you. Why don't you go away?" Delaney said, sounding weary.

"No, you don't have a claim on me," I said. "We're not related except by marriage. Your father to my aunt. No blood connection. But there's still a connection. I can't in all good conscience stand by and not try to help you. Your life might be at stake, and you don't seem to have any other friends. You need my help."

Before Delaney could respond, Jack spoke up. "Mr. Delaney, Charlie's right about the threat to your life. Unless you're ready to die, you need to listen to him. To both of us."

"I'm not in no hurry to die," Delaney said. "But I don't see what you two have got to do with it. No reason at all why someone would want me dead. I've been gone from Mississippi for nearly twenty years. I don't know anybody here no more."

"That's not true," Jack said. "I can think of at least two people you know and who will certainly remember you."

Delaney's glance shifted to Jack but then shifted back to the screen. "Don't know who you're talking about."

"Elizabeth Barber and Leann Finch." I watched him

closely for his reaction as Jack spoke the names. Delaney tensed but evidently realized what he'd done and immediately tried to relax.

Jack continued, "You worked for the Barber family for years. You knew their daughter, Elizabeth. Twenty years ago she would have been sixteen or seventeen. Leann Finch was her best friend. You must have seen them together at some point."

Delaney's gaze remained stubbornly fixated on the television screen.

"Did you recognize Leann Finch yesterday in the emergency room?" I asked.

I noticed Delaney's hands tighten on the white bedspread, and they stayed clenched. For a moment I felt bad. It wasn't my intention to browbeat him, but we had to get through to him.

"I don't remember any Leann Finch," Delaney said. "I remember Elizabeth, though. Beautiful girl." He closed his eyes and sighed. "Don't know whatever became of her."

"You remember what happened to her parents and her brothers, though," Jack said.

"Of course I remember." Delaney opened his eyes and snapped the words out. "And if you're here to try to make me confess to killings I didn't do, you might as well get the hell out of my room right now." He picked up the television control, and I saw him push the call button for the nurse.

"We're not here to accuse you. You had an alibi, as I recall, your mother," I said. "We do want to talk to you about the murders, though."

"The police will be talking to you about them," Jack said. "They know you're back in Mississippi now. I'm actually surprised they haven't been here already."

"They have been," Delaney said. "About an hour ago. Some woman deputy and a man."

"Did they ask you where you were the past twenty years?" Jack asked.

"Yeah," Delaney said. "Told 'em I was in Montana, working on a ranch until I got word that Mama was dying and asking for me."

"How did the nursing home know how to find you?" I asked.

"Mama knew where I was," Delaney said. "In case you're wondering why I didn't come home sooner, well, Mama didn't want me to. Thought I ought to stay away."

"Because of the Barber case," Jack said.

"If you say so," Delaney replied in an indifferent tone. "Excuse me, gentlemen."

Jack and I turned to see a nurse, a stocky woman around my age, standing in the doorway. She came into the room and approached the bed. "Are we doing okay, Mr. Delaney? Do we need another pain pill? You're not due for about another hour."

"No, ma'am," Delaney said. "I was hoping you would show these men out. I'm tired, and I want to sleep."

The nurse turned to face us, her expression apologetic. "I'm sorry. I need for you to leave now so my patient can rest. He's recovering from a real bad accident."

"Yes, we know," I said. "We're sorry, Nurse. We'll go now, but we'll come back another time when Mr. Delaney is feeling more rested." I smiled at the nurse before I walked out of the room. Jack was right behind me.

While we waited for the elevator, I said, "He was pretty cool, but he's hiding something."

"Agreed," Jack said. "I think it has to do with his mother. He didn't want to talk about her."

"No, he didn't," I said. We stepped into the elevator, and I punched the button for the ground floor. "I'm beginning to think Stewart was right on the money about Mrs. Delaney."

TWENTY-FOUR

"Who else would he be trying to protect, other than himself?" I asked.

"I agree with you, up to a point," Jack said. "He doesn't want to talk about his mother, but there could be someone else he wants to protect. After all, it wasn't his mother who tried to run him down."

"True," I said. "The only other person I can think of is Elizabeth Barber. Why would he be trying to protect her, though?"

"She could have killed her family," Jack said.

The elevator reached the first floor, and the doors opened. Jack and I stepped out. I examined the signs to be sure I remembered the way to the emergency room from there.

"This way." I turned to the left. Jack followed me through the corridors until we emerged near the main desk in the emergency room. I saw only a few people in the waiting room, and no one stood in line at the desk.

"I'll ask about Dr. Finch," I said.

Jack nodded and stood near the entry to the waiting room as I approached the desk. "Excuse me." I smiled at the young man on duty. "I was wondering if Dr. Finch is on duty today. I need to talk to her about my cousin. She saw him here yesterday."

The young man said, "No, she's not here today."

"Do you know when she will be on duty again?" I asked.

"Tomorrow, I think," the young man replied. "Let me look at the schedule." He focused on the computer, tapped a few keys, and perused the screen. "Yes, tomorrow, seven a.m. till five p.m."

"Thank you," I said. "Guess I'll have to wait until tomorrow."

"If your cousin was admitted, you can talk to the attending," the young man said.

I nodded and repeated my thanks.

"No luck?" Jack asked when I joined him.

"No, she's off today. Won't be in again until tomorrow morning," I said. "Looks like we'll have to leave her until later, unless you want to try to track her down at home."

"Let's at least see if we can turn up her address or a phone number." Jack pulled out his cell phone and began to tap on it.

"We can sit in the waiting room." I was aware that the young man at the desk was watching us, and I didn't feel comfortable with that.

Jack followed me, phone in hand, to a corner of the waiting room. We took seats next to each other against the wall. I watched as he continued his search for Leann Finch.

"I subscribe to one of the websites that gives you phone directory type of information," Jack said. "I found our Dr. Finch." He frowned. "The phone number must be unlisted, but I have her address." He showed me the screen, and I read the address.

"That's only a few blocks from here." I checked my watch. "It's not quite eleven thirty yet. She could be at church if she's a churchgoer. Since it's on the way, though, why don't we go there and see if she's at home? If she's not, we can go have lunch and come back afterward."

"Works for me," Jack said.

The drive to Leann Finch's street took only about three minutes. The neighborhood was a modest one with homes built mostly in the late 1940s, after the war, when Athena had a small growth spurt. Dr. Finch's street featured one-story bungalows with lots that kept the neighbors from getting too close. Most houses had plenty of trees shading them, and the whole block appeared to take pride in their yards. Every one on Dr. Finch's block looked manicured and well kept.

"Nice neighborhood," Jack said. "Reminds me of my former neighborhood in Tullahoma. I sold my house when I got married. My wife's place was actually bigger."

"They certainly do keep things looking neat and tidy," I said.

Most of the bungalows had carports, and Dr. Finch's was no exception. Her carport was empty. I pulled into her driveway in order to turn the car around.

"On to lunch," I said. "How do you feel about eating at the bistro?"

"Fine with me," Jack said. "The food there is great. If we lived in Athena, we'd be eating there a lot. Wanda Nell loved it the two times we ate there together."

"The bistro it is," I said. "It probably won't be crowded now. After the churches let out, there's often a wait for a table."

We arrived a few minutes later, and I found a parking spot on the square across from the bistro. I didn't see Helen Louise when we walked in. With Henry out, she was probably stuck in the kitchen. I hoped Henry had recovered and was back up to speed soon.

Jack and I both opted for a small salad and a serving of Helen Louise's signature quiche Lorraine. I recommended a favorite wine of Helen Louise's choosing. We each had one glass, though I could happily have had a second. With driving on the agenda in the immediate future, I had to limit myself to the one.

During the meal Jack and I talked about our strategy for tomorrow. I mentioned that I planned to bring Diesel with me, since he always accompanied me. "He can be an excellent icebreaker," I said. "People are always curious about him because of his size, and since Elizabeth Barber is a vet tech, he might help us get her to talk."

"I like that idea," Jack said. "From what I've heard, he's also a pretty good judge of character."

"I've discovered that when he doesn't want a person to touch him or won't go near them, that's an indicator there's something off about that person. Interestingly, he seemed fine with Bill Delaney." I paused for the final sip of my wine. "That's the one thing that holds me back from utter conviction that he killed the Barbers."

"That is interesting," Jack said. "But he's not one hundred percent infallible, surely."

"No, he isn't," I said. "Every once in a while, he likes someone who turns out not to be a good person, but I like to think he senses something good in them."

We soon finished our meal, and as always I was tempted by Helen Louise's rich, delicious cakes and pastries, but Jack declined. His waistline, I noted, was much trimmer than mine, probably due in part to his turning down incredibly fattening desserts.

Helen Louise left the kitchen briefly while I stood at the counter paying the bill—over Jack's objections, but I insisted. I introduced Jack, and then we had to go. The after-church crowd was arriving in full force, and Helen Louise had to get back to the kitchen.

We drove back to Leann Finch's house, and this time there was a car, a large dark SUV, in the carport. I parked the car on the street in front of the house, and Jack and I headed up the walk toward the front door. When we were close enough I glanced over at the SUV. I remembered the make and the model of the vehicle that hit Bill Delaney, thanks to Frank. Dr. Finch's SUV didn't match.

Jack had his finger on the doorbell but he didn't press it. "I hope she isn't in the middle of a meal. If she is, she might be ticked off and refuse to talk to us."

"There's nothing we can do about that," I said. "We'll have to take our chances and hope that she will be cooperative."

"Right." Jack pressed the bell, and we waited.

No more than thirty seconds after Jack rang, the door opened. Leann Finch, dressed in knee-length shorts, a sleeveless blouse, and sandals, appeared not in the least surprised to see us. Perhaps she had spotted us coming up the walk and was prepared for us.

"Good afternoon, Dr. Finch," I said.

"Good afternoon, Mr. Harris," she replied. "What can I do for you?"

"We apologize for disturbing you at home on your day off," I said, "but my friend, Jack Pemberton, and I would like to talk to you about my cousin, Bill Delaney, whom you treated in the ER yesterday."

Dr. Finch frowned. "I can't discuss a patient with you without the patient's permission, Mr. Harris. Besides, he's in the care of another physician now, who will know more about his status."

"I should have been clearer," I said. "We actually want to talk to you about my cousin's past."

"The Barber case," Jack added.

"Why do you want to drag all that up?" Dr. Finch scowled. "It all happened a long time ago, and it's best forgotten." She stepped back in order to close the door. "If you'll excuse me, I have things to do."

"Wait, Dr. Finch." I put a hand on the door to keep her from closing it. "The case was never solved. It *can't* be forgotten. Four people, two of them children, were murdered in cold blood. They deserve justice, don't you think?"

Leann Finch glared at me, and I knew she was angry now. I had hoped to avoid getting her riled up, but this might be the only way to get through to her and get her to talk about the events of twenty years ago.

"Come in, then." Dr. Finch stepped away from the door to let us enter the house. The interior was blessedly cool. I had begun to perspire, standing out on the doorstep with the midday sun blazing down on us.

The door closed behind us, and Dr. Finch led us into the room to the right off the short hallway. She motioned toward the sofa, and Jack and I seated ourselves. She chose a straight-backed chair on the other side of a low coffee table directly across from us.

"Thank you for talking with us," I said.

Dr. Finch shrugged. "Whatever. You claim to be Mr. Delaney's cousin. What's his connection to all this?" She pointed to Jack. "Your name sounds familiar."

Jack said, "I live in Tullahoma, and I'm a writer. I write true crime books. I've been interested in the Barber case for a long time. I recently met Charlie and discovered his connection to Mr. Delaney, and we're working together to try to solve the case."

"I know that Bill Delaney was the chief suspect in the early stages of the investigation," I said. "He had a strong alibi, however, and the police had to look elsewhere. They never did find out who the killer was."

"Yes, I know all that," Dr. Finch said. "Why are you so interested all of a sudden? Is there new information on the case?"

I noticed that she tensed slightly on the second question. Was she afraid of new information? If so, why?

"There's no new information that we're aware of," Jack said. "But the attempt on Bill Delaney's life has to mean that someone is a little rattled, wouldn't you say?"

"Attempt on his life?" Dr. Finch shook her head. "It was a hit-and-run, nothing more. Mr. Delaney was inebriated and stumbled in front of someone, and the coward drove off."

"There's more to the story," I said. "There were two witnesses to the hit-and-run." Did I imagine it, or did she tense up again? I waited for her to respond to my statement. When she didn't, I continued. "The witnesses were my daughter and son-in-law. My daughter, who is an observant person, was watching the street, and she saw the car coming down the street. According to her, it swerved in order to strike Mr. Delaney."

I watched Dr. Finch closely, and she maintained a blank expression. Nor did she protest again that the hit-and-run was only an accident. Instead she simply watched me and Jack, her glance moving back and forth between us.

"So you see," Jack said, "we have every reason to believe that Bill Delaney's life is in danger. You must have recognized him, at least by name, if nothing else. Can you think of anyone who would want to kill him?"

"I think you'd better ask Mr. Delaney that question. Yes, I recognized the name, but he was my patient. My immediate concern was to assess his injuries and do what was necessary to stabilize him." She rose from her chair. "Now I really must ask you to leave. I have a lot to do, and there's nothing more I can tell you."

I felt certain that she had plenty she could tell us, but at this moment, I didn't think we'd get any further. Still, I decided to ask another question.

"When was the last time you saw Elizabeth Barber or talked to her?"

This time I wasn't imagining the flash of fear I saw in her expression, though she did her best to disguise it quickly. "You have to leave, immediately, or I will call the police. Get out of my house."

TWENTY-FIVE

"Thank you for your time," I said to Dr. Finch as she herded us toward her front door.

She made no response to this other than to jerk her door open and stand beside it, glowering as we departed. Jack preceded me, and I had barely cleared the door when it slammed behind us.

"She's frightened," Jack said as we walked to the car.

"Yes, she is," I replied. "I think we succeeded in getting her rattled. I wonder, though, whether we'll be able to get anything further out of her." I unlocked the car and got in.

Jack waited until I had the car cranked and the AC blowing before he joined me. "I don't think we will, until we can go back to her with new information that will shake her up even more."

"You're right," I said. "Do you want to try Bill Delaney again this afternoon?" I drove down the street to the next intersection and idled there while Jack considered my question.

"I don't know that we'd have any better luck with him this afternoon," Jack said. "May be better to let him stew a bit longer, too, and go back to him with any new information we can get."

"All right, then. We'll go back to my house." I turned onto the cross street and headed home.

Neither of us spoke again until we reached the house and I pulled the car into the garage. "Come on in and have something to drink," I said. "Is there anything else you want to talk about today?"

Jack followed me into the kitchen where a happy, warbling feline met us right inside the door. "Stewart must have heard us drive into the garage, didn't he, boy?" Diesel chirped, and I gave him the attention he wanted while Jack responded to my question to him.

"I think I might as well go on home," Jack said. "We can make a fresh start in the morning. How about we meet at nine at the diner where Wanda Nell works? It's called the Kountry Kitchen."

"That's fine," I said. "Diesel and I will be there."

Jack gave me directions, and I offered him a bottle of water for the drive home. He accepted, and Diesel and I saw him to the door.

I turned to see Stewart standing halfway up the stairs as I closed the door.

"I saw your car," he said. "I let Diesel out so he could greet you. I think he must have heard the car because he meowed at me until I opened the door."

"He probably did," I said. Diesel chirped in agreement, or so I interpreted it.

"Has Jack gone?" Stewart asked.

"Yes, we accomplished what we could today," I replied. "I'm heading to Tullahoma in the morning. We are going to talk to various people and see what we can find out."

"I presume you'll be taking Diesel with you," Stewart said.

"Definitely. He's an excellent icebreaker."

"That's good, because Haskell is on duty tomorrow, and I need to be in Memphis for a good part of the day. Dante is coming with me." Stewart cocked his head to the side, apparently listening to something.

Now I heard it also. From upstairs I could hear frantic barking, steadily increasing in volume. Dante was unhappy about being left alone.

"Good grief, it's a wonder he doesn't shred his vocal cords." Stewart grimaced. "I'd better get back upstairs before he starts chewing something up. Talk to you later." He turned and ran lightly up the stairs.

I looked down at Diesel. "For such a small dog, Dante sure can generate a lot of noise." The cat weighed about three times as much as the poodle but was, despite his chatty nature, not really loud like the dog.

Going in and out of the summer heat today must have affected me more than I realized because I felt like lying down for a nap. "Let's go upstairs for a nap," I told Diesel.

The cat regarded me for a moment. He meowed twice and headed for the utility room. I figured he was going to the litter box and his water bowl. He would join me upstairs when he was done.

In the bedroom I kicked off my shoes, removed my belt, and stretched out on the bed. I intended to sleep no more than half an hour.

I fell asleep so quickly I never even knew when Diesel got onto the bed with me. I woke to the sound of knocking on the halfway open bedroom door.

"Charlie, it's after six, and dinner is ready," Stewart said.

I sat up on the side of the bed. "Thanks for waking me up. I didn't mean to sleep this long. Is it really after six?" Beside me, Diesel meowed.

Stewart laughed. "Yes, it is. I came by earlier, and you were seriously sawing some logs. I didn't know you snored like that."

"Must have been Diesel you heard," I said. "He snores." The cat warbled and chirped as if to contradict me.

"Not even Diesel could snore that loud. Y'all come on down." Stewart disappeared from the doorway, and a moment later I heard him going rapidly down the stairs.

I went into the bathroom and washed my face. That helped make me more alert. Making my way downstairs, I detected the scent of fried chicken as I descended. I quickened my pace. I would never tell Azalea this, but Stewart's fried chicken was even better than hers.

Haskell, in civilian clothes, had already taken his place at the table. Diesel and Dante had their eyes on Stewart, who was plating the chicken. There was a bowl of steaming rice, another of cream gravy, and a plateful of biscuits on the table. A glass of ice tea had been set at each place.

"Tonight I wanted good old Southern comfort food." Stewart set the fried chicken on the table and took his seat. "I didn't think either of you would mind."

"Never." Haskell grinned. "This is my all-time favorite meal."

Stewart batted his eyelashes at Haskell. "I know."

"I could never say no to a meal like this," I said. "My waistline is proof of that."

We began passing and trading the food, the cat and the dog watching every move. They both loved fried chicken and knew that they would get bites from Stewart. Haskell had been known to slip them each the occasional morsel as well. I needed to watch to be sure Diesel didn't overeat and pay for it later.

Conversation lagged as we ate. I had to remind myself to eat slowly and not shovel the food in the way I sometimes did with a meal like this. Watching Dante and Diesel gobble down chicken without taking much time to chew served as a reminder.

After several minutes of steady eating, Stewart spoke. "I told Haskell about your plans for tomorrow, Charlie. He has something he wants to tell you."

Haskell put his fork down and had a sip of tea. "Yeah, I reckon Pemberton knows this already, but if he hasn't told you, I thought you should hear it from me. It's about the sheriff over there in Tullahoma."

I had a feeling I wasn't going to like what Haskell was about to share. "What about him?" I asked.

"Name's Elmer Lee Johnson," Haskell replied. "He's mostly a by-the-book kinda guy, and he's not going to be too happy with you and Pemberton nosing around."

"When you say *not too happy*, are you talking about Kanesha's kind of *not too happy* or something worse?" Chief Deputy Berry had been reluctant in the beginning to trust or even tolerate me. She had never threatened me, not seriously, anyway. Would this sheriff take things further if we got in his way?

"I don't think he'd arrest you," Haskell said. "Unless you really step over the line, but I don't think you'll do that. I guess he's more like Kanesha that way. At least, that's what my buddy on the force there has told me."

"Thanks for the warning," I said. "Jack told me that he and his wife have had some experience with murder cases there, so I suppose they must have had to deal with Sheriff Johnson. Jack hasn't said anything about him that I recall."

"Then maybe it won't be a problem," Haskell said. "I just thought I should tell you what I know."

"I appreciate it," I said. "I don't plan on doing anything rash, and Jack strikes me as pretty level-headed."

"That's good," Stewart said. "It would be *so* embarrassing to have to call Sean to bail you out of jail." He laughed.

"Yes, it would be," I replied, repressing a shudder. Sean would not mince words with me, either. I felt a paw on my thigh and looked down into a winsome expression, that of a cat in need of chicken. I pinched off a bit of the breast I was eating and gave it to Diesel.

Stewart changed the subject, telling us about the latest scandal in the chemistry department at Athena College. One of his colleagues had earned a reputation for the number and abbreviated length of his dalliances with women on campus and in the town. I listened but my mind soon focused on another subject—tomorrow's activities.

I wondered what we might be able to elicit from the people we planned to interview. I knew, based on my recent experiences, that sometimes small details slipped by the attention of otherwise vigilant investigators, and those small details could lead to significant information. One or more of the people Jack had on the list to interview might have seen or heard something that could put a new twist on the case. I hoped fervently that Jack and I might uncover one or more of those details.

Stewart wrapped up his anecdote, and I came out of my reverie when he suggested fresh apple pie with ice cream for dessert. I badly wanted to say yes, but after the meal I had finished, I knew I'd regret it before the night was over. I declined politely, and Stewart didn't push me to change my mind.

"If you leave the dishes," I said, "I'll clean up the

kitchen once you've finished with dessert. In the meantime, I'm going to the den to watch a little television."

"Thanks," Stewart said. "I'll take you up on that."

"Come on, Diesel." I pushed back from the table. "I'm going to wash my hands, and then we're going to the den."

The cat meowed twice, and I wondered whether he was complaining about having to leave people eating or whether he was saying he was ready to join me. He did not need any bites of apple pie nor any ice cream, no matter what he might think.

In the den Diesel and I got comfortable on the sofa. He stretched out, his head against my leg. I turned the television to a channel that showed old comedies from the fifties and sixties, the ones I grew up with. They were comfort whenever I was upset or preoccupied with a problem. I could watch and listen to the familiar antics but still mull over whatever was troubling me.

Tonight, while Lucy and Ethel got themselves into yet another scrape, I thought about the Barber case. There had to be details the original investigators either missed completely or did not recognize as significant. I wondered if Jack knew who had worked the case twenty years ago. If one of them was retired by now, might he be willing to talk about it? Or maybe even an officer still in the department? Since Jack wanted to write about the case, maybe one of them would want to be in the book badly enough that he would cooperate.

I was certain Jack had already considered that, although he hadn't mentioned it to me. If he didn't bring it up in the morning, I would mention it to him and see what he thought. We needed to know more about the original investigation, that was all there was to it. Even if I had to ask the current sheriff himself.

The house phone rang and interrupted my thoughts. I

reached for the handset on the end table beside me. "Good evening, this is Charlie Harris."

"Mr. Harris, sorry to bother you this evening," a female voice responded. She identified herself as a nurse at the hospital. "Mr. Delaney is asking for you. He's pretty agitated, and he threatened to leave the hospital and come to your house if we didn't call. Can you come?"

"Certainly," I said. "Tell Mr. Delaney that I'll be there in twenty minutes."

"Thank you," the nurse replied. "I'll tell him right away."

I hung up the phone and patted Diesel's side. "Sorry, buddy, but I've got to go somewhere, and you can't come with me. You'll have to stay here."

Diesel meowed but followed me from the den without further complaint. Stewart and Haskell, along with Dante, were finishing their desserts. I explained that I had to go to the hospital and why.

"Don't worry about Diesel," Stewart said. "You go and see what's got the poor man so upset."

"Thanks," I said on my way to the back door.

As I backed the car out of the garage, I could feel my heart rate pick up. Was Bill Delaney finally ready to talk to me about the Barber case?

TWENTY-SIX

||||||||||||||||||||||||||||||||||||||||||||||||||||||||||||||||||||||||||||||||

The Barber case might be solved tonight. Bill Delaney must be willing to tell me what he's been keeping back, I thought. Otherwise why would he be so agitated and insist that he would leave the hospital if he had to in order to talk to me?

When I left the car in the hospital parking lot, I felt the heat close in on me. The humidity, even this late in the day, felt suffocating. I had to stop at a water fountain in the hospital and gulp down several mouthfuls of water before I began to cool down. I loved my life in Athena, but in the summer months I preferred to live as much of it as possible inside in the air-conditioning.

Thankful that the hospital was cool, I took the elevator up and soon I reached Bill Delaney's room. The door stood wide open, and when I stepped into the room I was shocked to find several people in scrubs and white coats around the bed. One of the nurses turned and noticed me.

She walked over to me and motioned for me to move out of the room.

"Are you Mr. Harris?" she asked when we were out in the hallway. "He had us list you as his emergency contact."

"Yes," I said. "What's going on? Is he going to be okay?"

"He had a heart attack," the nurse replied. "He was extremely agitated, and he kept asking for you. We assured him you were on the way, but the stress evidently triggered a cardiac event. He's stable now. Luckily one of the attendants was with him and recognized the signs."

"Will I be able to talk to him?" I asked.

"Not for a while yet," the nurse replied.

"All right," I said. "Can you at least let him know that I'm here? I don't want him to get agitated again."

"I'll talk to the doctor," she said. "Why don't you go down to the waiting room near the nurses' station and wait? Someone will come talk to you soon."

I nodded, and she turned away to reenter the room. I walked down the hall and found the small waiting area. I had it to myself at the moment. I chose a seat and pulled out my cell phone to call Stewart and let him know I could be at the hospital much longer than I had planned.

"Don't worry about Diesel," Stewart said. "Is there anything you need? You're not going to stay all night, are you?"

"Thanks, I'm okay," I said. "How long I stay depends on how he's doing. If at all possible, I'd like to talk to him. He obviously has something he needs to tell me, and I'm afraid he'll upset himself again if he can't talk to me."

"Call me back if you do need me to bring you anything," Stewart said.

I thanked him again and ended the call. I debated calling Jack Pemberton to let him know about this new development, but after brief reflection I decided I should wait until I knew what had upset Bill Delaney so badly.

A few minutes later a tall man in a white coat entered the room. He looked to be about forty, with dark hair graying heavily at the temples. "Mr. Harris?" he asked, and I nodded as I rose from my chair. "I'm Dr. Greenway, a cardiologist. I understand that you're related to Mr. Delaney?"

"Yes, I'm his cousin," I said. "How is he?"

"Not good, I'm afraid," Dr. Greenway replied. "Why don't we sit down for a moment?" He gestured toward the chair I had been occupying.

I resumed my seat, and he chose one across the small space from mine. "Mr. Delaney has been a heavy drinker for many years," the doctor said. "That has done a lot of damage, and his heart is not in good shape. Neither is his liver. Right now he is stable, but I'm having him transferred to the ICU immediately. I don't want to give you any false hope. The heart attack was relatively mild, and if he was in better physical condition, I'd say he had every chance of making a good recovery. As it is, however, I can't say how well he might recover from this. He might not."

"Thank you for telling me," I said, saddened by this news. "He evidently got agitated because he had something to tell me."

Dr. Greenway nodded. "Yes, he was mumbling until we sedated him. The same words, over and over."

"What were they? Could you make them out?"

"He was saying, 'Tell him to let it go,' and then 'I promised, can't break a promise.'" He shrugged. "That's what it sounded like to me. Do you have any idea what it means?"

"Some of it, perhaps," I said. "Once he wakes up—if he wakes up—can someone please call me immediately? It doesn't matter what time it is."

The doctor stood. "All right. I suggest you go home for now. There's nothing you can do."

"Except pray," I said.

The doctor nodded and smiled briefly before he left the room.

I sat there, still dazed by what had occurred, trying to assimilate everything and to make some sense of it. What did Delaney's words mean?

I understood *tell him to let it go*. He was talking about the investigation into the Barber case. He wanted me to leave it alone.

I promised, can't break a promise.

He was protecting someone, I thought. He'd made a promise not to reveal something. Whatever it was, it obviously meant a great deal to him. So much, in fact, that he had suffered a heart attack over it.

Who had he promised to protect with his silence?

Three candidates came immediately to mind: Sylvia Delaney, Elizabeth Barber, and Leann Finch.

What about *X*? The unknown person. There certainly could be one, someone Jack and I hadn't discovered yet, who was linked to the case.

Time to head home, I decided. I left the waiting room.

A couple of minutes later, sweating profusely from the unrelenting heat, I unlocked the car and rolled down the windows to let the air inside dissipate. The sun had at last started to go down, but the night wouldn't bring much relief from the heat.

I prayed for Bill Delaney on the drive home. I had begun to realize that Jack and I were partly responsible for

Bill Delaney's state of mind. His agitation over our interest in the Barber case had been significant enough to bring on a heart attack. Had we not been pushing him to confide in us, he probably wouldn't have been so upset, and the heart attack might not have happened.

Jack and I had no way of knowing, however, that something like this would happen. Neither of us was responsible for the state of Delaney's health. His poor condition was self-inflicted. A lifetime of drinking took a harsh toll on the body. Delaney's own lifestyle choices were largely to blame, as was the unknown person who had tried to run him down. Still, I felt uncomfortable knowing that my actions had exacerbated the situation. Should I get the chance, I would apologize to Bill Delaney for upsetting him.

Despite my regrets, I did not intend to stop seeking the truth. I thought about those two young boys and their parents. They deserved to have their murderer named. If Jack and I could help find the truth, we would and be glad we had. If Bill Delaney was innocent, then he deserved to be vindicated.

By the time I reached home, I had decided not to call Jack. I would wait until I heard another report on Bill Delaney. If he made it to the morning, I would run over there, before Diesel and I needed to leave for Tullahoma, to see if he was in any condition to have visitors. I would share everything with Jack when I met him in Tullahoma.

Diesel greeted me at the back door. Stewart sat at the table, reading a magazine. He laid it aside while I was petting the cat. "How is he?" Stewart asked.

"They put him in the ICU," I said. "He was stable, but the cardiologist said he's in bad shape. He might not make it." Diesel meowed and rubbed against my leg. He knew I was upset.

"I'm sorry," Stewart said. "Will they call you?"

I nodded. "If I have to go out during the night, I'll let you know."

"Of course." Stewart picked up his magazine and rose from the table. "Is there anything I can do for you right now?"

"No, thanks," I said. "I think I'm going to head upstairs and wait for Helen Louise to call."

"Okay. You know where I am if you need me." Stewart left the kitchen, and I soon heard him jogging up the stairs.

"Come on, boy," I said. "Upstairs."

Diesel scampered out of the room ahead of me. I turned out the lights downstairs, except for a couple that stayed on, one in the hall and another in the kitchen. Upstairs I found Diesel on the bed, and after I undressed I went into the bathroom for a few minutes. When I emerged, Diesel appeared to be asleep. As I neared the bed, he opened his eyes and trilled at me.

I joined him on the bed and stretched out beside him. I stared up at the ceiling, and Diesel put a front paw on my arm. He meowed softly, and I turned my head to look at him.

"I'll be fine," I told him. He blinked sleepily and seemed to relax. His paw remained on my arm, however.

Gazing at the ceiling again, I couldn't keep my thoughts away from Bill Delaney and my part in upsetting him to the point of a heart attack. I had always had a tendency to worry over things, particularly over something like this. I mustn't let Helen Louise know about this when we talked tonight, though. She would be tired after a long day, and I didn't want her to lose sleep over this. There would be time enough to talk to her tomorrow or the next day, depending on her schedule.

Despite my worries, I soon dozed off, to be woken later by Helen Louise's ringtone on my cell. I answered, and right away I could tell by the sound of her voice she was exhausted. We talked only a few minutes, and then I told her to go to bed and rest. After a final exchange of endearments, we ended the call.

I turned out the light and waited to fall asleep again. I tried not to let my mind dwell on Bill Delaney and succeeded enough that I finally did drift off.

My alarm went off at five thirty, and I woke quickly, at first thinking it was the phone. When I realized that I had slept through the night without a call from the hospital, I felt better. I hoped this meant that Bill Delaney's condition had remained stable. Surely they would have called if he had taken a turn for the worse.

The drive to Tullahoma would take about ninety minutes, and that meant I would allow an additional fifteen to twenty minutes in case of complications. As soon as I was showered and dressed, I hurried downstairs with Diesel at my feet. By then it was six o'clock, and Azalea would be here soon. I looked up the number for the hospital and called, asking for the ICU nurses' station.

Moments later I was speaking with a nurse. I identified myself and asked whether I would be allowed to visit Bill Delaney this morning. The nurse put me on hold but was back in less than a minute.

"I'm sorry, sir, but the patient isn't able to have visitors this morning," the nurse said. "He's still sleeping, but in stable condition. By the afternoon you might be able to see him. Just check back with us later."

"Thank you, I will." I hung up the phone and uttered a quick prayer of thanks that Bill Delaney had made it through the night.

Diesel, I noticed, was sitting at the back door, watching it intently. He was waiting for Azalea. He knew what her schedule was and often greeted her when she entered the house. Moments later the door opened, and she walked into the kitchen. Diesel chirped loudly, and Azalea laughed.

"Good morning, Mr. Cat, and how are you?" Azalea set her purse down on the counter while Diesel warbled and meowed to let her know he was starving and surely could eat some bacon. Azalea laughed again. "Good morning, Mr. Charlie. When are you going to feed this poor thing?"

"Good morning, Azalea," I said. "He knows that when you're here there could be bacon. You've spoiled him."

"Seems to me you're the one done all the spoiling," Azalea said. "Don't go pushing the blame on me." She looked down at Diesel. "You hold on, Mr. Cat. At least give me time to cook. You'd be turning your nose up at raw bacon."

As Azalea set to work getting breakfast ready, I told her that Diesel and I were heading to Tullahoma this morning. "We need to leave around seven thirty."

"Then I reckon it'll be toast instead of biscuits this morning," Azalea said.

"That's fine," I replied.

I headed to the den to check e-mail. By the time I was done, breakfast would be ready. Diesel remained in the kitchen. As long as Azalea was frying bacon, he wouldn't go anywhere.

I read my e-mail, surfed the Internet for a bit, then went back to the kitchen. Breakfast was on the table. Diesel and I ate alone this morning. Haskell was probably out the door before I got up, and Stewart was most likely at the gym.

After a quick trip upstairs to brush my teeth, I was

ready to leave. Diesel and I bade Azalea good-bye, and soon we were on the road for Tullahoma.

As I headed out of Athena, I hoped that this day would bring new and helpful information. We needed a break in the case, and we needed it soon.

TWENTY-SEVEN

I accomplished the drive to Tullahoma without incident and, as usual, arrived early—nearly twenty minutes early. Jack's directions led me easily to the Kountry Kitchen. I pulled into the parking lot and texted Jack that Diesel and I had arrived.

We would wait for him in the car. Since Helen Louise's bistro was the only restaurant where Diesel was allowed, I had to stay with him. Had the temperature outside been mild, I could have left him in the car for a few minutes. With the late July heat, however, I remained with him, air-conditioning running. I simply couldn't understand people who left their pets—or children—in hot cars. If they were that ignorant they shouldn't have pets—or children—at all.

Jack texted back to let me know he was on the way and would arrive soon. Sure enough, only seven minutes later, he pulled into the parking space next to me. As he got out of his car, I rolled down my window to greet him.

"Good morning, Charlie," he said as he came up to my

window. "How are you? And how is Diesel?" He bent to look into the backseat where Diesel sat, nose pressed to the glass.

"Fine," I said. "Why don't you join me in the car so we can talk?"

"That won't be necessary," Jack said. "Wanda Nell's boss, Melvin, said we can use his office so Diesel can come inside. There's a door around on the other side of the building."

"Sounds good," I said. "Better than sitting in the car burning gas." I turned the car off and got out. Jack moved back so I could get Diesel out, too. Diesel wore his harness with a leash attached. He hopped out of the car onto the pavement and we followed Jack.

As we walked I kept an eye out for anything on the paved surface of the parking lot that could harm Diesel's paws. The temperature wasn't high enough yet to make it unsafe for Diesel to walk on. I was relieved to see that the owner kept his parking lot clean. We made it around the front of the building and down the side with no problem. Jack opened a door near the middle of the side wall and ushered us inside.

We were standing in a cramped hallway. To the left I could hear the sounds of the kitchen. Diesel detected the smell of bacon, as did I. There were two doors in the inner wall, and Jack opened one of them and motioned for us to enter. The office contained a desk, a couple of chairs, and two filing cabinets. There was room enough for the three of us and maybe one other person. We settled into the chairs, Jack taking the one behind the desk, and Diesel sat on the floor next to me.

That one other person came into the office, an attractive woman about Jack's age. He got up to give her a quick kiss and then introduced me to his wife, Wanda Nell.

"Nice to meet you, Charlie," she said. "You, too, Diesel. Aren't you about the most gorgeous cat I ever saw?" She extended a hand to the cat, and he sniffed it. Then he licked her fingers, and she laughed. "I had a piece of bacon a minute ago."

"He loves bacon," I said.

Diesel meowed and looked up at Wanda Nell.

"Sorry, sir, no more bacon." She patted his head, then scratched it. He purred for her. "I guess I pass the test."

"You do." I smiled. "He's your friend now."

Wanda Nell smiled down at the cat. She petted him a moment longer, then turned to her husband. "Elmer Lee came in right before I headed back here. You want to talk to him?" She turned to me. "Elmer Lee Johnson is the sheriff. I've known him a long time. We don't always get along real well, though."

Jack laughed. "That's because you've shown him up more than once, honey."

Wanda Nell shrugged. "If he wasn't so dang bullheaded most of the time, he'd do better. Gets his mind set on one thing and it gets stuck there. Now, do you want to talk to him?"

"I don't think I'm up to dealing with Elmer Lee this morning," Jack said. "We will have to talk to him at some point, but I'd rather wait until we have something concrete to go on."

"All right, then," Wanda Nell said. "I'd better be getting back out there before Melvin comes looking for me."

"Please thank him for me for letting me bring Diesel in," I said.

"I will." Wanda Nell looked at her husband. "Y'all be careful today. Let me know how it goes."

"We will," Jack replied. "We'll probably be back here for lunch."

Wanda Nell nodded before she left the room, pulling the door shut behind her.

"Before we do anything," I said, "I need to fill you in on the latest with Bill Delaney. It's not good news."

"What happened? Did somebody try to kill him again?" Jack asked, obviously alarmed.

"No, no attempt on his life as far as I'm aware. He suffered a heart attack last night." I gave Jack the details, and his expression grew grim as he listened.

When I finished, Jack said, "Obviously we upset him badly yesterday, and I feel like crap now. I never thought something like this would happen."

"I feel bad about it, too," I said. "We did get him upset, but if he was in better physical condition, I don't think he would've had a heart attack. It's a terrible combination of circumstances."

"You're right," Jack said, "but that doesn't make me feel much better." He paused. "I think we need to go ahead, though, and try to see this thing through. If he's protecting someone, that means there's something no one knows about this case. We need to find out what it is."

"And who it is," I said. "They told me he was muttering about promising someone, over and over. I figure there are three candidates, his mother, Elizabeth Barber, and Leann Finch, for the person he was making the promises to. Of course, there's always the possibility X is someone who has a connection to the case that we don't know about."

"I agree," Jack said. "I thought we might start here in town this morning and go see Sylvia Delaney's neighbors. There's that one woman who still lives next door to the Delaney house. Her name is Jimmie Ann Cooper and she has a son who lives with her. Turns out she knows Wanda Nell, so I think we can get her to talk to us without too much of a problem."

"That sounds good," I said. "I hope she's not allergic to cats or afraid of them, or you'll have to interview her on your own."

Jack rose from behind the desk. "We'll figure it out as we go along. I hope you don't mind driving again."

"Not at all," I said. "We want to stay cool, after all. We don't know what hot water we might get into." I grinned, and Jack laughed. Diesel trilled and chirped, as if he understood the joke himself.

While I put Diesel in the backseat, Jack retrieved his notebook from his car. He showed me a small digital recorder he had. "I always ask if I can record, of course. A lot of the time, they don't mind, and it's helpful later on. I take good notes, but it's easy to forget to write something down."

Jack directed me, and within a few minutes we pulled up in front of a white frame house with a neatly groomed yard. The lots in this neighborhood were not large but were wide enough to give the illusion of distance between the houses.

"That's the Delaney house on the right," Jack said. "Let's get this thing started." He opened the door and stepped out of the car.

"Come on, Diesel, time to get to work," I said.

With Diesel on the leash, I followed Jack up the walk to the front door of Mrs. Cooper's house. Jack rang the bell, and moments later a woman answered. I reckoned she was about my age, early fifties. Short, with dark hair and a wary expression.

Jack introduced himself. "I believe you know my wife, Wanda Nell. She was Wanda Nell Culpepper before."

The wary expression disappeared and a warm smile replaced it. "I sure do know Wanda Nell. If she isn't the sweetest thing the good Lord ever created, I don't know who is. I heard she got married a while back but I haven't run into her since I found out. It's nice to meet you. Y'all come on in."

She looked past Jack and saw Diesel and me. Her eyes widened at the sight of Diesel. "Heavens to Betsy, I swear that's the biggest cat I've ever seen. He's not a bobcat, is he?"

I repressed a smile. I'd heard that question often. After I introduced myself, I said, "No, ma'am, he's a Maine Coon." I gave her the quick facts on Maine Coons. "He's very well-behaved, and his name is Diesel. Would you mind if he comes in with us?"

"Not at all," Mrs. Cooper said. "Y'all come on in. I hope y'all will ignore the state of my house. We don't have a lot of company, and I'm inclined to let things slide a little." She motioned for us to precede her into a room to the left of the entrance.

Based on years of experience of Southern housewives, I knew that when Mrs. Cooper asked us to ignore the state of her house that it would be pretty near immaculate. Even my late wife, Jackie, used to say similar things whenever we had company.

Sure enough, Mrs. Cooper's living room looked perfectly clean and well organized. She motioned us to the sofa. "Would y'all like something to drink?" she asked.

We took places on the indicated sofa, and Diesel stretched out on the floor by my feet. He had allowed Mrs. Cooper to pat his head a couple of times, and he rewarded her with a couple of warbles.

"No, thank you," I said. "I'm fine. Jack?"

"No, I'm good, Mrs. Cooper," he said. "I really appreciate you inviting us in." He waited for her to seat herself across from us before he continued. "I'm a writer, and Mr. Charlie Harris is helping me with the research for the book I'm working on now. The books I write are true crime, and I'm interested in a crime that happened here about twenty years ago."

"The Barbers, has to be," Mrs. Cooper said. "Oh my Lord, I haven't thought about them in a long time, although I do sometimes see the Barber girl in the paper. She's married to a businessman, Campbell's the name, I think. So nice to know she made a good life for herself after all that tragedy, don't you think?"

"Yes, ma'am," Jack said. He shot me a glance. Obviously, getting Mrs. Cooper to talk wasn't an issue here. "I don't know if you knew the Barbers, but your neighbor's son worked for them. Bill Delaney."

"Sylvia's son," Mrs. Cooper said. "I hated when she had to go into the nursing home. She was the sweetest person, and we had a lot in common, both being widows with sons to raise. That was a terrible time for her with everybody pointing the finger at Bill." She shook her head. "Sylvia stood up for him, though. Just the way I would if somebody was accusing my son of doing something terrible like that."

"Did you know the Barbers?" I asked.

"Not to say really *know* them, no," Mrs. Cooper said. "A lot of people sure knew who Hiram Barber was, let me tell you. People would duck out of the way if they saw him coming down the street. Mean as a rattlesnake, and crazy to boot. I never could figure out how he ever talked Betty into marrying him. I went to school with Betty's younger sister. She was an Eaton. Do you know the Eatons?" She looked at Jack but didn't wait for an answer. "Betty must have seen something in him nobody else ever did, but I bet she wished she'd never married him after he started getting crazier and crazier."

Jack was busy scribbling in his notebook. He hadn't

had the chance to ask Mrs. Cooper if he could record the interview. I hoped he knew shorthand, otherwise he'd never keep up with the spate of words.

"I'd see her in town sometimes but she would never talk for more than a minute or two. Always afraid Hiram would come along and have something ugly to say to her. He was always running her down. I'd've scratched his eyes out if he tried that with me, but Betty wouldn't stand up to him."

The import of Mrs. Cooper's description of Betty Barber finally sank in with me. Before she could launch into further speech, I asked, "Do you think Hiram Barber abused his wife and children?"

"I'm sure he did," Mrs. Cooper said. "He was just the type of man who would. Like I said, he got crazier and meaner. Betty never would admit it, but I bet he slapped her around."

Jack and I exchanged a quick glance. This could be a piece of the new information we'd been hoping for. I asked another question. "Do you think the sheriff's department knew about this?"

"Nobody ever asked me," Mrs. Cooper said. "Back then people didn't talk about stuff like that much."

"I don't think they knew," Jack said. "My source never mentioned it, and I'm sure he would have if he'd known about it."

The situation Mrs. Cooper described left me in little doubt that Hiram Barber was abusive. The question was, had that played a role in the murders?

TWENTY-EIGHT

I was so lost in thought, considering the ramifications of Hiram Barber as an abuser that I nearly missed Jack's next question.

"You mentioned Mrs. Barber's sister, a Miss Eaton," Jack said. "I don't know her. Does she still live in Tulla-homa?"

Mrs. Cooper shook her head. "No, she died a few years back. The way I heard it, she had breast cancer but wouldn't go to the doctor. Waited too late, and by then they couldn't do much for her."

"That's really sad," I said. "Why wouldn't she go to the doctor?"

"Her church." Mrs. Cooper grimaced. "One of those groups that don't believe in doctors. Some mess like that. Beats me what some people will believe."

"Are there any other family around? The Eatons, that is, who would know more about Betty Barber before she married?" Jack asked.

"Most of them have either died or moved away that I know of," Mrs. Cooper said. "Though I can't say for sure."

"We'll have to see if we can track any of them down," I said.

"I'd like to talk to you about the night of the murders," Jack said. "Do you remember that night?"

"I do," Mrs. Cooper said. "It was a quiet night here, like most every night. This has always been a nice neighborhood. Things get a little rowdy on the Fourth of July and New Year's Eve, people barbecuing and stuff. Setting off fireworks, even though it's illegal."

I was thankful that Mrs. Cooper was willing to talk but she was a bit too chatty about inessential details.

"Who was here in the house that night?" Jack asked.

Mrs. Cooper seemed to take a moment to think. "My heavens, who would be here. Me and my son. My husband died about a year before. Killed in a car accident out on the highway."

"I'm so sorry," I said.

Mrs. Cooper nodded. "My son was only seven at the time. He misses his daddy still."

"I can imagine," Jack said. "According to Mrs. Delaney's testimony her son came home drunk that evening, passed out, and never left the house. Did you hear him come home?"

"I sure did, him banging on the door for poor Sylvia to let him in." Mrs. Cooper sniffed. "Too almighty drunk to even find his own house key."

"Do you remember what time that was?" I asked.

Mrs. Cooper tilted her head to one side and gazed at the wall while she considered the question. "Near as I can remember it was around seven, maybe a little earlier."

"Did you hear anyone leave the house after that?" Jack asked. "For example, did you hear their car leave?"

"No, I didn't," Mrs. Cooper said. "I went to bed at nine like I always did back then, because I had to be up to get ready for work and get my son off to school." She paused a moment, as if another thought had struck her. "I wouldn't have heard anything, I reckon, because my bedroom is on the side of the house away from them."

"What about your son?" I asked. "Did he hear anything?"

"My goodness gracious, I don't know." Mrs. Cooper appeared surprised at the idea. "Nobody ever asked him. I know I sure didn't. I didn't want him knowing too much about the whole thing. Didn't want him having nightmares. He had trouble sleeping after his daddy was killed, and I can't tell you how many nights I had to go into his room because he was having a bad dream."

I felt great sympathy for the boy. Losing a parent at any age is tough, but especially so when you're a child.

"Could we talk to your son about that night?" Jack asked.

"I don't see why not." Mrs. Cooper rose from her chair. "I'll go call him. He's working in his room." She walked into the hallway and called out, "Ronnie, can you come here a minute? We need to talk to you." She returned to her chair. "He'll come if he doesn't have those headphones on. Wears them a lot because it blocks out noise so he can concentrate."

Jack and I exchanged glances. It sounded to me like Ronnie Cooper was in his room playing video games. I had expected Mrs. Cooper to tell us he was at his job.

Moments later a tall young man entered the room. He was so tall he had to duck his head to get in the door. I reckoned he must be about six foot six or seven. He was solidly built, dressed in athletic shorts and a sleeveless T-shirt that showed off a muscular physique. I had been expecting a couch potato, but Ronnie Cooper looked like a pro athlete.

"Good morning." He had a deep voice. "What's going on, Mom?"

"Sit down, honey," Mrs. Cooper said. "We don't want our visitors getting neck strain looking up at you. These gentlemen are Mr. Jack Pemberton and Mr. Charlie Harris, and that big kitty there is Diesel."

Ronnie seated himself in a chair near his mother. He leaned forward and extended a hand to Diesel. The cat rose from his relaxed stretch by my feet and went over to the young man. Diesel sniffed his fingers for a moment, then Ronnie began to stroke Diesel's back. The cat started purring, and I knew Ronnie Cooper had passed the Diesel test.

"He's beautiful," Ronnie said. "Maine Coon, right?"

"Yes, he is." I was surprised because not that many people I had encountered had seen one before, let alone knew the breed.

"Ronnie's real smart," Mrs. Cooper said, beaming. "He's a computer programmer, and he works from here for a company in Memphis. He telly-somethings. What is it?"

"Telecommute," Ronnie said. "I go into the office about three times a month for meetings, but most of the time I work from home. What can I do for you, gentlemen?"

Jack took the cue and launched into an explanation before Mrs. Cooper could get going on one. He gave Ronnie a quick summary of our interest in the Barber case, and when he finished, Ronnie nodded.

"I remember it now," he said. "Haven't thought about it in years, though."

"All Ronnie's ever been interested in is computers and cars," Mrs. Cooper said. "You should see what's parked in my garage right now. He won't tell me what he paid for it, but I know it must be expensive. I'd be afraid to drive it."

"I told you I didn't pay full price for it, Mom," Ronnie said, a note of exasperation creeping into his voice. "I took over the payments from a guy at work who got over-extended." He looked at Jack and me. "Lamborghini. I wouldn't have bought it, but the deal was irresistible."

Jack whistled, and I almost did. Lamborghinis were some of the most expensive cars made. Ronnie must be doing well to be driving one, even if he had taken over the payments from someone else.

"I hate to hurry you guys along," Ronnie said, "but I've got to get back to work soon. What is it you want to ask me?"

"It's about the night of the Barber murders," Jack said. "Do you remember when it happened?"

Ronnie shrugged. "Sure, kids at school were talking about it."

"They want to know if you heard anything from next door that night," Mrs. Cooper said. "Ronnie's bedroom is on that side, next to their driveway."

I watched as Ronnie ceased petting Diesel and leaned back in the chair, eyes closed. After a moment his eyes popped open. "I remember," he said. "They had an old banger of a car. The engine made a whistling noise." He turned to his mother. "Remember, Puck used to bark when she heard it."

"Puck was our rat terrier," Mrs. Cooper said. "Lord, I loved that dog. Smartest thing on four legs I ever saw."

"She was a great dog," Ronnie said. "She slept with me back then. I used to have a lot of trouble sleeping, but I grew out of it eventually. Anyway, like I said, Puck would bark if she heard that car going in or out of the driveway next to my room." He frowned. "I think that was the night she woke me up twice because of the car."

"Can you be sure?" I asked, excited that this could really shake things up if he had heard the Delaneys' car leaving during the night. "That was twenty years ago."

"I've got a good memory," Ronnie said. "But if you want proof, I can probably show you."

"How?" Jack said.

"Notebooks." Ronnie got up from his chair and headed from the room, once again ducking to clear the doorway.

Jack and I looked to Mrs. Cooper for an explanation.

"He's been writing in his notebooks since his daddy died," Mrs. Cooper said. "The counselor at school said it might help him, and I guess it must've done because he still does it. Except now he does it on his computer, I think."

Jack and I nodded. One of Laura's friends in elementary school had done the same thing, I remembered, after her mother died.

"It might take him a minute or two," Mrs. Cooper continued. "He probably knows exactly where that old notebook is. You should see his room. Everything neat, always, never anything out of place. I guess he learned it from me." She glanced around the room with what I took to be a complacent air. The room was indeed neat. She obviously took great pride in her housework.

Mrs. Cooper again offered us a drink, but we both declined. Before she could get started on another anecdote or long-winded observation, Ronnie returned, papers in hand. He resumed his seat and brandished the pages.

"I scanned all the old notebooks and converted them into searchable PDFs," he said. "Makes it easier to find things, like what you're looking for. I checked the date of the murders online, and then I found the corresponding date in my notebook. It's all here, in case anybody needs proof." He leaned forward to hand me the pages.

I accepted them, and he said, "The part you're interested in starts near the bottom of the page."

I leaned toward Jack so we could read together. I found the section Ronnie indicated and began to read the precise but childish scrawl.

9:53 pm Puck barked and woke me up. Heard the car next door go by. Engine whistles. Wish old man Delaney would let me look at it. Could probably fix it for him but he won't listen. Wonder where he's going? Out to buy beer, maybe. Mom says he gets as drunk as Cooter Brown all the time. I asked her who Cooter Brown was and she didn't know.

There was another entry on the second page that occurred about two hours later.

12:18 am Puck barking again. This time I heard old man Delaney coming back in the car. Hope he stays home now so Puck stops waking me up.

That was the extent of it. Proof that either Bill or Sylvia Delaney left the house that night.

Bill Delaney's alibi just went up in flames.

TWENTY-NINE

Either way you looked at it, I decided, Bill Delaney had no alibi. That is, of course, if the murders occurred between ten and midnight. I realized that we were ignorant of one of the most important facts in the case. What time were the Barbers killed?

"Can we keep these?" Jack brandished the two pages.

Ronnie Cooper shrugged. "Sure, I don't think there's anything I don't want anyone to know."

"You might be questioned about them again by official investigators," Jack said. "At some point Charlie and I will have to share what we've found out with them."

"No problem," Ronnie said. "Now, if that's all, I'd like to get back to work." He looked at me and Jack.

"I can't think of anything else at the moment," I said.

"Neither can I. Thanks for your help. This is an amazing find," Jack said. "I can't believe no one knew about this before."

"Nobody ever asked," Ronnie said. "I never thought

about it myself." He rubbed Diesel's head. I marveled that my cat had remained near Ronnie the entire time. Ronnie rose from his chair.

"Hang on a sec," Jack said. "Sorry, I just thought of something. You wrote these things in your notebook as if it was Bill Delaney driving the car that night. Did you actually see him in the car?"

"It had to be," Mrs. Cooper said. "Sylvia couldn't see well enough at night to drive. She was scared to death to even try."

Ronnie shot an exasperated glance at his mother. "I can answer for myself, Mom. Yes, it was Bill Delaney. My bed was right under the window back then, and I looked out right after Puck woke me up. Both times. There's a streetlight nearby, and there was enough light for me to see him at the wheel of the car."

"Thanks for clarifying that," Jack said.

"And thank you, Mrs. Cooper, for telling us about Sylvia Delaney's problem with driving at night," I added. "All this information is a great help."

"I'm going back to work," Ronnie said. "You know where to find me if you have any more questions." He left the room, and his mother gazed fondly after him.

"He's such a hard worker," she said. "Puts in I don't know how many hours every day. Between going to the gym and work, he doesn't have time for much else." She sighed. "I don't reckon I'll ever be a grandmother unless that computer of his can have a baby."

I smothered a laugh at the thought. Mrs. Cooper seemed genuinely serious, but there was nothing I could offer to comfort her, other than a platitude. Jack seemed at a loss for words, too. Really, I thought, how could you follow up a statement like that?

"Can you think of anyone that Betty Barber might

have been close enough to that she would have confided in them about what was going on at home?" Jack asked.

Mrs. Cooper shook her head. "Not that I can think of, other than maybe one of her neighbors. I'd say you might try their church, but I think Hiram got angry with the preacher, and they stopped going."

"Do you have any idea why he was angry with the preacher?" I asked. Could there be a clue in that? I wondered.

"Probably because Hiram wasn't tithing the way he should, and the preacher probably complained." Mrs. Cooper rolled her eyes. "Hiram always put on like he was so poor he couldn't even pay attention. He sure didn't spend money on his wife and kids. He wouldn't hardly pay his hands much, either. I don't know how he kept anybody working on the farm. Anyway, he had enough money to pay his share to the church. He was too cheap to do it."

This was consistent with what we'd already heard about Hiram Barber. I wondered if he had always been so obsessed with money or had something happened to trigger this behavior?

Jack rose from the sofa and tucked his notebook in his jacket pocket. "Mrs. Cooper, thank you so much for talking with us this morning. You've been a great help."

"Yes, you certainly have." I rose, too, and Diesel returned to my side. I picked up the end of the leash, and he rubbed against my leg.

"Well, I guess I'm happy I could help," Mrs. Cooper said. "Seems like Ronnie was more help than I was, but either way, I'm glad. You're welcome to come back anytime." She stood and walked toward the door. "I was able to retire thanks to Ronnie, so I'm at home most of the time nowadays."

After a few more comments about how happy she was

to help and how welcome we were to come back, we were able to get away from Mrs. Cooper and head to the car.

"Good grief, that woman can talk," Jack said when we were seated inside with the air conditioner blasting. "And thank goodness she did. Ronnie, too."

"Yes, thanks to Ronnie we know that Bill Delaney was out of the house for two hours that night," I said. "What we don't know, of course, is when the murders took place. We really need to find that out."

Jack frowned. "According to the information released to the press, Elizabeth Barber came home from her friend's house —Leann Finch's house—around seven the next morning. That's when she found the bodies. They could have been dead twelve hours or more by then, of course."

"Unless they were killed between ten and midnight," I said. "That would narrow down the time frame to between nine and seven hours, roughly. About how long would it take to get from here to where the Barber farm used to be?"

Jack thought about it for a moment. "At that time of night, with almost no traffic, and if he was driving fast, less than twenty minutes. Maybe even fifteen. As the crow flies, it's only about ten miles, but it's off the highway on country roads that are full of curves."

"So that could put the time of death to between half past ten and half past eleven," I said. "Give or take a few minutes. Is there any way you could get hold of the autopsy results?"

Jack shrugged. "All I can do is ask. But there might be an easier way."

"And that would be?" I asked.

"Go straight to Elmer Lee Johnson and tell him what we've found out, maybe bargain a little with him to find out about the time of death," Jack replied. "What do you think?"

"I don't know the man," I said. "You do. How do you think he'd respond to a proposition like that?"

"On a good day he might go for it," Jack said. "I'm sure he'd like to be able to close the case. It would put him one up on his predecessor, his old boss."

"And on a bad day?" I asked, not sure I wanted to hear the response.

"He'd cuss us out and threaten to throw us in jail for interfering in the official business of the law." Jack grinned. "He's not too fond of me, you see. I told Wanda Nell he's jealous, because he's had a thing for her for years, going back to when she was married to his best friend, Bobby Ray Culpepper."

Even though it was none of my business, I was about to ask Jack what had happened to Wanda Nell's first husband, but he saved me the trouble.

"Bobby Ray got himself murdered a few years ago. He and Wanda Nell were already divorced, and Elmer Lee had a big mad on over her dumping his best friend. He treated her like the chief suspect, but frankly I think the whole time he wanted her for himself. He was just too stubborn and too loyal to his dead best friend to do anything about it. He thought the world of Bobby Ray, who was, basically, a no-good good ol' boy. He ran around on Wanda Nell most of the time they were married."

Jack obviously didn't think much of the late, unlamented Mr. Culpepper. Couldn't say I blamed him, given what he'd told me. This was more than I really needed to know about his wife's life, but I supposed it did help explain the sheriff's potential attitude toward Jack and anyone associated with him.

"I have never understood men like that," I said. "I know there are a lot of them out there, though. Look, about talking to the sheriff, it's up to you. I'll go along with what you think is best."

Diesel, from his vantage point in the backseat, added his opinion. He meowed loudly. Jack laughed.

"Okay, I get the hint. Decision time. Let's go talk to Elmer Lee," Jack said. "The sheriff's department is off the square in beautiful old downtown Tullahoma."

"Off we go, then," I said. "Just tell me how to get there."

Jack gave me the directions, and in about ten minutes we pulled up in front of the sheriff's department. We got out, and I took Diesel's leash in hand.

"If he's out of the office," Jack said, "I'll see if we can make an appointment with him for sometime today. I think it's best to get this over with as soon as we can."

"I agree." Diesel and I followed Jack into the building. We hung back while Jack approached the desk and asked to talk to the sheriff. The woman at the desk picked up a phone and talked to someone. After about thirty seconds, she put down the receiver and nodded.

Jack turned and motioned for Diesel and me to join him. "We're in luck," Jack said, "he's here and can see us now. Thanks, Thelma." He smiled at the receptionist, and she grinned back at him.

"You're welcome, Jack," she said, batting her eyelashes at him. "Anytime."

Jack chuckled, and I smiled at Thelma as we left the desk. Her eyes grew big when she finally caught sight of Diesel. I kept smiling and following Jack down a hallway.

He paused in front of an open door and knocked on the door frame. "Come on in," a gruff-sounding voice said.

Jack entered, and Diesel and I went with him.

"Thanks for seeing us, Elmer Lee," Jack said. "I know you're busy, but we think this is important." He stood aside and motioned me forward. "This is my colleague, Charlie Harris, and this is Diesel."

Sheriff Johnson rose from behind his desk and walked around to shake my hand. Then, to my surprise, he squatted until his face was almost level with the cat's. He held out a hand to Diesel and let him sniff. After a moment, Diesel butted his head against the hand, and the sheriff scratched the back of Diesel's head. The cat responded with a couple of happy chirps. The sheriff rose from his squat and looked at me.

"I know who you are, Mr. Harris. Kanesha Berry has talked about you at the Mississippi Sheriffs' Association meeting. I been knowing her for a few years. She speaks pretty highly of you."

"I'm happy to hear that, Sheriff Johnson," I said. "I would also like to thank you for talking with us this morning."

Johnson nodded and moved back around his desk to resume his seat. He waved a hand to indicate that we should sit. Jack and I pulled chairs in front of the desk, and Diesel sat between us.

Johnson leaned back in his chair and regarded Jack. "So what is this all about, Jack? What have you got your nose stuck into this time?"

"The Barber case," Jack said.

The sheriff's eyes narrowed. "How come you got interested in that?"

"Perhaps I should explain," I said. "I recently made the acquaintance of Bill Delaney." I noticed that Johnson stiffened slightly at the mention of the name. He obviously recognized it immediately. "It turns out that his biological father was married to my late aunt. He apparently only found out who his father was when his mother, Sylvia Delaney, passed away recently."

"Where is Delaney now?" Johnson asked.

"In the ICU in the Athena hospital." I gave him a quick summary of the situation. "I haven't had a chance to call the hospital to get an update since this morning when they told me he was still in stable condition. He's in bad shape physically, though, so his long-term prognosis isn't good."

"Why are you so interested in the Barber case?" Johnson asked again.

"Because of Bill Delaney," I replied. "I know he was suspected, but his mother gave him an alibi that no one could break."

"That's true," Johnson said. "I was a young deputy at the time, and I worked on the case. His mama was a tough lady. Looked sweet as they come but tough. But again, why are you poking into this?"

How could I explain that I felt a responsibility toward Delaney because of my aunt? I wasn't sure whether Johnson would buy it. I settled for a simpler answer. "I need to know the truth because of his connection to my family."

Johnson shrugged. "Okay. So are y'all here to ask me questions about the case? What's going on?"

"We have information that could help break the case, once and for all," Jack said. "We're ready to give it to you, but we want something in return."

"What information could you possibly have?" Johnson sounded skeptical.

"Information about an alibi," Jack said.

Johnson stared hard at both of us, his eyes narrowed again.

Jack continued, "In return for that, we want to know the details of the autopsies."

Johnson laughed. "You don't want much, do you? Do you seriously think I'm going to give you information like that?"

Jack sounded confident when he replied. "If you want to hear what we found out, you will."

They looked like two combatants about to engage. All I could do was sit there with my cat and wait to see who emerged victorious.

THIRTY

||||||||||||||||||||||||||||||||||||||||||||||

Evidently Elmer Lee Johnson's curiosity won out over his desire to deny Jack the information we wanted to barter. "All right, Jack, I'll let you see the autopsy report." The sheriff leaned forward and put his elbows on his desk. "So what's this big new information about an alibi? You talking about Bill Delaney?"

"Yes," Jack said. "Charlie and I came from interviewing the Delaneys' next-door neighbor, Mrs. Cooper, and her son, Ronnie. Do you know them?"

Johnson snorted. "Everybody in town knows Ronnie Cooper and that expensive car of his. What did he have to say?"

"Not anywhere near as much as his mother did. That woman sure can talk," I said. "But what Ronnie told us will probably surprise you." Diesel meowed, and Johnson looked startled. Then he grinned.

"I heard that cat acts like he knows what you say." Johnson shook his head. "Next thing you know, he'll be reading a book. Okay, now, what did Ronnie Cooper tell you?"

"He heard—and saw—Bill Delaney leave the house that night around ten and come back a little after midnight," Jack said.

"He couldn't've been more'n about seven or eight back then," the sheriff said. "How can he remember that far back and know what he's talking about?"

"He's been keeping a notebook since around the time his father died, maybe a year before the Barber murders. He's an impressive young man, I have to say."

Jack took up the narrative. "He told us the Delaneys' car had a distinctive whistle in the engine. His bedroom is the one next to the driveway for the Delaney house. Did you know that?"

Johnson shook his head. He was starting to look intrigued. "Go on."

"The Coopers had a dog that would bark every time it heard the engine whistling," I said. "The dog woke Ronnie up twice that night, and Ronnie recorded it all in his notebook. Jack, why don't you show the sheriff the pages?"

Jack pulled the folded papers from his pocket and handed them across the desk. Johnson took them and unfolded them.

"Down toward the bottom of the first page," I said.

Jack and I remained quiet while the sheriff read. When he finished, Johnson dropped the papers on his desk, slammed his fist on top of them, and uttered an obscenity. I flinched at it, but I understood his emotion.

"How the hell did we miss this twenty years ago?" Johnson shook his head. "Delaney was out of the house after all. His mama sure put on a good act, though. She swore up and down he was out of it all night, sleeping it off in his room."

"He might have fooled her into thinking that," I said. "Maybe Mrs. Delaney really thought he *was* in his room."

Johnson shrugged. "Too late to ask her now, but I'm sure the hell going to talk to Delaney the minute he's able."

"Now do you understand why we want to look at the autopsy reports?" Jack asked.

Johnson glared at Jack. "Of course I do. Time of death. You want to know if the Barbers were killed during that window of time."

"Exactly," I said. "There was maybe a little more than an hour when Delaney could have killed the Barbers. If he had left the house another time, the Coopers' dog would have alerted them. So the key time is between ten and midnight, minus the time it took him to go back and forth from home to the Barber farm."

"Wait a minute," Johnson said. "What time did Delaney get home the first time? I can't remember what his mama said."

"According to Mrs. Cooper," Jack replied, "it was around seven. He was drunk all right, so drunk he couldn't find his own house key. He was making all kinds of noise, beating on the door and yelling to be let in."

"He couldn't've been that drunk if he was going out again at ten o'clock, driving a car," the sheriff said. "I saw him a few times when he was bad drunk. He'd conk out and the trumpets of Jericho couldn't wake him up."

That was an interesting point, one I hadn't considered yet. What if Delaney pretended to be drunker than he was? Could that be an argument for premeditation?

"The autopsies," Jack said, his rising impatience obvious. "Come on, Elmer Lee, we made a deal."

"I know that," the sheriff replied, sounding testy. "I can tell you what you want to know, though, about the time of death." He paused. "About the *times* of death, that is."

"What do you mean?" I asked. "Weren't all four of them killed within a short span of time?"

Johnson shook his head. "From what we could tell at the time, it looked like they had been. We thought Barber was shot first, then his wife and the boys. Turned out that was all wrong."

"So Barber didn't die first?" Jack asked.

"No, siree, he didn't," Johnson replied. "He was the last to die. In fact, he probably didn't die until over two hours after his wife and the boys were killed."

Jack and I exchanged startled glances. This wasn't something either one of us would ever have suspected.

"That's bizarre," I said. "What was going on during those two hours? Was Barber out of the house during that time, with the killer waiting for him after he murdered the family?"

Johnson shrugged. "We don't know. Between that and the shotgun disappearing, we couldn't figure out what the hell happened in that house."

"What about the times?" Jack asked. "Did the pathologist establish the relative times of the killings?"

"That I can answer," Johnson replied. "Mrs. Barber and the boys were killed somewhere between approximately seven and nine o'clock."

"So that means Barber was killed sometime between nine and eleven?" I asked.

Johnson nodded. "Roughly. The house was cold. Barber's daughter told us he wouldn't let them turn on heaters until the outside temperature got down under thirty-five degrees. It was a cold night, probably in the forties, and the house wasn't insulated worth a damn."

"So the cool temperatures slowed down the postmortem processes," Jack said.

"Yeah," Johnson said. "Now, the interesting thing about what you found out is that Bill Delaney has an alibi for the murders of Miz Barber and the boys."

"But not for Hiram Barber," I said. "Wouldn't you think the same person killed all of them? It stands to reason, doesn't it?"

"Normally, I'd say so," Johnson replied. "But Delaney could have killed ol' Hiram, couldn't he? The timing fits with what Ronnie Cooper says in his notebook."

"That's true," Jack said. "But don't you think it's more likely that Hiram Barber wasn't home when his wife and the boys were killed? The killer waited for him to come home and then killed him, too."

"Probably," the sheriff said. "But then where was Hiram Barber while his family was killed? We talked to everyone we could find near the Barber farm, and nobody remembered seeing him after about five o'clock that evening. Nobody heard the shots, either."

Jack shrugged. "Just because they didn't see him doesn't mean he wasn't elsewhere at the time."

"You got me there," Johnson said.

"Elizabeth Barber reported the deaths the next morning, didn't she?" I asked. "Around seven?"

"Call came in at seven minutes past seven," Johnson said.

"I must say you have an incredible memory to pull all these details out of your head," I said.

"I've studied that case on and off for years," the sheriff said. "I've pretty much memorized most of the details. Always hated the fact that we weren't able to crack it."

"Now that this new information has come to light," I said, "will you reopen the case?"

"I'd like to," Johnson said. "First I have to find the

money to pay for the investigation. I can't just reassign people to this when I've already got men working overtime as it is to cover all the shifts."

"I hadn't considered that," I said.

Johnson sounded bitter when he replied, "The almighty budget runs things these days. I'm the one who gets the blame when we run over, and I'm not looking to lose this job in the next election."

"So for now, what's the plan?" Jack asked. "It doesn't sound like you're going to reopen the case."

"I can't right now," Johnson said, "much as I'd like to. If I'm going to ask for the money to run an investigation, I have to have more to go on."

"What if we keep digging and find more?" Jack asked.

Johnson shrugged. "Then I reckon if you found something big enough, I could get the money."

"So you're okay with us continuing?" I asked.

"As long as you don't break any laws," Johnson said. "I can't stop you from talking to people. Now, if they call me and complain about harassment, that's another story."

Jack looked at me, and I nodded. He turned back to face Johnson. "Then I think Charlie and I are going to keep talking to people. But first, the autopsy reports?"

"Normally something like that would be in the files in storage," Johnson said, staring at the wall past us. "But sometimes I keep copies of things right on top of my desk." His gaze drifted to a metal tray on one corner of his desk and then back to the wall. "If you'll excuse me, gentlemen, I need to step out for a minute."

"Sure thing," Jack said.

The moment Johnson cleared the door, Jack was on his feet, examining the contents of the metal tray. He soon extracted a file and shoved it partially down the back of his pants. His jacket would keep anyone from seeing it.

I was amused, both by Jack's quick action and by the sheriff's method of sharing information with us. We got what we wanted, and in the long run he might get what *he* wanted, a conviction in a cold case.

By the time the sheriff walked back into the room, Jack was in his chair, relaxed and leaning back, his left leg crossed over his right. Johnson didn't give any indication that he suspected one of us had removed the file. He never glanced at the metal tray.

When he was seated again, he said, "Well, gentlemen, I think I've told you everything I can. Is there anything else you want to tell me?"

"I can't think of anything else right now," Jack said. "Charlie?"

I shook my head. "Same here."

"Guess we'll be going," Jack said. "Thanks for your time, Elmer Lee."

I echoed Jack's words, and then we walked out of the office. Diesel preceded us. He sniffed as he walked and his head went side to side as he checked out interesting sights and smells. We got several startled looks, and a couple of deputies grinned when they saw me with a large cat on a leash. We didn't stop to talk to anyone and proceeded out to the car.

"Where to next?" I asked once we were settled in. Jack stuffed the autopsy folder under the seat.

"Depends on how hungry you are," Jack said. "We could have lunch now, and then head out to talk to one of the Barbers' neighbors. I thought Mitzi Gillon would be a good person to talk to. I taught her grandson last year."

"Let's eat first," I said. "Diesel is probably ready for some water, and I noticed a small section of grass by the diner where I can let him do his business if he needs to. I suppose we can eat in the office?"

"Probably so," Jack said. "Let's go back to the diner. Do you know how to get there from here?"

"I'm pretty sure I remember," I said. "Tell me if I make a wrong turn, though."

My memory and sense of direction didn't fail me, however. We soon arrived at the diner. This time I parked in front, and I took Diesel around the side to see if he needed to do anything. Jack entered through the front to let his wife know we were back.

By the time Diesel finished sniffing and selecting a place to urinate, Jack stood at the open side door waiting for us.

"Good news," he said. "Melvin's going to let us eat in the back dining room. They're not too busy at the moment, so we can sit in there, shut off from the front. Nobody will know there's a cat back there with us."

"Sounds good," I said. We followed Jack to the back dining room, where I found a bottle of water and a large bowl. I filled the bowl for Diesel, and he lapped thirstily at the water.

Served by Wanda Nell, Jack and I dined on a variety of vegetables, cornbread, and fried chicken, all excellent. Diesel had a few bites of my chicken and was happy.

Thirty minutes after we arrived at the diner, we headed out for the Gillon farm. Jack directed me, and the drive took about twenty minutes. As he'd mentioned earlier, once we left the highway, we drove along paved country roads that curved frequently. It would be difficult to drive fast here without having an accident at some point.

We turned off the road onto a paved driveway that led to the Gillon farm. We drove through a stand of trees about a hundred yards from the road, and when we emerged on the other side, I could see that we were at the foot of a gentle slope. A large frame house, painted a pale green, with a porch on the front and one side, stood atop the rise.

I brought the car to a stop on a circular driveway in front of the house. We got out of the car and approached the front door. Jack rang the bell while Diesel and I stood slightly to one side.

After a few seconds the door swung open and a small girl, probably no more than four or five, stood there. Diesel warbled loudly because he likes children. The girl looked at the cat. Her eyes widened in terror. She screamed and slammed the door.

THIRTY-ONE

///

"This doesn't bode well," I said to Jack. Diesel had shrunk back against me when the little girl screamed. She was obviously afraid of cats, and she had probably never seen one as large as Diesel.

"I'm sure everything will be okay." Jack rang the bell again.

This time an elderly woman, small, plump, with gray hair in a neat bob, opened the door. She looked at us and said, "That's not a cougar. Come back here, Britney. It's just a big ol' kitty cat. No need to be afraid."

The woman, whom I presumed to be Mrs. Gillon, looked at Jack. "You're Mr. Pemberton. You taught my grandson, Larry, last year."

"Yes, Mrs. Gillon, I did." Jack smiled. "We're sorry we frightened your granddaughter like that."

"Great-granddaughter," Mrs. Gillon said. "Larry's older sister's baby. And who are you?" She looked straight at me.

"My name is Charlie Harris, and this is my cat. His

name is Diesel. I'm really sorry we frightened Britney. He's very gentle and loves children."

Britney peered around her great-grandmother's skirts and gazed fearfully at Diesel. "Just a kitty cat?" she asked, her voice tremulous.

"Yes, he's a kitty," I said. "He lives with me. He even sleeps on my bed with me. Would you like to say hello to him?"

The girl hesitated. Mrs. Gillon said, her tone patient, "Go ahead, honey. He's a nice kitty. He's just big."

Britney moved from behind Mrs. Gillon and slowly approached Diesel. He eyed her warily, afraid she might scream again. She reached out a hand. Diesel extended his neck so that he could sniff at her fingers. Britney giggled. "He tickles," she said as she drew her hand back.

Diesel chirped, and Britney giggled again. "What a funny sound."

"He makes a number of different ones," I said. "That's a happy sound. He's telling you he's very pleased to meet you."

"Can I pet him?" the girl asked.

"Yes," I said. "He likes having his head rubbed."

Britney extended her hand again and gave Diesel a tentative pat on the head. He chirped again, and she stroked more confidently. After a moment Diesel warbled for her.

"Funny." Britney giggled.

"All right, honey, now that you see this big kitty is sweet and friendly, let's ask these gentlemen into the house. It's hot out there on the porch, and it's not polite to keep company waiting," Mrs. Gillon said.

"Yes'm," Britney replied. "Please come in." She moved behind her great-grandmother to let us inside.

"Thank you," Jack said.

Along with Jack, Diesel and I followed Mrs. Gillon

and Britney into the living room. I could see that Mrs. Gillon wasn't obsessive about having everything appear immaculate like Mrs. Cooper, but this room had a more comfortable air to it. Clean, but not everything precisely in place.

We took the seats indicated, and Diesel stretched out beside my chair. Mrs. Gillon sent Britney to play in another room. When the child was out of earshot, she said, "Gentlemen, I'm an old woman, and I don't think this is an ordinary social call. So I'm asking you up front what it is you're here about."

"I appreciate your directness, Mrs. Gillon," Jack said. "I'm not sure if you're aware of this, but in addition to teaching at the high school, I also write books."

"Books about murder," Mrs. Gillon said. "I've read all of 'em. You're good. You make it all seem real, like I know the people in the book."

Jack's face reddened slightly. "Thank you, it's very kind of you to say so."

Before he could continue, Mrs. Gillon looked at me. "What about you? Do you write about murder, too?"

"No, ma'am. I'm helping Jack research a cold case," I said.

"You want to talk about the Barbers, don't you?" Mrs. Gillon asked.

"Yes, we do," I said. "If you don't mind talking to us about it, that is."

"Why should I mind?" Mrs. Gillon asked. "Happened twenty years ago. It was a terrible, terrible thing, but nothing I could do about it." She shrugged. "I've wondered ever since who was to blame, and I'd like to know. If you can figure it out, I'd sure like to hear about it."

"We are doing our best to solve the case," Jack said. "You may be able to help us by telling us what you know about the Barber family. The more we know about them, the more likely we'll be able to find clues that could solve the case."

"Murder begins at home," Mrs. Gillon said. "I reckon that's what you mean."

"In a way," I said, pleased that Mrs. Gillon cut right to the heart of things. "Unless some stranger wandered by and decided to kill the family, they were murdered by someone they knew."

"I reckon it's possible a tramp happened by and did it," Mrs. Gillon said. "Hiram kept cash in the house, and word got around. But if there'd been any indication of a tramp in the area, one of the farmers around here would have seen the signs and warned everybody. That didn't happen."

"So we're back to the Barbers and someone who knew them," Jack said. "How well did you know the family?"

"Tolerably well, I'd say. Knew Hiram since he was a boy, about the same age as my middle child, Larry's daddy. They played together some, but Hiram was always accusing Larry of hurting him and cheating when they played games. Hiram's mama would come storming up here, demanding an apology." Mrs. Gillon chuckled. "She never got one from me, that's for sure. That Hiram was a whiny, selfish brat, and his mama made him that way. I finally told Larry he couldn't play with him anymore."

"We've heard that Hiram was hard to get along with," I said.

"He was that, and then some," Mrs. Gillon said. "He took after his mama, unfortunately. His daddy was a good man. He just picked a lemon from the tree of life when he married that no-good woman."

"That's unfortunate," Jack said. "It sounds like Hiram didn't have a happy childhood."

"No, he didn't," Mrs. Gillon said. "They finally had to put his mama in Whitfield, she got so bad. Died there when Hiram was about eighteen. His daddy died a year later and left him to run that farm by himself."

The state mental hospital, I thought. That was bad.

"What about Hiram's wife?" I asked. "Did you know her before she married him?"

"Betty Eaton," Mrs. Gillon said. "Betty's mama and me were good friends a long time ago. Betty was a pretty girl, sweet with it. She never should have married Hiram. Bad decision, but I guess she felt like she had to after her boyfriend up and joined the Marines and left her like that."

"Who was her boyfriend?" Jack asked.

"The one they thought killed 'em all," Mrs. Gillon said. "Bill Delaney."

I hadn't seen that coming, but I remembered Bill telling me he'd joined the Marines. I explained my connection to Delaney to Mrs. Gillon.

When I finished, Mrs. Gillon said, "And now you want to know if he's a killer. Can't blame you for that."

"What do you think?" Jack asked. "Did he kill the Barbers?"

"I never thought so," Mrs. Gillon replied. "He was a good man, he just couldn't keep away from the liquor. Like to broke his mama's heart, I'm sure."

"How did he come to work for Hiram?" I asked. "Didn't Hiram know about his wife and Bill Delaney?"

"Sure he did," Mrs. Gillon said. "But Hiram didn't pay much, and I'm guessing Bill Delaney, with his reputation, was desperate for work, so he was willing to work for next to nothing."

"Plus he was able to see Betty again," Jack said. "That's interesting."

"How long had he worked for Hiram?" I asked.

Mrs. Gillon frowned. "Let me see now. Seems to me that he started working there a year or so before the twins were born." Her expression darkened. "Those poor little boys. Such a hard life. Hiram gave that girl anything she wanted while Betty and the boys had to beg for scraps."

"We've heard she was pretty spoiled," Jack said.

"She was," Mrs. Gillon said. "She got paid back, though, for every thoughtless word or thing she ever did. She was like a different girl after she found her family murdered."

"An experience like that was bound to have a profound effect," I said.

"For the better, in this case," Mrs. Gillon said. "Elizabeth realized she wasn't the center of the universe, although even if her father hadn't been killed when he was, she would have found out before long."

"What do you mean?" Jack asked.

"She wanted to go to college to be a veterinarian," Mrs. Gillon said. "But there was no way Hiram was going to let her go away from him. She would have spent the rest of her life on that farm unless she just up and ran away from him."

"She didn't end up as a veterinarian, though," I said.

"No, she didn't," Mrs. Gillon said. "She was able to go to college, after all, once she sold the farm. But then she met that boy over at State and got married. I hear she helps out at one of the vet's offices in town, though."

"Yes, she does. Now, if we can go back to Hiram and the way he treated his wife and sons," Jack said, "I'd like to ask you if you ever heard or saw anything that might lead you to think he was abusive."

Mrs. Gillon glanced toward the door. "Excuse me a minute." She got up from her chair and walked toward the door. "When I look out of this room, somebody better not be lurking in the hall." She paused near the door.

I heard the sound of scurrying little feet. Mrs. Gillon certainly had sharp hearing. I hadn't heard Britney sneaking down the hall.

Mrs. Gillon returned to her seat. "That child is nosy, and I have to be careful of what I say around her. Now, you were asking me if Hiram abused his family."

"Yes, ma'am," Jack said.

"I don't know that he ever laid a hand on a single one of them," Mrs. Gillon said. "I never saw any signs of that. But he abused them in other ways. He was always running Betty down, and when those boys started second grade— that was right before they were killed—he started in on them. Always talking about how stupid they were. He quit going to church because he was too cheap to tithe, and he wouldn't let Betty go, either. He kept her there on the farm most of the time. I hardly ever saw her the last year of her life."

"What were the boys' names?" Jack asked. "I don't remember."

"Matthew and Mark," Mrs. Gillon said.

My heart ached for Betty Barber and the boys. The more I heard, the more Hiram Barber sounded like a monster. I wondered, however, whether he was mentally disturbed or whether he knew exactly what he was doing. I asked Mrs. Gillon that.

"Considering his mama died at Whitfield, I'd say there was a good chance he was downright crazy," Mrs. Gillon said. "But there wasn't much anybody could do, the way things stood. Nobody knew exactly what went on in that house except them. We had our suspicions, and Peggy Finch even talked to the sheriff about it one time. You know her daughter's a doctor. She and Elizabeth Barber were real close back then."

"Yes, ma'am," I said. "I actually know Dr. Finch. Did the sheriff do anything after Mrs. Finch talked to him?"

Mrs. Gillon shook her head. "Not a blessed thing. He patted her on the head and told her it wasn't his business to come between a man and his wife. It was the husband's right to run his household the way he saw fit." She snorted. "Fool. After I heard that I never voted for the old jackass again."

I was appalled, though not surprised, at the former sheriff's response to Mrs. Finch's report. There were still far too many people who were willing to overlook abuse in all its forms for the same reasons.

"He was pretty bad," Jack said. "A lot of people were happy when he got voted out of office." He glanced at me. "I don't think I have any more questions. What about you, Charlie?"

"None that I can think of right now," I said. "Mrs. Gillon, we really appreciate this. Your candor and willingness to talk to us has given us a much fuller picture of the family."

"I'm glad to do it," Mrs. Gillon said. "I've had those two boys and Betty on my conscience for twenty years. I want to see justice done for them."

Jack and I rose, and Mrs. Gillon got up to see us to the door. "That cat of yours has better manners than my grandchildren and great-grands," she said. "Where are y'all going next?"

"I thought maybe we would see if Mrs. Finch would talk to us," Jack said. "They live on the other side of what used to be the Barber place, I believe."

"Yes, go about four miles on down this same road. You can't miss it. Great big, gaudy mailbox that looks like a sailboat," Mrs. Gillon said. "Don't ask me why it's a sailboat, though."

We thanked her again. I glanced down the hall before we walked out the door and saw Britney watching. I waved. She giggled and waved back.

Once we were in the car Jack said, "We've been lucky so far, finding people willing to talk. Let's hope our lucky streak lasts with Mrs. Finch."

"Amen to that," I said.

We were destined for disappointment, however. When Mrs. Finch opened the door, she barely gave us time to mention our names. She looked at me, then at Diesel, and said, "My daughter said I can't talk to you" and shut the door in our faces.

THIRTY-TWO

We got back in the car, and I headed for Tullahoma. There was no point in trying to get Mrs. Finch to come to the door again. Jack pulled the folder with the autopsy reports from beneath his seat and opened it. He started looking through the papers. I had decided that if there were any pictures included, I wasn't going to look at them. I felt haunted enough already by the thought of those two innocent boys, their lives taken away.

I forced my thoughts away from autopsies. "We've learned a lot," I said, "though it would have been helpful to talk to Mrs. Finch about that night."

"Yes, it would have. We need to find out more about what went on with Elizabeth Barber and Leann Finch that night. I wonder if the Finches can really swear to the fact that neither of the girls left the house that night," Jack replied. "We'll have to try Dr. Finch again. After we, or maybe you, talk to Bill Delaney again, if that's possible. We're getting close to the truth, I can feel it."

"Closer, anyway," I said. "I wish we could find out where Hiram Barber was during those two hours."

"That seems impossible at this point," Jack said as he turned a page. "What do you think about Elizabeth Barber as the killer?"

"I've considered her, certainly," I said. "What do you think her motive was?"

"Freedom from that family," Jack said. "And probably money. According to Mrs. Gillon, Elizabeth wanted to be a veterinarian, and that means four years of college and four years of vet school. That's a big investment in both time and money. Without her family's support, she'd have had a tough time accomplishing any of it."

"I can see her maybe killing her father," I said. "He was the one who intended to hold her back. Again, according to Mrs. Gillon. I wish we could verify that with someone else. But her mother and her brothers? That's much harder for me to grasp."

"With her father dead, would her mother have been able to run the farm? Elizabeth might have been stuck there," Jack asked. "Killing them all was a completely ruthless thing to do, but she might have seen that as her only choice to get totally free."

"Say she did do it, and for the reasons you've stated," I said. "Did she do it alone?"

"Maybe," Jack said. "But why did Bill Delaney leave home for two hours? What was he doing? Maybe it was something completely unrelated to the murders."

"Could have been," I said, "though I'm having a hard time imagining what else it could be. Especially since Mrs. Gillon told us about Betty and Bill. I think he must have gone to the Barber farm that night."

"Maybe."

I glanced at Jack for a second then focused again on driving. He seemed intent on a particular page.

"Have you found something?" I asked.

"Possibly," he replied. "Mrs. Barber, Matthew, and Mark were killed execution style, but Hiram was shot in the back."

"Perhaps Hiram tried to flee from the killer, whereas the others were too afraid to try," I said.

"Could be." Jack suddenly closed the folder and stuck it back under his seat. "I hope whoever killed them rots in hell for eternity." He seemed overcome with emotion. He turned his head away and looked out his window.

I gave him time to collect himself. I knew how he felt. As we approached the city limits of Tullahoma, I spoke. "Where do you think we should go next?"

Jack turned his head and faced forward again. He cleared his throat before he responded. "Let's try the vet clinic. Stay on the highway. It's on the edge of town to the west. Just about five miles from here. It'll be on the right. You can't miss it."

"What's the plan when we get there?" I asked.

"One thought I had was that we take Diesel in and tell them he needs to see the vet. You'll have to think up why. I don't know that much about cats and their habits."

Diesel heard his name mentioned, and he meowed and chirped as if to ask what we were talking about.

"It's okay, boy," I said. "Jack, I'm sorry, but I don't feel comfortable with that. We'll have to come up with something else. Why not just go in, ask if Elizabeth is there, and ask to speak to her?"

"Let me think about it," Jack said. "I imagine Leann Finch has already warned her about us, though, so that approach might not get us anywhere."

He fell silent, and I didn't interrupt his ruminations.

A few minutes later we reached the western side of Tullahoma, and I easily spotted the vet clinic, thanks to its large sign. I turned off the highway into the parking lot. As I looked for a parking space, I noticed a large, dark SUV. With rising excitement I realized it matched the description of the SUV that had struck Bill Delaney.

I drove closer to it so I could see the make and model. Once I did, I saw that it was a match. I stopped the car and nudged Jack. "Look at that SUV," I said. "It matches the one that hit Delaney. What do you want to bet that it belongs to Elizabeth Barber?"

"I think I'd lose that bet," Jack replied. "I've got an idea. Park next to it. It's parked away from other cars, so the owner has to be one of those people who can't stand the thought of their car getting scratched."

I did as Jack asked. "What's your idea?"

Jack unbuckled his seat belt. "I'm going in there and tell the receptionist that I accidentally scraped the side of that SUV. I'll ask to talk to the owner. I doubt Elizabeth Barber knows what I look like, so I won't give my name. I'll ask her to come out and look at the damage, and I'll say my insurance information is in the car."

"Then once you get her out here, I can tell her that her SUV matches the description of the one that hit Bill Delaney," I said. "That ought to shake her up a little. I can hint that my daughter and son-in-law actually got a picture of it with part of the license plate."

"Are you sure you feel comfortable with telling a lie like that?" Jack asked. "A few minutes ago you didn't seem okay with it."

"It does bother me, but if Elizabeth Barber tried to run Bill down, my scruples can take a brief vacation."

"Good man," Jack said. "Okay, I'm going in."

I watched as he crossed the parking lot and entered the front door of the clinic. Then I turned to Diesel. "I want you to lie down and be a good boy, Diesel. I don't want this woman to see you and be alerted too soon. We're going to act like we're taking a nap. Okay?"

Diesel meowed and stared at me for a moment.

"I'm going to lie down, too," I said. "Nap."

Diesel meowed again and stretched out on the seat. He knew what the word *nap* meant. I twisted so that I could lie across the front seats and got myself into position. I didn't turn the car off because it would get too hot. I hoped the SUV's owner would be too upset to notice until it was too late.

I don't think we had to wait more than six or seven minutes before Jack appeared with a striking woman in scrubs that did little to disguise a shapely figure. She was shorter than Jack and had bright red hair pulled back and twisted into a bun on the back of her head. She was gesticulating in an angry manner.

Jack maneuvered her into the area between my car and hers. He got on the other side of her and drew her toward the front of the SUV. That allowed me to sit up, open the door, and effectively trap her between the two of us.

She was in such a state, continuing to flap her arms about, that she evidently didn't hear me open the car door. She was still facing Jack.

". . . some sort of prank. You look way too old to be pulling this kind of crap. I've got work to do."

"I'm sure you do." Jack looked over her head toward me. "Charlie, I'd like you to meet Elizabeth Campbell. Elizabeth *Barber* Campbell."

She whirled to face me, her expression furious. "What the hell is going on here? Who are you people?" She pulled a cell phone out of a pocket of her scrubs. She started to tap in a number.

"I'm a friend of Bill Delaney's," I said. "The man you tried to run down on the square in Athena recently."

That hit home, I could see. She almost dropped the phone. Then she recovered. "I don't know what the hell you're talking about. I'm going to call the police." She started to tap on the phone again.

"Go ahead, by all means," I said. "I'll be happy to report to them that we've found the hit-and-run driver that the Athena police have been looking for."

She stopped tapping and stared at me. I could see the fear creeping into her expression. I didn't need anything more to tell me that she was guilty.

"This is ridiculous," she said. "I was nowhere near Athena that day. You can't prove any of this."

"And what day would that be?" Jack asked.

She realized her slip but tried to bluster. "Whatever day you're talking about, I wasn't in Athena. I haven't been in Athena in a long time."

"Not even to visit your best friend, Leann Finch?" Jack asked.

Elizabeth Barber—I couldn't think of her by any other name—backed up against her SUV and glanced wildly back and forth between Jack and me.

"You might be disappointed to hear that you didn't kill Bill Delaney, though you did put him in the hospital," I said. "That was a pretty dirty trick, you know. Going to see him that day, getting him drunk, and then trying to run him down."

Her eyes widened again, and I took grim satisfaction in the fact that my hunch had proved true. She had been in Bill's apartment that morning. The lipstick Diesel had found on the floor belonged to her, I was sure of it.

"Too bad you lost your lipstick while you were there," I said. "My cat found it, but I left it there. I'm sure the police in Athena will be happy to test it for fingerprints. What do you want to bet they'll match yours?"

All at once her legs seemed to give way, and she slid down the side of the SUV until she was sitting on the pavement. Tears started streaming down her face.

Jack and I exchanged startled glances. I hadn't expected this. I thought she would continue to brazen it out. A cynical thought flashed through my mind, however. She might be trying this tactic in order to garner sympathy. Best not to be taken in by it. I glanced at Jack again, and I could see by his expression of disbelief that he'd had the same thought.

"Why did you do it, Elizabeth?" I asked, my tone gentler than she probably deserved. "Did you really want to kill him?"

THIRTY-THREE

||||||||||||||||||||||||||||||||||||||||||||||||||||||||||||||||||||||

While Jack and I waited for a response to my question, I could hear Diesel in the car meowing loudly and scratching at the window. Elizabeth Barber, her hands now over her face, continued to cry.

Since Diesel sounded more frantic as the seconds ticked by, I opened the door and let him out. He meowed again and climbed onto Elizabeth's legs and butted his head against her hands. Obviously startled by the sudden weight on her legs and the pressure against her hands, she let her arms fall. Diesel butted his head against her chin. Elizabeth wrapped her arms around my cat and buried her face in the side of his neck.

Jack and I watched as the cat's ministrations proved effective in calming the distressed woman. We waited as the sobs diminished in volume and Elizabeth's breathing appeared to be normal again.

An unfamiliar voice from behind me startled me. "What's going on here? Liz, honey, are you all right?"

A small woman, no more than five feet tall and whippet thin, pushed by me to get closer to Elizabeth. "Is something wrong with the cat? I got worried when you didn't come back."

"I'm okay, Louann." Elizabeth raised her head from Diesel's neck. Her reddened eyes and tear-stained appearance apparently did little to reassure her coworker, however. Louann glared at Jack and me in turn.

"What did y'all do to her car? The damage must be really bad for her to carry on like this."

"My car is fine," Elizabeth said. "They brought me some bad news, that's all."

"Judging by the way you look, honey, it must be pretty dang bad news. Who's that cat belong to?"

"He's mine," I said. "Come on, Diesel, let the lady get up now."

Diesel warbled as if in protest. Elizabeth offered a watery smile as she stroked his head.

"It's okay, Diesel," she said softly. "I'm okay."

The cat meowed and climbed off her legs. He moved next to me, and I stroked his head. Elizabeth slowly raised herself off the pavement. Jack extended a hand to help her, but she ignored it.

"You come on back in the clinic," Louann said. "Wash your face and have something to drink. Your makeup's all streaky."

"Thanks, but I'll be fine," Elizabeth said. "You go on back, Louann, and I'll be there in a minute. Go on now, I mean it."

Louann shot hard glances at Jack and me before she moved away, but she headed back to the clinic after one more plea to Elizabeth to come back inside. Elizabeth ignored her.

"You said Bill Delaney is in the hospital," she said, addressing me. "How is he?"

"Not good," I said. "His health was already bad, and that's going to make it more difficult for him to recover from this. He's in the ICU now."

"I'm sorry he was hurt," Elizabeth said.

She still hadn't admitted that she was responsible. I thought we had shaken her enough that she would confess to it, but she was evidently made of sterner stuff than I expected.

"I'm sorry he's in the hospital," she said. "I hope he's okay. There's nothing I can do to help him. I really have to get back to work." She made as if to push past me, but I didn't budge.

"You do realize that we are going to have to tell the police that we have identified your SUV as the one that ran Bill Delaney down," I said. "Don't you have anything to say about that?"

"I'll talk to the police if I have to," Elizabeth said. "I don't see that it's any business of yours. I told you already that I wasn't in Athena."

"There were witnesses," I said, "who saw the whole thing."

That startled her. The mask of defiance slipped for a bare second but then was back.

"It's nothing to do with me," she said. "Whoever they saw that day, no one can prove it was me."

"I guess you'll just have to wait and see," Jack said. "Several of the businesses around the square have security cameras, and some of them run twenty-four hours a day. I'd be willing to bet one of them caught the whole thing. Including the license plate of the SUV in question."

I did my best to hide my surprise at Jack's statement about the video cameras. As far as I knew, there were no such cameras around the square.

Jack's bluff shook her. Her body stiffened at his words,

but she didn't reply to him. Instead, she pushed me out of the way and hurried back into the clinic.

"That was some performance," Jack said. "Those tears may have fooled your cat, but they didn't fool me. That woman is stone cold."

"Maybe." I wasn't completely convinced that Elizabeth Barber's display of emotion was totally calculated. Diesel responded to genuine emotion, not put-on feelings. He had seen Laura acting out tragic scenes from her favorite Shakespeare plays in my living room, and even as Juliet lay dying on my sofa, he didn't budge an inch. At least some of what we saw Elizabeth Barber doing was genuine. Whether it was remorse, sympathy, or fear, I didn't know. Perhaps it was a combination of all three.

"What now?" I asked.

Jack shrugged. "I think it's time to go back to Elmer Lee and tell him everything we've heard. And especially about this SUV." Jack tapped his knuckles against it. "I'm going to record the license plate." He pulled his cell phone out of his pocket.

Diesel and I stood aside and let him get by to the rear of the SUV. He took a couple of pictures of the license plate. "Let's have a look at the front. Which side hit Bill Delaney?"

"It would have been the passenger side." I moved to the front of the SUV, and Diesel and Jack followed me. I bent to examine the front more closely. I couldn't really see anything that indicated the vehicle had hit anyone. I moved aside to let Jack have a look.

He took my place and squatted to put himself at eye level with the bumper and the lights. I envied his knees the ability to do that without making noise. Mine creaked anytime I had to squat or get down on my hands and knees. Getting back up was also not pleasant.

Jack stayed in his squat for what seemed like several minutes. I was perspiring under the heat of the afternoon sun, and I knew Diesel must be getting uncomfortable. I put him back in the car where it was air-conditioned. I wanted badly to join him, but I would wait until Jack was finished.

Finally he stood. "Find anything?" I asked.

Jack shrugged. "I'm not sure. I think there may be some fibers snagged in the light surround, but it's hard to tell without some kind of magnification. I'll report it to Elmer Lee. It'll be up to the Athena police, I guess, to have it examined."

"If they'll accept what we tell them. That reminds me, that bit about the video cameras around the square was a bluff, wasn't it?"

"Mostly." Jack grinned. "But you never know. Let's head to the sheriff's department. I'm about to burn up out here."

Finally. I opened my door and slid into the wonderfully cool air. I wished I had a cloth of some kind to wipe my head with. The sweat would soon dry, however.

Before I drove away, I decided on impulse to call the hospital in Athena to check on Bill Delaney. I told Jack what I was going to do, and he nodded.

Within a minute I was connected to the nurses' desk in the ICU, and I asked for an update on Delaney's condition after identifying myself.

This time I was talking to a man who told me that Delaney's condition had improved somewhat. He had rallied a bit and was alert and able to eat on his own. If he continued to improve they would be moving him out of the ICU later in the day, or by the next morning. I thanked the man for the update and ended the call.

I shared the information with Jack as we headed back

to the sheriff's department. On the way I was thinking about what I should do next. I decided I should go on home. Jack could easily handle the talk with the sheriff. I said as much to Jack.

"Sure," he said. "In that case, head for the Kountry Kitchen. I can pick up my car and go to the sheriff's department from there."

Within a few minutes we reached the diner and I pulled into the parking lot behind Jack's car. Before he got out I reminded him to take the folder of autopsy reports. I didn't want to be tempted to look in the folder if I went home with them.

"I think we accomplished a lot today," Jack said.

"Much more than I ever expected, frankly," I replied.

"We're getting close," Jack said. "Keep me posted on Bill Delaney. Are you going to try to see him tonight?"

"I think I will," I said. "I don't want to risk causing a setback, though, so I'll have to be careful."

"I'll let you know what Elmer Lee has to say," Jack said.

"Please thank your wife for everything. It was a pleasure to meet her," I said.

"Will do. She enjoyed meeting you and Diesel." Jack opened the door and got out. He closed the door and bent to wave good-bye to Diesel. The cat meowed.

I decided to fill up the car before we left Tullahoma, and I found a gas station on the way. With the tank full, Diesel and I headed for home.

As I drove, I mulled over all that we had learned today. I tried to assimilate it all and put it into a plausible pattern. I came up with several scenarios, each of which might explain everything. The question was whether any of them contained the actual truth of what happened that night.

We made record time on the drive home, and I was surprised to see that it was only four thirty-three when we walked into the kitchen. Given all the activities of the day, I felt like it should be past my bedtime.

Azalea greeted us and asked how the day had gone. Before I could respond, Diesel started warbling and chirped, with a couple of meows thrown in. Azalea stared at his face in fascination, as if she understood every single sound.

"Is that so?" she said when Diesel finally stopped. He meowed once before he padded away in the direction of the utility room. Azalea looked at me. "I swear that cat thinks he's a person like you and me."

"I wouldn't argue with you on that." I chuckled. "I imagine what he was trying to tell you is that we had a pretty busy day. We talked to several different people today, and we learned a lot."

"You reckon you got everything figured out now?" Azalea asked before she turned back to the stove. She stirred the contents of a pot that was emitting a tantalizing scent.

"In a way," I said. "The problem is there are several potential answers, and I'm not sure which is the correct one. What is that you're cooking?"

"The filling for a couple of pecan pies," Azalea said. "Mr. Stewart's been pestering me for one. Says he can't make them like I do."

"I don't imagine anyone can." I was never a huge fan of pecan pie until I tasted Azalea's. She refused to divulge her secret recipe, however, despite all Stewart's blandishments.

"What's for dinner?" I asked.

"Roast beef," she said. "Over there." I followed the direction of her nod and saw the Crock-Pot on the counter. I sighed happily. Azalea made the most tender roast I've ever eaten. It would practically melt in your mouth.

"When will it be ready?" I asked.

"Around six," she said. "I have to leave before then, but it'll turn itself off. Stewart said he'll whip up some mashed potatoes and gravy to go with it, and there's a pot of green beans in the fridge that just needs warming up."

"Sounds wonderful," I said. "I'm going to the den for a while but I'll see you before you go."

She nodded, and I headed from the room.

A few minutes later I was comfortably settled on the sofa with my laptop and Diesel stretched out beside me. I opened my e-mail program and waited for it to load. My cell phone rang and I picked it up from the end table beside me. Jack Pemberton was calling.

"Hi, Jack," I said. "How did it go with the sheriff?"

"It went fine," Jack replied. "Look, I'm calling from my car. I'm tailing Elizabeth Barber, and she's headed for Athena. I bet she's planning to go to the hospital. She might be intending to make another attempt on Bill Delaney."

THIRTY-FOUR

"Surely she can't be that crazy," I said. "She has to know that it would be incredibly risky to try to kill him again."

"Who can tell with her?" Jack said. "I can't really figure her out."

"How far away are you now?" I asked.

"I figure we'll be in Athena in about an hour and a quarter, roughly," Jack said.

I thought fast about what to do. "Did you tell the sheriff we are pretty sure she was the driver in the hit-and-run?"

"I did," Jack said. "I'm not sure he completely believed me, though."

"Have you alerted him to the fact that she's left town?"

"Not yet," Jack said. "I wanted to call you first. I'll call him and let him know. I think he needs to get in touch with the police there."

"I agree. I would try it myself, but it would have a lot more weight coming from a sheriff than from me," I said.

"I'll head to the hospital and keep an eye on things. He may still be in the ICU, and that's good. It would make it harder for her to get to him without anyone seeing her."

"Sounds good," Jack said. "I'll call you when we get close to Athena."

I thanked him and ended the call. I shut down my laptop and put it aside. "Diesel, I'm afraid I'm going to have to be gone for a while. I don't know how long, and you can't come with me."

As expected, the cat meowed, but I simply couldn't take him with me. The hospital did allow visits with therapy animals, but the animals had to be registered with the hospital, along with their handlers. Diesel and I weren't part of the program, although I had looked into it. Now I wished I had signed us up. Diesel would be good with patients. He wouldn't have any trouble passing the behavioral tests they gave the prospective therapy pets.

Too late to worry about that right now. I would simply have to leave Diesel at home. Azalea would be leaving soon, and I had no idea whether Stewart would be here to look after him. If Stewart wasn't available, I'd have to take Diesel to Laura's house. He would love that because he could be near the baby.

I texted Stewart to inquire and heard back quickly. He was sorry, but he wouldn't be home until around six. That meant Laura's house. I called her, and Frank actually answered her phone.

"Hi, Charlie, what's up?" he said.

"I need a babysitter," I replied. "Would you and Laura mind looking after Diesel for a few hours? If it's convenient, of course."

"Sure, bring him on over whenever you're ready," Frank said. "We're not going anywhere tonight, and Diesel can help look after little Charlie. It's amazing to me how he watches over the baby."

"Yes, it is. He loves that baby almost as much as I do," I said. "Thanks. I'll be over in the next twenty minutes or so."

"Come on, boy," I said as I ended the call. "We're going to see Laura, Frank, and baby Charlie."

Diesel perked up at the mention of those names. He hopped off the sofa and hurried ahead of me to the kitchen, anxious to be on the way.

Azalea was pouring the pecan pie filling into pie shells when we walked in. "Azalea, I'm going to have to go to the hospital for a while, and I don't know how long I'll be. I'm taking Diesel over to stay with Laura and Frank while I'm gone."

"Everything will be fine here, Mr. Charlie. You go on and do what you need to do," Azalea said.

"Thanks. I'll see you in the morning."

Diesel was already at the door, waiting for me to open it so he could get to the car. He was like an impatient child. I got him into the car, and moments later we were backing out of the garage and on our way.

The drive to Frank and Laura's house took only a few minutes. I wanted to get Diesel there and be on my way to the hospital. I had a sense of urgency that I had to keep under control, otherwise I'd get pulled over for speeding. Elizabeth Barber couldn't possibly have reached Athena yet, much less the hospital, but I was anxious about Bill Delaney's safety. I forced myself to drive at a more reasonable speed, and we made good time.

I explained my errand to Frank. He looked concerned, but I told him I was certain there would be police officers there if they were needed. I was thinking that surely Elmer Lee Johnson would take this seriously enough that he would communicate with the police department here. And surely they in turn would take this seriously enough to send someone to keep an eye on Bill Delaney.

"Just be careful," Frank said. Diesel had already disappeared inside the house, eager to find Laura and baby Charlie. "We'll take good care of Diesel."

"I know you will, and I will be careful. Thanks again." I left him and hurried back to my car.

By the time I reached the hospital barely half an hour had passed since Jack's call. More like twenty-five minutes, I reckoned, so Elizabeth Barber couldn't get here for another forty minutes or so. I didn't think she would drive recklessly. She wouldn't want to attract police attention.

I made my way to the floor where the ICU was situated. The visiting hours were posted, and the next visiting time was from seven to eight this evening. It wasn't five thirty yet, so I couldn't go back for more than an hour and a half. In the meantime, however, I could call and find out whether Bill Delaney was still there or had been moved into a room.

I was about to call when a man in scrubs came out of the ICU and started down the hall. I stopped him. "Excuse me, I'm sorry to bother you, but I'm here to visit a patient in the ICU. I realize it isn't visiting hours, but is there any way I could possibly go in to check on him?"

The man turned out to be the same one I had spoken to earlier, I realized when I heard his voice. "You can go back for a couple of minutes," he said. "What's the patient's name?"

"Bill Delaney," I replied. "I believe I talked to you earlier about him. I'm his cousin, Charlie Harris."

"Right, I remember," the nurse said. "You'll be happy to hear that he's been released from the ICU. In fact, they just took him to a room. I believe it's room 227."

"Thanks, that is great news," I said, although Bill would now be more vulnerable outside of the ICU. "One more question, if you don't mind. Has he had any visitors today?"

The nurse shook his head. "No, nobody outside of hospital staff."

On a sudden hunch, I asked another question. "Did one of the staff happen to be Dr. Finch? Leann Finch?"

"Actually, yes, she did come in and check on him probably an hour ago. Only stayed a couple of minutes because she had to get back down to the ER."

By now the nurse was clearly eager to get away from me. I thanked him, and he hurried off down the hall.

Room 227, he said. Two floors down. I headed for the elevator.

When I reached the second floor, I pulled out my phone and sent Jack a text to inform him that Bill was out of the ICU and in a room. I headed down the hall toward 227.

The door stood open. When I looked inside I saw two women in the room with Bill Delaney. They appeared to be working with monitors and IV equipment. I stepped back to wait until they were finished. I wanted to talk to them before I entered the room. I didn't want to pop in on Bill without knowing more about his status now.

His heart must be stronger than they thought, I decided, if they moved him out of the ICU this quickly. That didn't mean, however, he should be subjected to any sudden shocks. I would have to be really careful when I approached him. I prayed that the realization that I hadn't left things alone wouldn't cause another setback. Surely it was all weighing on his conscience, whatever his role in the murders had been. I thought I knew what it was, but I couldn't be sure unless he or Elizabeth Barber was finally willing to tell the truth about that night.

While I waited, I thought about the fact that Leann Finch had visited him briefly this afternoon. She was far too smart, I was sure, to try to harm him right there in the ICU, though she might have been willing to risk it. It boded well that he had been released from the ICU.

I had figured that Leann Finch's role in all this was that of the supportive best friend. Willing to lie and cover up for Elizabeth Barber, but not an active participant in what went on in the Barber house that night. That she was protecting Elizabeth, I had no doubt. I didn't believe she was protecting Bill Delaney, except whenever protecting him meant protecting her best friend.

I had to wait almost another ten minutes before the two women came out of Bill Delaney's room. I waited until they were several feet away from his door before I spoke to them. I focused on the nurse. The other woman was a personal care assistant.

"Excuse me," I said. "I'm Charlie Harris, Mr. Delaney's cousin. I arrived a little while ago to find out that he was released from the ICU. That must mean he's doing a lot better."

"He mentioned you, Mr. Harris," the nurse said. "I know he wants to talk to you, but he was falling asleep when we left the room. I'd give him at least half an hour before you try to talk to him. He needs as much rest and quiet as possible."

"But he is stronger now," I said.

"Yes, he's really improved, according to his cardiologist," the nurse replied. "He's not ready to give up just yet." She pointed down the hall. "There's a waiting area down there at the end of the hall. If you've got time to wait, you can stay there. Like I said, give him at least half an hour to sleep before you go in."

"Thank you, Nurse, I will." I smiled and let her go. I

headed down the hall to the waiting area. I noticed as I passed Bill Delaney's room that the door was partially open. I resisted the urge, however, to look inside. I would follow the nurse's instructions and not go in for half an hour.

I discovered that I could position one of the chairs at an angle that allowed me to keep an eye on Delaney's door. I settled in to wait. A check of my watch assured me that I ought to be able to get into the room before Elizabeth Barber would arrive at the hospital. I hoped that a police officer or a deputy would arrive before her. I wasn't really afraid of her, but I knew that an officer in uniform would be a much better deterrent than I would.

About twenty minutes later, Jack called. "We're just getting into Athena," he said. "Looks like she's heading toward the hospital, as predicted. Probably be there in less than fifteen minutes. How is he?"

"I haven't seen him yet," I replied. "I'm in the waiting area down the hall. I've been watching his room. No one's gone in there for the past twenty minutes. There's no policeman anywhere around that I can see."

"Maybe one will still turn up by the time we get there," Jack said. "Elmer Lee surely got in touch with the police there."

"He may have done," I said, "but they might not have considered the threat level high enough. Who knows? Text me when you actually get to the hospital. I'm going to slip into his room and hide in the bathroom."

"Will do."

I ended the call.

Eleven minutes later I received a text from Jack.

In the parking lot. Entering hospital now.

I texted back simply *OK*.

I walked down the hall to room 227 and peered inside. Bill Delaney appeared to be asleep. I slipped into the room.

The bathroom was immediately to my right. The bathroom door faced the bed. It was closed. I opened it carefully and positioned myself inside with the door nearly shut. I had a good line of vision to the bed. I was ready for Elizabeth Barber.

THIRTY-FIVE

I had to admit later, when I was relating the story to my family, that I felt rather foolish lurking in the bathroom like one of the Hardy Boys on a stakeout. With no policeman in sight, however, I felt I had to do something to protect Bill Delaney. I could have tried to bar Elizabeth Barber from entering the room, but at the time I didn't really believe she would be so brazen as to try to harm Delaney again. Not when she knew that Jack and I were planning to give her name to the police as the hit-and-run driver.

I waited, trying not to fidget or make any noise. Delaney seemed to be sleeping soundly, and I didn't want to wake him until it was necessary.

As I surveyed the portion of the room I could see from inside the bathroom, I noticed a large cabinet on the other side of the bed next to the window. It looked large enough for a person to hide inside, depending on whether it contained any shelves and how they were arranged. That might have been a better place to hide, had I noticed it earlier, because it was closer to the bed.

I was almost tempted to leave the bathroom and go investigate the cabinet, but I realized there might not be enough time. Elizabeth Barber could walk into the room at any moment. I couldn't risk it.

Seconds later I was glad I hadn't. I heard footsteps, light but obvious. Someone was coming into the room. I tensed as I waited for Elizabeth Barber to come into view.

I almost gave myself away with a gasp of surprise when I saw that the person who had entered was male and in uniform. The police had taken this seriously after all. Then I realized that the officer wasn't wearing a police uniform. He was a sheriff's deputy. That meant that Kanesha Berry was aware of the situation and taking action. As I watched, the deputy moved quietly around the end of Bill Delaney's bed to the closet. He opened the door to the right and slid inside the cavity there. He pulled the door nearly closed.

Thankful that an officer of the law was present, I relaxed slightly. Now we both waited for Elizabeth Barber to appear.

The seconds ticked by. Where was she? I wondered. I would have thought she'd be here by now. Maybe something—or someone—held her up long enough for the deputy to get into place.

Or maybe, I thought, she went to talk to Leann Finch first. Why, I wasn't certain, but maybe to consult her for some reason.

Another minute passed, and then another. Then, finally, the sound of more footsteps coming into the room.

I recognized the red hair, although Elizabeth Barber had tried to cover most of it with a scarf. The tendrils that had escaped the scarf gave her away. She had a handbag with a long strap over her left shoulder.

I tensed again, watching to see what she would do. She stopped close to the bed, left hand on her bag, the right on the bed rail.

"Bill, can you hear me?" she said in a low voice. "Wake up, I need to talk to you."

She reached out as if to touch him but hesitated. Her hand rested on the rail again.

"Bill, please wake up, it's me, Lizzie," she said, her voice slightly louder, the tone more urgent.

The form on the bed began to stir. The bed had Bill's torso raised at a slight angle, perhaps ten degrees. I couldn't see his whole face but I could see when his head moved.

"Lizzie, what are you doing here?" Bill's voice sounded hoarse. "If they find you here, you'll give everything away."

"I had to come, I couldn't help it," Elizabeth Barber said. "I'm so sorry, Bill, I don't know what I was thinking the other day. I guess I just lost my mind for a minute. I didn't really want to kill you."

Bill grunted as he shifted in the bed. "I thought you trusted me."

"I did," she said. "I mean, I do, but you promised you'd never come back."

"I had to, Lizzie. Mama was dying, and she wanted to see me before she passed on. I couldn't deny her that. I owed her that much. *You* owed her that much."

"Yes, you're right," Elizabeth said, sounding tired. "If it weren't for her, we would have all been in trouble."

"Mama hated lying worse than anything," Bill said. "But she understood why I asked her to. When she found out what happened, I swear she would have killed him all over again if she'd had the chance."

"He was a monster, he deserved to die," Elizabeth said,

her voice heated. "But I'm not here to talk about him. I wanted to let you know how sorry I am, and I hope you'll forgive me."

"Of course I will," Bill said. "I may not be around much longer anyway, so it won't matter. Then you'll always be safe."

"No, I won't, Bill," Elizabeth said. "I've done a lot of soul-searching since I tried to run you down. There were these two men today who confronted me outside the vet clinic. They're not going to let it go. They're pretty sure they know what I did. I think it's time to tell the truth and be done with it."

"Is that what you really want?" Bill asked.

"Yes," Elizabeth said. "Would it be okay if I gave you a hug? I remember you used to give the best hugs."

"I'd like that," Bill said. He held up his arms.

Elizabeth's hand slipped inside her bag as she began to lean over the bed. The hand came out with a syringe, her thumb on the plunger. She was ready to plunge the syringe into his neck, but the sheriff's deputy burst out of the cabinet in time and knocked it out of her hand.

I emerged from the bathroom at the same time and grabbed her before she could run out of the room. She started screaming, kicking, trying to stomp my feet, anything to get away, but the deputy subdued her and got her hands behind her back. Another deputy entered the room and helped cuff her.

I hit the call button. When someone answered, I said, "Get in here fast. I think Mr. Delaney might be having another heart attack."

I wasn't sure whether Bill was actually in distress. He had a peculiar expression. His eyes were closed, but they popped open when I leaned over and called his name.

"Are you okay? Are you in pain?"

He didn't answer my questions. All he said was, "You didn't have to stop her."

The experience with Elizabeth Barber shook me pretty badly. It would be a long time before I could get that scene out of my mind, if ever. Even with her arms behind her, cuffed, she still struggled to get to Bill Delaney. Her ranting, obscenity-laden words sounded like those of a madwoman. Her paternal grandmother's legacy to her and her father, no doubt. Blocked from being able to kill Delaney, she seemed to lose all contact with reason.

I stayed at the hospital until nearly eight o'clock, answering questions for both the police and the sheriff's department. Kanesha Berry was there herself, and Elmer Lee Johnson turned up halfway through my session with Kanesha.

I told them what I thought happened on that night twenty years ago when the Barber family was murdered. They were somewhat skeptical, but I was pretty sure I was right. The only two people who could confirm my suspicions were Bill Delaney and Leann Finch. I wondered whether they would be willing finally to tell what happened that night.

After a rough night with not much sleep—sleep haunted by Elizabeth Barber's mad ranting—I got up the next morning hollow-eyed and tired. Azalea's breakfast perked me up. By the time I arrived home the night before, I couldn't eat anything. And for me, not being hungry or wanting to eat was a definite sign of abnormal distress.

I made up for those lost calories with a second helping of grits and a fifth biscuit with grape jam. Diesel feasted happily on bites of bacon. Azalea didn't press me to talk. She could tell I wasn't in the mood to discuss the events of the previous night.

By nine I was dressed and ready to go. I explained to Diesel that, once again, he would have to stay home. I was going to the hospital, and I couldn't take him. He protested with the usual indignant meows and trills, but Azalea offered him a little more bacon to distract him. For once he didn't fuss. I slipped out the back door and drove to the hospital.

Jack was waiting for me in the lobby. We were going to see Bill Delaney to ask him if he would tell us the whole story.

"I'm sorry that you had to witness such a terrible scene," Jack said. "I can only imagine how bad it was."

I nodded. I didn't really want to talk about it right now, and Jack appeared to sense that. He let it drop. He did ask, however, whether I thought Bill would talk to us.

"I don't know," I said. "I'm hoping that he's thought about it and decided to let the truth be known. I think I know what happened, but I want him to confirm it."

"What do you think happened?" Jack asked as we stepped into the elevator. I had checked earlier, and Bill Delaney was still in room 227. I took that as a good sign. I was afraid he would be back in the ICU.

I answered Jack's question without going into any details. To my surprise, he didn't scoff at my solution. "Interesting," was all he said.

We strolled down the hall to Bill's room. The door was open, and I could see Bill sitting up in bed watching television. I knocked on the door, and his head turned toward us. He shrugged when he saw us, but he didn't tell us to go away. Instead he turned the television off and motioned for us to come in.

We bade him good morning, and he returned the greeting, though he eyed us a bit warily, I thought.

"Mind if we sit?" Jack asked.

"Help yourselves," Bill said.

Jack brought chairs to the bedside for both of us, and we sat.

"You know why we're here," I said.

Bill nodded. "You want the whole story." He sighed. "I spent a lot of last night thinking about it, and I guess I should set the record straight. I realized I wasn't quite ready to die after all. I keep thinking about my mama. She hated to lie, but she went along with it. I didn't tell even her the whole truth. I reckon I'll tell you, though."

"We're listening," Jack said. "Do you mind if I record you?"

Bill shrugged. "Don't see why not. Go ahead."

Jack pulled out his digital recorder and turned it on. He placed it on the nightstand next to Bill's bed. "Interview with William Delaney," he said, then added the date and the location. He also included the fact that I was there as a witness. "Go ahead."

Bill looked at me. "Do you already know what I'm going to say?"

"I think I know some of it," I replied. "I know that you didn't murder anybody. I think you still loved Betty Barber too much to harm her or her children."

"No, I didn't kill them," Bill said. "I was trying to rescue them from Hiram. That son of a bitch deserved to die, and I'm not sorry he did."

"You were trying to rescue them?" Jack asked.

"Yeah," Bill said. "Betty was desperate to get away from Hiram and get the boys out, too. Hiram treated her bad, and the boys, too. He was getting crazier all the time, like his mama did before they sent her to Whitfield. I was going to get them that night after Hiram fell asleep. Betty was going to put something in his milk to make sure he slept."

"Was Elizabeth in on the plot?" Jack asked.

"She was," Bill said. "Told me she wanted her mama and the boys to be safe." He scratched his chin. "She arranged to spend the night with her friend Leann so she'd be out of the house. We didn't want her father to know that she knew anything about it.

"I'd arranged to get there about ten thirty. Hiram was usually in bed by eight, and I figured by ten thirty he should be sound asleep. Mama knew about this part of the plan, of course. I pretended to be real drunk when I got home that night, and Mama would tell everybody I passed out and never left my room—in case Hiram came nosing around.

"I parked my car a couple hundred yards down the road leading to the house." He reached for a cup off the nightstand and drank from it. "When I got to the house, I had this feeling something was wrong. Everything was too quiet. I let myself in the front door like I'd said I would do. Betty and the boys were supposed to be waiting for me just inside. They weren't there, so I started looking for them. I walked into the kitchen, and the first thing I saw was Elizabeth standing there, looking at her father, this horrible expression on her face. Hiram was sitting in a chair with a shotgun across his knees. He seemed dazed.

"Then I caught the smell. Blood. So bad it gagged me." He paused to drink again from his cup. His hand trembled a little. "Elizabeth saw me. 'Look what he did,' she said. She pointed, and I looked over. Betty and the boys. Dead."

"I'm so sorry," I said. "I know this is painful for you."

Bill nodded. "For a minute there, I didn't know where

I was, or who I was. All I could think of was killing Hiram. I went for him. Elizabeth grabbed the shotgun. I pulled Hiram out of the chair. He came to enough to realize I meant to hit him. He twisted himself out of my arms and turned away. Had his back to Elizabeth. That's when she shot him."

Jack looked at me. So far everything I had told him earlier matched Bill's account.

"Do you believe Hiram actually killed his wife and sons?" Jack asked. "Couldn't it have been Elizabeth?"

"No, I know he did it," Bill said.

"How can you be so sure?" I asked.

"I just know," Bill replied. "Elizabeth told Hiram I was coming to take Betty and the boys away from him. They were my sons."

"That made him go crazy and kill them?" Jack asked.

"Partly," Bill said. "Elizabeth also told him I was the boys' father. He'd always suspected they weren't his, I think, and Elizabeth telling him she knew it for a fact pushed him over the edge."

THIRTY-SIX

IIIIIIIIIIIIIIIIIIIIIIIIIIIIIIIIIIIIIIIIIIIIIIIIIIIIIIIIIIIIIII

"Yes, Sean, you're right," I said, trying not to sound long-suffering, though I wasn't sure I was completely successful. "If I hadn't gone to the hospital the deputies would have handled things very well on their own." I was thankful Sean had at least waited until we finished our Sunday dinner before he brought up the subject. I don't think I would have been able to eat otherwise.

"I know you think I'm nagging, Dad," Sean said. He sounded aggrieved.

"Well, you are," Laura said. "You talk to him sometimes like he's an adolescent."

"Thanks for the support, sister dear." Sean leaned back in his chair and crossed his arms over his chest.

"She's right, sweetheart," Alex, Sean's wife, said. "I can hear you sounding just like that about fifteen years from now with our child." She smiled at him.

Sean's gaze softened as he looked across the table at his wife. He might fuss at me, but he wouldn't fuss at Alex.

"Go on, Charlie," Stewart said. "Before Sean launches into another lecture on proper behavior for grandfathers." He grinned.

"Ha-ha," Sean said.

"I did feel a little foolish hiding in the bathroom," I said, "but I couldn't take the chance. If the deputy hadn't shown up, and I hadn't been there, Bill would have died."

"What was in the syringe? Were you able to find out?" Haskell asked.

"A powerful tranquilizer, with a dose strong enough to bring down a couple of bull elephants," I said. "Lethal to Bill, obviously."

"She was desperate," Helen Louise said. "Despite the fact that she murdered her own father and tried to kill another man, I do feel sorry for her. She was not quite sane."

"Sane enough to kill people to get what she wanted," Haskell said. "And she nearly got away with it. I wonder how long it would have been before she turned on someone else, like her husband or her children."

That didn't bear thinking about. I felt desperately sorry for Campbell and the children. I imagined he would be watching his children closely from now on for signs of their mother's extreme behavior.

"The one I feel really sorry for is Bill Delaney," Laura said. "He thought he was going to be able to save the woman he loved and his sons from a monster." She shook her head, and I could see tears running down her face. Frank obviously noticed, too. He left his chair and went around the table to comfort her.

"I agree, honey," I said. "To me, that is the real tragedy in all this."

"Why did Delaney protect Elizabeth all these years?" Sean asked. "I don't understand that at all. Why didn't he turn her in?"

"I asked him that," I said. "He told me he couldn't. He didn't want her to go to prison. It wouldn't have been self-defense with her shooting him in the back. If Hiram had intended to kill her, she would have been dead by the time Bill arrived. She was Betty's daughter, and he felt he had to protect her. It was all he had left that he could do for Betty."

"Did he tell you what he did with the shotgun?" Stewart asked.

"He drove out to Tullahoma Lake and threw it in. Even if the sheriff's department had looked for it there, I doubt they would have found it. It's a big lake," I said.

"Did Dr. Finch know all of this?" Alex asked.

"I'm not sure how much she really knew," I replied. "I believe she knew Elizabeth was planning to help her mother and brothers escape from her father. I also believe Elizabeth told her that Bill Delaney killed Hiram in revenge for Hiram murdering her mother and the boys. Elizabeth swore her to secrecy because she said she didn't want Bill to go to jail."

"She was still trying to protect her all these years later, I suppose," Helen Louise said. "Now *that* is a best friend for you."

"She loved Elizabeth like a sister, and that's why she was feeding Elizabeth information on Bill's condition, although that is unethical," I said. "I don't think she ever realized that Elizabeth had such a dark side to her personality."

"She was pretty good at keeping it hidden," Haskell said.

"For the most part, yes," I said. "I didn't trust her, although the act of contrition she put on at Bill's bedside almost convinced me I was wrong. That was before she tried to kill him, of course."

"Was she afraid he would finally tell the truth to someone?" Frank asked. "After he'd been silent for so many years?"

I shrugged. "That's my guess. She didn't trust him. He promised never to come back, apparently, and then he did. That spooked her."

"I'm thankful she's off the streets," Laura said. "I'd hate to think of her loose out there."

"And hopefully she'll stay off the streets," Haskell said. "Depends on the kind of bond the judge sets. Right now she's in our jail waiting to go before the judge to be indicted."

"She's here, in Athena?" Laura sounded alarmed.

"Yes, for the attempted murder of Bill Delaney," Haskell said. "It will take a while before the other charges are brought. Delaney will probably face charges, too, though they might go easy on him because of his health and the fact that he's now cooperating with the investigation."

"The main thing is she's where she can't harm anyone else," Alex said. "What I don't understand is why Elizabeth hated her father so much? Especially since he supposedly spoiled her. Was she abused, do you think?"

"I suspect she might have been. If she was, it will probably come out at the trial," I said.

"How is Bill Delaney doing?" Helen Louise asked. "Have you made a decision yet on inviting him to live here?"

"He's doing better than I expected, after everything that happened," I said. "He could live three days, three weeks, or three years, but he won't be living them here. I invited him to stay here. He thanked me, but I could see that being around me would remind him too much of recent events."

"So what is he going to do?" Laura asked.

"He's going back to Tullahoma," I said. "Turns out he has more than enough to live on. He is pretty frugal with his money. He has a little apartment there, and a couple of his old Marine Corps buddies are still around. He told me he has realized he isn't so ready to die after all. The fact that Elizabeth tried to kill him again convinced him he shouldn't try to protect her anymore."

"I'm glad to hear he's got a home," Helen Louise said. "He might not be able to find much happiness in the time he has left, but perhaps he can find peace of a sort."

I smiled at the woman I had grown to love so much. In her articulate, sensitive way, she had voiced my own thoughts beautifully.

"I think it's time we changed the subject to a happier one," I said. "I'd like to hold my grandson for a little while, if that's okay."

Laura glanced over to the bassinet by the wall. Diesel lay beside it, ever vigilant should baby Charlie start to cry.

"I think he's probably ready for a meal anyway, so why don't you give him a bottle, Dad?"

"I'll get one from the fridge and put it in the warmer," Frank said.

I nodded my thanks, and he headed to the kitchen. I went over to the bassinet and picked up my grandson. He was already stirring a little, and Laura was right. He would soon be demanding to be fed. I returned to my chair and held him in my arms. Diesel came with me and sat beside my chair. He had to be sure I was taking proper care of the baby.

Looking at baby Charlie, at that perfect little face and head, I was able to push away the dark thoughts brought about by recent events. I held the future in my arms, and I would do everything in my power to see that it was a future full of love, light, and laughter.

Keep reading for a sneak peek at

THE PAWFUL TRUTH

the next Cat in the Stacks mystery!

What did you get yourself into?

That thought had run through my mind several times over the past few days, but never so often as it had during the ten minutes I waited for class to start.

Staring at the eager young faces and listening to the chatter of voices rise and fall around me, I felt increasingly out of place. I had not failed to notice the covert glances, the occasional grimaces, and the *what is he doing here* tilts of the head in my direction. Not much subtlety.

Stop being so self-conscious, I chided myself. *You have every right to be here, even if you are three decades older than the rest of the class. Focus on why you're here, and remember the excitement you felt when you finally decided to do this.*

Good advice, I realized, and I felt the tension begin to ebb away. I had long been fascinated by medieval history and sometimes wished I had majored in history, rather

than in English, during my undergraduate days here at
Athena. I had heard great things about the young professor who taught this course on the history of England from
the end of the Roman occupation until the Norman Conquest. He offered a second course that picked up with the
aftermath of the Conquest through the accession of the
first Tudor monarch, Henry VII. When I saw the course
listed for the spring semester, I decided to give myself a
belated Christmas gift and sign up to audit it. If all went
well with the first one, I would sign up for the second one
the next time it was offered.

Dr. Warriner's courses always filled quickly, I had
learned. I managed to squeak in before the class closed
admissions. I hoped he lived up to his reputation because
I was so interested in the subject and anticipated filling in
the gaps in my knowledge.

A late arrival caught my eye when she slipped into an
empty seat to the left a row ahead of me. A voluptuous
blonde with a head of curly hair, she appeared to be in her
thirties. Still younger than I, but at least there would be
one other older student in the class. As if she felt my spec-
ulative glance on her, she turned to look my way.

A cool, assessing gaze met mine. She smiled briefly,
then turned back to face the front of the classroom. That
one glance revealed a stunning face, with makeup so ex-
pertly applied that she appeared cosmetics-free. Perhaps
Dr. Warriner's reputation had drawn her in as well, I
mused. Or she might be a graduate student.

Conversation ceased suddenly as a tall, muscular man
strode into the room and to the front of the classroom.
Had I not already seen Carey Warriner around campus a
few times, I would have been more struck by his appearance. I heard the slow exhalation of sighs around me, and
I glanced around. The female students raked him with

their eyes, and I understood why. Warriner was easily the most handsome man I had ever seen in the flesh.

Broad-shouldered, he stood at least six foot four, and his chiseled features brought to mind the stars of Hollywood's Golden Age. With his sleeves rolled up to expose bronzed forearms, he favored the class with an engaging smile as he surveyed the room. Perhaps it was my sometimes overactive imagination, but I thought the smile slipped briefly when his gaze rested on the attractive blonde to my left.

The smile quickly returned, however, and he perched on the corner of the long table at the front of the classroom. "Good afternoon, everyone. I am Professor Warriner. Welcome to my course on the history of early medieval England."

His beautifully modulated baritone elicited a few more audible sighs from around the room, and his smile broadened. He appeared appreciative of this reaction. He reached for a folder he had laid on the table beside him.

"First things first, of course," he said. "Let's get the dull stuff out of the way. When I call your name, please raise your hand."

He extracted a piece of paper from the folder and began to read the names. The blonde lifted her hand to the name *Dixie Belle Compton*. Talk about a Southern name, I thought. *Dixie Belle*. I noticed that Warriner did not look at the students when he called this name. Perhaps he already knew her? That would explain the brief change of expression.

I was so engrossed in contemplating this, I nearly missed my own name. I jerked my hand up, and Warriner nodded. He soon finished his roll call and laid the paper aside. He rose from his perch and went to the board. Here he wrote his e-mail address. Turning back to face the class, he said, "You will use this to submit your written assignments. You will find the syllabus for this course, if you haven't already, on my page on the history department website. This course requires a substantial amount of reading, some of it translations of primary sources, some of it monographs by historians covering particular subjects." He paused to the sound of a few subdued groans.

"This course is no sinecure," he continued. "If you don't know the meaning of the word, I suggest you look it up. You will have to work, and work diligently, if you expect to do well in this class. If you aren't willing to work, I suggest you go ahead and drop the class today." He paused for a moment as he assessed the class with a measuring glance. "I am passionate about my subject, and while I don't expect my students to share my passion to the same degree, I do expect dedication to your work in this course. There will be no online instruction in this course. I prefer the old-fashioned methods, and that means I expect to see you in class at every scheduled meeting, on time, and ready to participate. Do not be late."

Warriner's uncompromising expression did not daunt me. In fact, I admired his standards, well familiar with them from my own college years here, thanks to several of my toughest professors. I had to admit to a certain amount of surprise, however, because of the prevalence of online education these days and the use of chat rooms and so on for group assignments.

I heard the rustle of movement around me. No doubt a few students were squirming a bit, and I wondered how many of them would return for the second class. Might as well weed out the less serious students right away.

"Now," the professor said, "on to the scope of this course. We begin with the departure of the Romans in the fifth century of the Common Era. We will not discuss in detail why the Roman Empire abandoned its province of

Britannia. That is the subject of a course taught by my colleague, Professor Fischer."

A hand shot up from the front row.

"Yes, what is it?" Warriner asked.

"Um, I was wondering, you know," a lanky young man said, his words hesitant, "if you're going to talk about King Arthur? I mean, you know, this is the period when he lived, right? Once the Romans left, you know." He stammered to a halt, and he appeared to shrink under the now harsh gaze of the professor.

Warriner stood and folded his arms over his chest. He surveyed the room before he again focused on the student with the question. "This is not a course on fantasy and myth. A professor in the English department teaches a course on English folklore. I suggest you take that if you want to read about Arthur and his knights." He paused briefly. "Now, back to reality. There could well have been a warlord in the aftermath of Roman withdrawal who attempted to take control of parts of Britain, but if he existed at all, he was nothing like the legends that have grown up around the fantasy of Arthur."

I felt the tension in the room. Perhaps the young man had hit a sore spot with Warriner by asking his question. Based on my own reading—admittedly limited—I agreed with the professor, as much as I enjoyed tales of Arthur and the Round Table. I loved the movie *Excalibur*, for example, but I viewed it as fantasy, as I did Mary Stewart's enthralling Arthurian tetralogy about Arthur that I had read years ago.

Warriner suddenly smiled, and the tension I had felt dissipated. "I get a similar question every time I teach this course," he said to the student, "and thank you for getting it out of the way so quickly. Now we can begin to focus on the real meat of the course."

The professor spent several minutes discussing the assignments for the course, including assigned readings and the reports to be written about them; the number of tests, including the final exam; and the research paper due by the end of the course. Students could choose their topic, but he must approve them, and for those who needed help, he had a list of suggestions they could consult.

He paused for questions, and after he had answered three, he began his lecture. I had my pen and notebook ready. Many of the students, I had already observed, had brought laptops or tablets with keyboards with them. At first I found the clicking and tapping of keys and screens distracting, but I quickly became absorbed in Warriner's lecture. My hand began to cramp after about twenty minutes. As accustomed to the keyboard as I was, I had not written this much by hand in years. I decided I would bring my laptop from now on.

I did my best to keep up with my note-taking, but occasionally I found myself so intent on the lecture I forgot to write anything. Warriner spoke with passionate interest in his subject and shared fascinating details about life in fifth-century Britain. His lecturing style made the past come alive, and I enjoyed every moment that he spoke. The bell rang far too soon.

"We'll continue the topic on Friday," Warriner said as students began to gather their belongings and stow away their devices.

I flexed my cramped writing hand and then massaged it. While other students filed out of the room, Warriner did not move from his position at the front. I glanced up to find him regarding me. "Mr. Harris," he said, "I would like to talk to you, if you have a moment."

"Certainly." I stuffed my notebook and pen in my briefcase and rose from the desk to join him.

Warriner perched again on the table and regarded me with a frown. For a moment I wondered if I had somehow offended him, or if he didn't care for older students in his classes.

"Is there a problem?" I asked.

The professor shook his head. "Not at all. I am wondering, however, why you are auditing my class rather than taking it for credit. Though we have not met before today, like everyone at Athena I am aware of your reputation for assisting in local murder investigations. Surely you're not intimidated by the intellectual demands of the course."

"No, it's not that," I said, somewhat defensively. His tone had not been dismissive or in any way negative, and I suddenly realized that my initial reaction was due to my own insecurities, not his remarks. "I haven't been in the classroom for over twenty-five years, and though I am thoroughly interested in the subject, I'm not sure I want to work that hard."

"Doing well in this course takes effort and ability," Warriner said. "Don't underestimate yourself. I think you should consider taking the course for credit."

I shrugged. "I'll think about it, but I don't believe I'll change my mind. If you'd rather I dropped the class because of that, I will, though I'd be deeply disappointed."

Warriner flashed a smile. "No need for that. How about this? You turn in the first two assignments, let me see what you can do with them. If neither of us is satisfied with the results, I won't push you into taking the class for credit, and you can audit."

I considered that for a moment. I wondered why this mattered to him, but I had to admit he intrigued me with his offer. "All right, I'll do that."

"Good." Warriner nodded and rose from the desk. "Then I'll see you here on Friday."

I nodded and turned away. At the door I almost ran into Dixie Belle Compton, who had apparently been lingering there. She brushed past me and strode into the room. She jostled my arm, and I dropped my briefcase. She didn't pause in her progress, and I suppressed a rude comment.

As I bent to pick up my briefcase, I heard Warriner say, in a savage but carrying undertone, "What the hell are you doing in my class?"

Miranda James is the *New York Times* bestselling author of the Cat in the Stacks Mysteries, including *Six Cats a Slayin'*, *Twelve Angry Librarians*, and *No Cats Allowed*, as well as the Southern Ladies Mysteries, including *Fixing to Die*, *Digging Up the Dirt*, and *Dead with the Wind*. James lives in Mississippi. Visit the author at catinthestacks.com and facebook.com/mirandajamesauthor.

Ready to find
your next great read?

Let us help.

Visit prh.com/nextread